CONQUER ALL OBSTACLES

A NOVEL BY

JO-ANNE VANDERMEULEN

THE LAURUS COMPANY
NORTH TEXAS

Scripture quotations, unless otherwise indicated, are taken from the Holy Bible, New International Version®, NIV®. Copyright ©1973, 1978, 1984 by Biblica, Inc.™ Used by permission of Zondervan. All rights reserved worldwide.

"**Conquer All Obstacles**" is a complete work of fiction. Any resemblance to persons' names (living or dead), which means characters; events, which means incidents or places; are used fictitiously or are products of the author's imagination and is entirely coincidental.

This title is also available in hard cover and eBook.
Visit www.JoConquerAll.com

CONQUER ALL OBSTACLES
PUBLISHED BY THE LAURUS COMPANY
P. O. Box 2071
Lake Dallas, TX 75065

Copyright © 2009 by Jo-Anne Vandermeulen

All rights reserved. No part of this book may be reproduced in any form or by any means, electronic or mechanical, including photocopying, recording, or by any information storage and retrieval system, without permission in writing from the publisher, except for brief quotations in critical reviews and articles.

Cover Photo: Grace Metzger Forrest
Text and Layout Design: Nancy E. Williams
Edited by: Nancy E. Williams, Diana L. Meadows

ISBN-13: 978-0-9841680-1-9
ISBN-10: 0-09841680-1-X

PRINTED IN THE UNITED STATES OF AMERICA

Dedicated to ALL ...

*who have struggled with mental illness,
family and friends who have been affected by this disease,
and
to those women who are overcoming the trauma of violence.*

YOU can CONQUER ALL OBSTACLES.

ACKNOWLEDGEMENTS

*We all have choices.
Today, I choose NOT to be a victim.*

I praise the Lord, my Shepherd, for I am never alone.
Without Him, I am nothing.

*"Even though I walk through the valley of the shadow of death, I will fear no evil,
for you are with me; your rod and your staff, they comfort me."*
Psalms 23:4, the Holy Bible, New International Version (NIV)®

To my family, friends, followers, and fans—a community filled by love—I thank you for your support. I am truly blessed.

- I would like to give a special thank you to my editors, Nancy E. Williams and Diana L. Meadows of The Laurus Company. Their skills, input, and personal encouragement have been invaluable throughout the publishing process.

I also want to thank the following very special people:

- Billi Wagner, my critique partner from the Yahoo! Group, "It's Your Story."

- Lana Sebastian, my local reader from Yorkton, Saskatchewan.

- Helen Strong from Rocanville, Saskatchewan, my grade twelve English teacher and coworker for 15 years, the woman who had faith in me all along, spending hours line editing my earliest works.

—Jo-Anne Vandermeulen

NOW

Chapter 1

NOW

Gladstone Central Hospital
Mental Health Division
Gladstone, Saskatchewan

The needle scribbled over the paper near Tara Robstead's right ear. The sound reminded her of fingernails scraping down a chalkboard. Engulfed in total darkness and feeling tape pinching her forehead, she pictured a machine hooked to her scalp assigning instructions to the instrument.

Turn that damn machine off, she yelled from the confines of her mind. Her pulse hammered inside her head like an air pump expanding her skull, but her body was like an unresponsive carcass.

Could use some blankets in here. Can anyone hear me? Hey, fellas, you trying to conserve heat in this building, or what? Her body remained motionless, strapped to the stark white hospital bed.

The door creaked open, as if pushing against the silence. Soft footsteps advanced, then stopped.

A sheet covers nothing. Might as well be naked. Guys, I feel like a specimen here. Eyes, I command you to open. Open now!

Nothing.

So dark.

Why am I here? Hello?

A soft hum came from above her that seemed to be growing louder. *Would somebody please fix that annoying light fixture?*

Answer me, damn it! Who are you? The machine by Tara's left ear took on an extra beat.

I need to see who this person is. I need to be prepared.

What if it's him? Beads of sweat formed above her upper lip.

Why don't you speak so I'll know who you are? Not that I can distinguish voices. All of the voices sounded muffled, as if caught in the tunnel of a lead pipe.

I want to contribute to the conversation he must be having with himself. That is, if it is him.

The needle stopped. A rhythmic beat pulsed. The door creaked open again.

I should give that door a name. Anything that makes that much noise deserves a name. The confident click of not one but two pairs of shoes announced their entrance.

I know, I'll make this a game and call it "Blind Woman's Trivia." I'll get more points for guessing the identity of people who enter my domain—my castle. Yes, I like that much better. Appear before the draw-bridge, and you shall enter on my command. You are allowed to play the game only if I can properly identify you.

"Any change, Doctor Frances?" a deep voice asked.

No, no! You have to play by the rules. Can't use names unless you are ready to quit. Okay, Doctor Frances, you're out of here. You must now only watch us having fun.

"I am afraid it doesn't look good," Doctor Frances responded. "If she fails to respond in the next few hours, we will have to try her on some other mood stabilizers. If increasing the valproic acid is ineffective, we will have to try electroconvulsive therapy."

Come on, guys! You said that the last time you came in here. Don't sound so pessimistic. I'm going to have to deduct points if I don't get some good news here.

"You're going to shock her brain? But she looks like she's just sleeping," the third voice, a new visitor, responded.

"Some patients don't appear sick even though their illness is severe." Papers rattled near her right ear as Doctor Frances examined the data on the accordion stack of paper accumulating neatly under the printer. "It's what makes this form of mental illness so difficult. Patients can go on living what appears to be a productive, happy life while masking the true anguish that fights constantly in their mind. We will increase her medication before we apply any electroconvulsive therapy."

"I just never would have guessed that her moods were associated with a mental illness," the new visitor added, a tinge of bewilderment in his voice.

Tara heard footsteps, then shuffling steps around her bed. She caught a whiff of Brut cologne and knew it belonged to the man with the deep voice. He had been there often. He raised his arms, stretching over her head. *Must be checking on intravenous bags or tubes, or something like that,* Tara mused.

Guys, you know you can talk to me. I'm right here. As for Doctor Frances, you can't play anymore. And as for the other man, my new visitor, I'll have to give you ten points for remaining anonymous. You sound like a nice man, but I've been wrong before. In fact, that's what got me here in the first place. I'm always wrong.

"I feel I never paid enough attention. I should've been there for her," the new visitor spoke. She felt her blankets tighten, as if his fists curled around the end of the layered cotton sheets, then a slow release as the fabric tucked evenly around her shoulders. "I should have seen it coming."

Her arm was lifted. Pressure cuffed around her wrist.

Doctor Frances continued, "I really think we have to be careful not to place blame. Instead, it would be more productive to understand bipolar disorder. Symptoms are not always obvious. The patient may appear to be relatively asymptomatic—or normal, if you will—or the patient may have the more recognizable manic episodes, where they experience a soar of high energy one minute and dive to an extreme low mood the next. Unless the patient chooses to reveal their honest feelings and thoughts, the severity of their mental state can go undiagnosed for years. They may appear healthy and actually be quite ill. They may take on denial as a form of reality and refuse to admit anything is wrong.

How come I can't seem to see it coming? I try so hard to look for clues, anything that would indicate danger. But, no, I just walk right in and sit right down. Hey, I think there's a song about that.

"Walk right in, sit right down."

Damn, I can never remember the words. Can always get the tune though.

"In Tara's case," Doctor Frances continued, "her negative test results lead us to conclude that she has been in mental denial. In her mind, she detects danger most of the time. She learned to hide her true inner state as a coping mechanism."

"But for her to be lying there for no apparent reason. I don't understand why she doesn't snap out of it." The new visitor's voice quivered as he spoke.

"At times, it only takes a single terrifying event to trigger deep depression at a level this severe, especially if one is already suffering from post-traumatic syndrome."

"How long will she be like this?"

"I cannot give you an answer right now. As doctors, we are often left perplexed. When the EEG results don't correspond with the symptoms, it is very difficult to determine the severity of the condition; it is truly trial and error finding the proper treatment. We have started Tara on a low dose of valproic acid, which is a mood stabilizer. If there is no improvement, we will increase the dosage as the day proceeds."

There was a long pause and a heavy sigh.

"I have to be honest with you. Recovery lies in the will of the patient. It is up to her if she wants to get better or not," Doctor Frances said.

You mean I have all the control? You seem to think I'm sick. Well, I am. I'm sick and tired of living with all these psychos in my life.

Rick? Is that you? Are you my visitor? Tara swallowed hard, the action causing the tape to tighten across her forehead.

It better not be ... Oh, my God! I thought he was dead. Devin? Her heart rattled in her chest like a drum roll before a hanging. *I can't do this again. Don't make me. I can't. I have nothing left.*

Her limp hand dropped, and she heard the click of a pen and

some scribbling. Someone touched her eye and pulled the eyelid upward, forcing it to open. "Without a proper diagnosis, there is no treatment. With no treatment, there is no cure," Doctor Frances explained.

Well, if that's all it takes, I can tell you everything right now. But, first, where did that light go? I think I know who my visitor is, but I can't be sure. If you'd just pry up these heavy lids for a second more, I know I could identify my mystery visitor. As for what's wrong with me, I can tell you everything you need to know. You just need to listen to me. I can recall everything that happened. But, no, that's not what you want to hear, is it?

The wand screeched wildly on the machine beside her head, the needle scraping faster than before.

"Is there anything I can do?" the new visitor questioned.

"You had better leave now," Doctor Frances said with a firm tone. She imagined his handsome head turned toward the monitor, watching the needle tracing madly up and down the page. "Later, when we get Tara settled, I will need you to come back and talk to her."

You want to know how I'm feeling? God, I hate that word—feeling!

Suddenly, what sounded like running sneakers pounded the tiled floor. *Great, now my castle is a gymnasium? The basketball player is going in for a lay-up before the net. He shoots, and the orange orbit remains suspended in the air ...*

My new visitor is leaving? I thought you wanted to know how I was feeling. Come back. Come back! I need to tell you what happened to me. You need to take some of the blame. This isn't all my fault!

"We need some help in here," Doctor Frances' stern voice called loudly, along with some garbled and incoherent words.

Get the whistle out of your mouth so I can understand you. And stop blowing it, I'm right here.

"Code sixty-six," Doctor Frances yelled.

You want me to talk to you? How can I talk to you when I can't even wake up? ✧

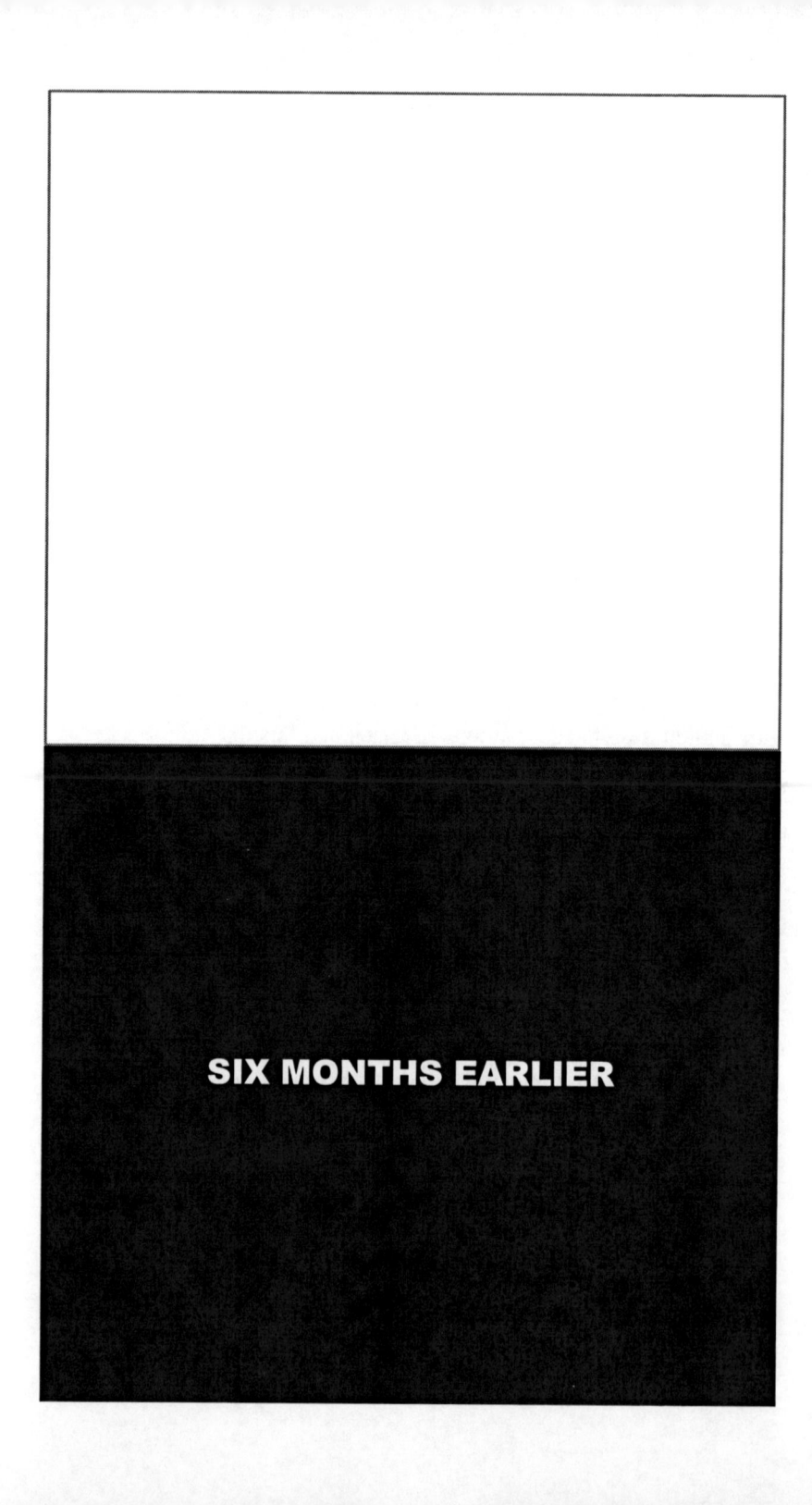

SIX MONTHS EARLIER

SIX MONTHS EARLIER

Tara Robstead's lungs fought for air as she watched the man she loved slump in defeat. The meeting had ended ten minutes ago when the twenty-five teachers they worked with had stomped out of the library. She chose to stay. Tara wouldn't see it any other way after what Josh Henderson had done for her. But did he realize she was still there, sitting in her faithful position front row center?

"I'm here for you if you need to talk," she spoke from across the empty room. Her loud voice bounced off the pasty cinderblock walls lined with bookshelves. "It's not your fault that Alex insisted on a need for more cutbacks."

Unlike her strong voice, Josh's voice had cracked when he delivered Alex's news to the room full of teachers. Remembering the tears that had threatened to spill from his moist eyes, Tara lowered her chin as she prayed for strength, unsure if the whispered words were for him, herself, or both of them.

Her mind slipped back to their first encounter. The clear images sprang to life.

Her tears wouldn't stop ... his arms opened, wrapping around her shaking body ... she didn't want to leave Rick, but she had no choice.

Tara sank back in the cheap stacking chair. An oversized cannonball remained in her gut. If only the cumbersome weight in her boss's stomach could shift, Josh could breathe for both of them.

Josh's deep, heavy sigh broke the silence in the room. "How can a new Assistant to the Director be better for the students," he cleared his throat, "if I have to cut another teacher? My promotion shouldn't affect others like this."

"But you had no choice," Tara countered, realizing she was stuck to the smooth surface of the chair as she tried to rise. She lifted her legs one at a time before extricating herself from the seat. Sitting in the same spot for two hours had taken its toll on her cotton outfit. Her fingertips brushed across the thin fabric of her mini-skirt, releasing it from its suction hold on her bare thighs. "You had to listen to Alex."

Glancing down as she stood, she noticed multiple creases in the front of her matching flowered blouse. The electric fans placed at each room's entrance only pushed around the dry summer air and did nothing to lessen the heat in Saskatchewan's Prairie Region. It wasn't until now that Tara realized how hot she really was. She sucked in her stomach and pressed the fabric down against her moist body and into her belted waist until the skirt and top looked like one.

She stepped around the clutter of chairs that had been pulled out from the rectangular table and stood within inches of Josh's deflated posture. He seemed to see only the sheet of paper before him. Tara's eyes traced to the spot where he stared: *"PROMOTION."* At the bottom of the neatly typed page was the name of the Director of Education: Alex Conway.

More images popped into her active mind.

His tears mixing with hers ... mingling stories of tender loneliness and broken hearts ... hugging ... kissing ... naked bodies connecting, quenching an uncontrollable need ...

"I like your tie," Tara's soft voice hinted playful sarcasm. Perspiration rolled down from her long neck, trickled down her cleavage, and cupped around each breast. She thought of the last time they had made love. Her nipples instantly grew hard.

Josh moved as if her words had awakened him from his hypnotic state. He reached up for his glasses and danced them off his face, the life in his expression gone. His usually twinkling brown eyes appeared distant, until they began a slow crawl up Tara's body.

"Is that a smirk I see on your face?" Tara whispered, feeling more like a teenager than a woman of thirty-five.

Thoughts of what she might have done in her younger years to raise his mood washed through her mind: Standing and waving her arms in the air like a fan during a Roughrider football game, painting her face green and screaming at all the horrific calls, and wearing a watermelon as a hat.

Now, maybe she should shake green and white pom-poms at her side and scream through a megaphone: *It's time to blow this Popsicle stand! So, you lost this one,* she visualized her hip snapping out to the side and the entire fabric of her skirt flipping up over both butt cheeks, *and I still love you!* Tara covered her mouth to stifle a giggle.

Josh chuckled as if he read her mind. "Now, how can I not smile when I have a goddess in front of me?" The deepness of his voice contrasted the expression he wore just a few seconds before.

"You are just too kind." Tara's lips parted, her tongue slowly traced the fullness of her bottom lip. A gush of desire filled her, igniting her face to a beam.

"You were awesome," she quickly changed the subject, so as not to draw too much attention to herself. This was neither the time nor the place.

Joshua's head dropped and shook back and forth. "I really hate my job sometimes." His form remained bowed, his chin disappearing into his chest. He seemed to be examining the sheaf of notes in front of him, but she knew better. His tailor-made navy suit seemed to sag, pulling his broad shoulders down with his mood. He raked his long fingers through his thick, full head of dark brown curls.

Tara moved closer to him. She gently placed her hand on the back of his neck. "Hey, someone's got to do it, and I thought you were marvelous." The clean scent of his shampoo permeated her nostrils, and she could feel his heat radiating into her palm. She imagined how she could really take his mind off his work.

He raised his head, pulled his tall frame out of his chair, and stood in front of her. "I think your words are just a little biased," his gaze slid to hers, "but thanks anyway." He lifted a stray lock of her black hair that was curling around her chin and gently tucked it behind her left ear, being careful not to disturb the diamond stud piercing at the top. "You are so beautiful, more like an angel."

Her eyes closed. She tingled under his gentle touch, as if under a magical spell.

He pulled her against his firm body. Could he feel her heart thumping through her blouse? She swallowed and opened her eyes.

His lips were relaxed and slightly parted. His head leaned down.

She yearned to graze her lips across his for just a taste of him. Reality became nonexistent. Everything was forgotten except the memory of his lips on hers.

And then he stopped.

Tara remained standing, poised to meet his kiss.

It was as if a warning alarm had fired in Josh. His eyes grew wide. He stepped back from her trance. "I've got to go pick up my boys." He stared at his watch, more out of habit than necessity.

"What?" She stepped back.

"You know my family comes first." A muscle worked on the inside of his jaw, just like it always did when he was angry.

"This isn't about your kids." Angrily, she placed her hands on her slender hips and widened her stance. "So don't try to use them as your excuse." Tara pushed past him, and Josh stumbled back against the chair.

"When are you going to tell me the truth? What is the real reason we can't be seen together? Why can't you just admit what's bothering you?" Bending down, she began flipping the stacks of paper on the tables they had used in their meeting, bouncing them as if handling a deck of cards at a Blackjack table.

She glared back up at his wide eyes and open mouth. "All I ask from you is a little love and respect," she spat through clenched teeth. "You got the loving right, I have to admit, but the respect? When are you going to think about me and my needs for a change? And I don't mean in the bedroom!" Her hands were moving in fast motion, scooping spoons, napkins, pens, and anything she could grab to fire into a pile. "When are you going to start looking at yourself and get honest about what *you* want in life, so you can stop lying to yourself and to me?"

"Now wait a minute here." His hands gestured like a cop directing traffic. "You know the deal. What if someone were to walk in?"

She stopped. "And so what if someone did? I'm sure your buddy, Alex, wouldn't scratch you off the precious application list for Assistant Directorship." She glared and then began stacking chairs. The noise escalated, competing with their voices.

"When will you learn? The world doesn't revolve around only you. I have other responsibilities." His hands caught her wrists.

Tara couldn't move, numbed by the sudden forced restriction. Her inner ears felt as if she had just dived twelve feet under water; the pressure felt as though it would burst her eardrums.

"This promotion means everything to me." He stared directly into Tara's eyes.

Tara struggled for control. "What makes you think changing jobs will help your boys when you'll be working longer hours and will be home less?" The words came out through her clenched teeth.

Never taking his eyes off of hers, his grip tightened. "Just leave my stuff alone," Josh ground out the syllables. "I can do it myself!"

Words and even the odd physical blow to her body she could handle, but not being constrained. When she heard a man's deep, threatening voice, it was as if her world was going to collapse, leaving her in the rubble—the same garbage she'd crawled out from under following her twelve years of marriage. Never would she be able to ignore the condescending tone of someone being mad at her.

Tara's hands trembled. She yanked her fists free from his grasp. Twirling around, she marched toward the closed door in the same manner her coworkers had done earlier. Stopping, she turned back and shouted, "You know, I just don't get you," pointing a finger with a waggle. She looked at him with a wide-eyed glare. "*If* you are really standing up for what is right, then *why* are you not standing up for what is right *here*?" Her arm made a sweeping wave across the room where he had just delivered his bad news to the teachers. "I can't stand here and watch this brick wall spring up between us anymore."

In just three strides, she reached the exit. In one continuous motion, she flung the door open, marched through it, and slammed it shut.

The loud bang reverberated within her head while she watched a half dozen pairs of shoes rock on the boot rack, domino each other, and tumble off the top shelf. She pushed out the breath she was holding and watched the wooden plank wobble and vibrate in the same frequency as her racing heart.

Tara needed time to cool off. Josh walked out of the library and down the long, vacant hallway that was walled with steel lockers. The click of his dress shoes echoed with every step. The only shred of light seeped from under the bottom of her fifth grade classroom door. He stopped, knocked three raps, paused, two more, then continued on down the hall, following the red glow of each exit light.

Entering the staff room, he went directly to the crusted coffee pot that had been left stinking on the burner. He rinsed the container under the tap and then switched off the machine.

The window air conditioner roared as he walked into the darkness of his ten by twelve foot office and made his way around four heavy chairs that circled a round conference table. He walked past his desk that was cluttered with open folders, stacked textbooks, and piled one-inch binders, and sank into the worn green couch located on the adjacent wall next to the heavily draped window. Resting his head back, he closed his eyes. He would just wait. How many times this week had she yelled at him, expressed her hatred, and tried to change his way of thinking? He couldn't possibly think of only her. Could she not see what this promotion would mean for his boys? If only she would listen and just back off, life would be a whole lot easier.

Josh rose, walked behind his desk, and sat down. He stared at the four by six inch framed photograph of the parents standing behind the two children propped on chairs in typical staged fashion. Could those four smiles work miracles and fool others, or were they just trying to convince themselves?

In the breast pocket of his dress shirt, he felt for his glasses and put them on to again view this image of a perfect foursome.

He barely recognized his own family.

Sure, the picture had been taken over seven years ago, but the boys looked so small. Had they really been that young for what seemed like a snapshot taken only yesterday? Where had the time gone? Nathan now rose above his own father, and Michael's arms, when stretched over his head, could graze the ceiling as if dunking a basketball. Josh chuckled while studying their expressions: Nathan's cute smirk as he got the final jab into his brother's ribs, and Michael's serious expression as if afraid the legs might give out beneath his perch.

Then there was Margaret standing beside him. He frowned, and his breath caught in his throat. It must have been a good day for her. She looked presentable from this distance, wearing her usual smug expression. Only if standing right next to her would someone have a clue. Only then could they see her glassy, blood-shot eyes, the red nose, and smell the stench of alcohol on her breath.

Josh glared at his own reflection and shook his head. He had been beaming into the lens with pride and contentment. How could he have spent all those years living a lie? His motto, "Fake it 'til you make it," got him where he was today. It had worked for him then, but would it work for him now? Perhaps it was time for a change. Maybe it *was* time to confess his secret passion, as Tara had said, and become honest with himself and everyone around him. Lay the cards face up on the table, and let the chips fall where they may. For once, it would be nice to have a genuine smile in a photo.

His gaze returned to his boys. In another year, Nathan would be going to college. Matthew would go in two more years. Josh swallowed hard as he thought of the promises he had sworn to keep.

He laid his head on the desk and squeezed his eyes shut. The bills had piled up. Finding money to deposit into their education fund every month became more and more difficult.

Lifting his head, Josh picked a paper off the stack. He read the Assistant Director job description. Doing the math with the increased income released the tightness in his chest and sent a flutter stirring high and tight within his stomach. Being Assistant Director of Education for the final years before his retirement would solve all of his financial problems and allow him to meet the goal he had always intended for his sons. His family would be set for life.

But what about Tara and all of the promises he had made to her? His chin dropped to his chest. What did he have to look forward to but another decade of pretending he was content without her in his life?

He had no choice. He just couldn't have both.

A knock interrupted Josh's thoughts as he quickly shoved the paper under the stack of files. Three more slow raps, a pause, and then one more could faintly be heard over the loud roar of the air conditioner.

"Enter." His voice sounded gruff as his eyes focused on the backside of the closed door of the principal's office. He could not swallow the lump in his throat.

"Come in." His voice softened as he tried to concentrate on the firm decision he had made.

Slowly, the door opened. Tara's form gracefully slid through, her arms hidden behind her. His breath sucked in.

The backside of her body closed the door. The lock clicked.

He held his breath as he examined the long muscular legs that traveled forever up from her high heels to the curve of her hips, right up to her voluptuous breasts.

There was more to her than her obvious beauty. Josh envisioned her perfectly straight teeth and her full lips drawn back into a wide smile. Her entire face glowed after they had spent time together. The striations of darker blue in her irises sparkled when she stared adoringly into his eyes as if he were the only man alive. She hung on his every word, causing him to feel that what he had to say was of the utmost importance. She always seemed to know how to respond to make him feel like a man.

Tara prowled slowly around the dark office. She seductively dipped her chin, causing the black strands of bone straight hair to swung forward and cup around her oval face. She paused in front of the diplomas hanging above the bookshelves, examining each as if she were actually reading the fine print.

Every time she was near him, he dissolved like a sugar cube in water. He soaked in the sweet taste of their combined concoction.

Her hands were clasped behind her back. She totally ignored his presence, but continued to advance.

His heart raced, pulsated inside his ears. His mouth was instantly dry as he caught a whiff of her sweet rose fragrance mixed with heat like an aroused feline beast. He imagined his whiskers catching on her soft hair as he breathed in all of her sensuality.

She was so close.

Through the thin fabric of her blouse, he could see her breasts lift as she inhaled. His mouth watered, and he swallowed the moisture. His hands wanted to grab her and squeeze her firm muscles within the short grey skirt.

He stood and stepped closer to her back. "I'm sorry," he whispered into her ear, nuzzling his nose into the blanket of softness. His body pressed firmly against hers. She released a heavy sigh as her body shook.

"When are you going to tell her?" Tara spoke without turning around, as if speaking to the walls.

His arms hugged her body. Her head fell forward and then tipped back to rest on his shoulder.

"Let's talk later," he whispered. His lips grazed up the side of her long neck. The soft skin pulsed under his tongue. He nibbled her lobe and could hear his own breath quicken in rhythm. Never before had a woman affected him in such a manner. It was pure lust. A sensual heat of madness swirled in his groin. His body burned.

Her fingers found his belt, button, and then his zipper. She traced her full lips with her tongue and then gasped as she found him at full erection.

He bulged with hunger as he pressed himself against the back of her skirt. He wanted nothing in the way, only to feel her moistness surrounding him, her muscles tightening and constricting as she took him in and swallowed him whole.

"I need you." His warm breath exhaled into her ear. His head was dizzy, as if in another world with only one thought on his mind: how he would love to take her right here, right now. But, no, he wanted that ultimate pleasure of pure passion—seeing her fully satisfied.

"Slow down, baby." He breathed heavily down her neck. He kissed the side of her throat, tasting the salt. Releasing his hold, he placed his palm over her mouth to silence her panting. "Shhh," he murmured in a deep voice, cupping his hand over her lips. His two fingers entered her mouth. She caressed down both tips with her rough tongue and then sucked hard.

Another moan escaped. She shifted her hips back, pressing harder as if she couldn't get enough.

His fingers found the buttons on her blouse. Expertly, he guided each button through its hole. A soft kiss at the back of her neck for each release added to the slow and gentle rhythm.

His moist breath reflected back onto his face.

Her hot skin quivered.

Reaching under her blouse, he fingered the bra hooks open. Slowly, he traced the contours of her breasts, while the backs of his hands spanned out as if to remove the day's creases from the garment.

A deeper groan escaped from her throat.

Now, everything about her was inside his head as his traveling mouth rode over her tiny goose bumps. Her skin tickled the palm of his open hand. He released a button, and her skirt fell to the floor.

He spun her around and effortlessly lifted her onto the edge of the solid mahogany desk. Leaning into her, he kissed her hard. His teasing tongue flicked and contacted hers.

Sliding his hand up the inside of her thighs, he sank to his knees and kissed the exact path his hand had previously explored. The soft flesh on her legs muffled his ears as his lips reached her center.

She was soaking. The most ultimate pleasure had just begun.

Everything about her tantalized all of his senses at once, all in perfect rhythm—touch, smell, taste, and sound; so sweet.

Her breathing quickened.

His lips sucked while his tongue flicked her swollen nub.

Her body rocked with each stroke, vibrating into his hands that were cupped firmly around her buttocks. She gasped as her body tightened and shuttered.

Josh rose up, standing tall between her quivering thighs. Tara's arms were around his neck, and the motion pulled her body against his. She wrapped her legs tightly around his waist, hugging his body. His cock plunged deep inside her hot, dripping cavern. Rocking back and forth, his manhood throbbed quicker by the second.

All muscles taut, she arched her back, and lifted her hips. She knew exactly what to do. With one arm she reached behind her and cleared a spot on the top of his desk, never missing a beat.

He rose above her and entered her again. All momentum focused inside. Her internal vise pulsated, milked him in spastic motion. He pumped his entire being into complete oblivion. The rush exploded inside his head and erupted from the length of his manhood. Jolts of electricity sparked his entire body into a seizure of stars.

He was still, floating somewhere between this world and another. Stroking his back, Tara giggled between short bursts of air.

"What's so funny?" Josh asked, still trying to catch his breath.

"We've been sneaking around for over two years, and I don't even know how you like your eggs cooked."

Josh turned to straighten his disheveled clothing.

Tara stood naked and grabbed his arm. A stern disapproving look replaced the smirk. "I deserve my 'happily ever after,' too." The tears glistening in her eyes were close to brimming over. He had never seen her cry, not even while telling him the horrific stories of what she had experienced with Rick, how much work she had to do to make up for his lack of parenting, and the bruises that were left on her body when she didn't measure up to his standards.

"I'm going to tell her soon." Fastening his belt, he smoothed his hair back, tucking the unruly curls behind both ears. He deserved happiness, just as much as she.

Her hand clutched tighter around his forearm, a deep crease formed between her eyebrows, and her full lips pressed into a fine line.

"I promise." His thumb moved up the bridge of her dainty nose, smoothed the wrinkle with gentle umbrella-shaped strokes, and then moved onto the forehead and through the follicles of her hairline. Her eyes fluttered closed, and her grip loosened on his arm.

He couldn't let her go.

Suddenly, there was a loud knock on the door. The voice on the other side yelled, "I know you're in there!" The door rattled as if it would soon come off its hinges. "Let me in."

"Oh, my God, it's her," Josh mouthed to Tara. His heart pounded like a sledgehammer, and his body lost all of its strength. He felt as though he might pass out. ✧

NOW

NOW

Gladstone Central Hospital
Mental Health Division
Gladstone, Saskatchewan

This is jail—total confinement. There's no comfort when I'm wrapped like a cocoon. Tara wanted to cry, but couldn't.
Why does everyone insist on cuddling me? The doctors, nurses, and even that nice sounding man keep tucking me in. I'm no baby. I want some answers. Her muscles refused to move. It was an effort to breathe.
I can manage anything in life. I'll prove they're wrong. I can do it.
She imagined herself a smiling clown, simply juggling three balls. The circus music blared through the speakers, and dust entered her nostrils, along with the stench of fresh manure.
Isn't life a simple and manageable act to please the audience?
The spectators rose in the stands, grinned, and clapped their hands, until she heard a synchronous rumble of astonished gasps escape from the hundreds of mouths. Their bulging eyes stared and waited for the show to go on. *I won't let you down. I'll give you what you want.*
"Throw in the last ball," the clown yelled toward the audience.

A shadow in the sidelines flinched.

She squinted past the halogen lights, trying to recognize the bulky form, unsure if he was someone familiar or another stranger entering her ring. Again, Tara called to the mysterious human form, *"Hey, Mister, what are you waiting for? They're all waiting."*

Slowly, he shook his head no in response to her command.

"Come on, toss it to me, I can do this with my eyes closed." Tara's voice took on a teasing quality, as if she was daring someone to walk the same tightrope she had just crossed.

The man shrugged and then attempted to lift the massive black ball in his muscle-bound arms. He looked like a competitor lifting very heavy dumbbells in a weight-lifting competition. His legs wobbled under the extreme weight.

Tara tossed the three balls, rolling them rhythmically in the air. *"Your job is easy: just wait for my signal, then throw it to me,"* she called over to the man.

"Hey, musicians, you forget the drum roll?" The crowd grew silent. The fluorescent spotlights stopped wandering over the walls of the circus tent and beamed solely on her. Beads of sweat drenched her forehead, threatened to roll down her face. She concentrated on the three balls juggling before her eyes. A sideward glance, one more signal, her chin bounced up and down in time to her flipping hands.

She stopped. *"I need to hear some banging on those drums,"* she yelled over her shoulder to the orchestra who looked as if they had been paused with a remote and had decided to watch rather than do their job. *"Don't you guys know what I want? Do I have to do everything myself?"*

"Get this stupid coat off of me. Now!" She dropped the three balls beside her bare feet that were black with filth. Her toes disappeared into the soft dirt. She tugged down on her coat and wiggled to bring her elbow back up through the body.

"Who's sewn my cuffs together?" There appeared to be no opening as Tara continued to struggle with the jacket.

No matter how hard she tried to pull her arms through, the material stuck. Now it wasn't her arms that moved, it was the fabric. As if alive, the material cinched together like a boa, clutching tighter and tighter around her wrists.

Her eyes grew wide. Her hands were stuck down at her sides, strapped in long bandages of cotton fabric. She gulped for air. Now she couldn't exhale. The cloth wound tighter and tighter around her body, squeezing the air from her lungs.

She was trapped. ✦

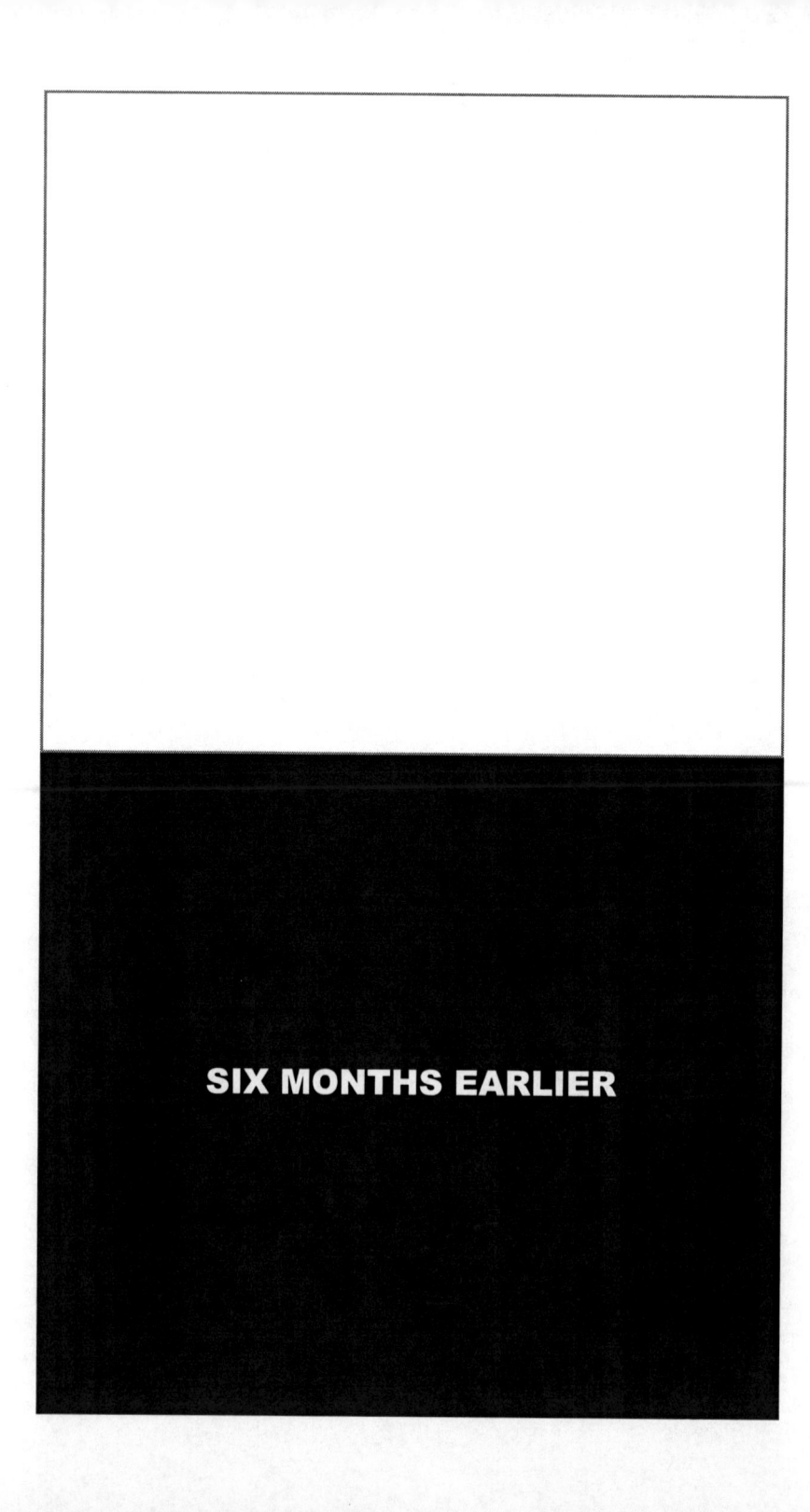

SIX MONTHS EARLIER

Chapter 2

SIX MONTHS EARLIER

When Josh and his sons arrived home that night, he could barely get the back door open. Sets of sneakers, boots, and an overflowing garbage bin obstructed their passage. Josh pushed harder, and some of the bags fell to the floor.

The boys quickly disappeared into other parts of the house. Josh exhaled loudly as he walked to the foyer and set down his briefcase and laptop in their usual spot. He was weary, and he could feel it in every muscle of his body. The confrontation earlier that evening had been one he wished he could remove from his memory forever. His worst nightmare had become reality. How foolish they had been to risk getting caught. Josh grimaced at the humiliation and fear he had felt.

Glancing in the entryway mirror, he grabbed a tissue from the box he found on the floor, moistened it with his tongue, and wiped the lipstick from his cheek. He stopped and glared at his reflection. The mirror told lies, just as the photograph on his office desk had done. Josh attempted to smile at the reflection. The face grinned back, but he found no happiness in the image he saw there. He wondered how he would be able to keep his freshly made promise to emit a genuine smile into the lens of the next camera that took his picture.

Before rounding the corner, he ran his fingers through his hair again and tucked the stray curls around each ear. Could he live without Tara in his life? He felt empty.

It was precisely nine o'clock when Josh collapsed into his chair at the dinner table. He tried to make himself breathe normally. Scanning the table, the white cardboard food cartons on the blue tablecloth reminded him of a sparse marina with white-sailed ships. White paper plates, like barges, anchored the tossed utensils, and the plastic cups bobbed around the three settings. Wishful thinking, he knew, as much as he would like to escape right now.

Noticing his two sons' plates, Josh realized that paying the delivery boy had cost him valuable time in supervising the distribution of their meal. Obviously, the boys had rationed by their hungry stomachs, and the contents were now being gobbled down as if it was their last meal, more like sharks tearing at their prey before they could even smell the blood.

Nathan placed a packet of soy sauce between his lips, licking off the dribble on the side of the plastic. Lifting his square chin high into the air and extending his neck, he looked more like a seal balancing a ball with its nose as he sucked the packet until the plastic shriveled and turned clear.

Across from him, Michael's face scrunched as he watched his brother, two years his elder, displaying the vulgar table manners. "You're disgusting!"

Nathan's face peered over the last of the empty containers. "Waste not, want not." He beamed and then stretched to retrieve his vibrating cell phone. Checking the display, his eyes bulged and his tongue flicked in and out through his pursed lips, mimicking the character in a rerun horror flick they had watched last month called, *The Fly*.

"Who's texting you now?" Michael asked.

"None of your business. Now go be a goodie-goodie and take out the garbage like Daddy told you."

"Slow down a tad," Josh mumbled, grabbing the third empty grease-stained box.

A tongue spat out of Michael's mouth intended for Nathan but was left with no audience. Nathan's head was down, fingers grazing crazily over the keypad.

"Boys, I said take a break!" Josh's hand slammed down onto the table. Both heads simultaneously snapped to attention, fingers froze, and cutlery stopped moving.

"Do we have to go over the rules every time we eat?" Josh sat straighter at the head of the table. He glared out past the empty mate's chair and turned his head from side to side, looking into the eyes of each of his sons. Their matching brown manes swayed as their heads shook, and their eyes lowered.

Michael was the first to look up. His head tilted, and his hazel eyes never left his father's. "Sorry, Dad." His voice squeaked with the early signs of manhood.

"And, Nathan, what about you?"

Nathan had turned seventeen just last week. That would make six years of store-bought birthday cakes. Had it only been seven years since Maggie had spoiled them rotten?

Josh stopped chewing and sniffed the air. The putrid smell of old food and soured milk hit his nostrils as he remembered entering his four bedroom bungalow home earlier that evening and tripping over the spilled contents from the large garbage bin placed at the back door.

Never, in her vocabulary, would they have *ordered out*, nor would her house have looked this disastrous. She wouldn't have heard of it. Only full-course, homemade meals were served at her fancy table. Josh knew the hours she had spent in the kitchen meticulously preparing their food. Yet, the work was always worth the effort, as Josh tried to remember the joy on her face as she served her family.

In his memory, every night at exactly six o'clock, she would announce that everyone was to gather 'round the table as she proudly presented the meal on a platter.

He narrowed his eyes and tried to picture his wife before she became ill. Her face would beam as she anticipating the glorious praise from her hungry family. She was more than beautiful when her arched eyebrows peaked. Her dusk blue eyes darted from face to face as she toyed with the tips of her apron strings. She just sat, waiting for the desired responses, knowing the plates would be scraped clean. Leftovers were unheard of at the Henderson table. Only when she had witnessed their smiles and nods of approval did she dare pick up her fork.

After she became ill, it was no longer Margaret but Josh who loved the looks of anticipation from his kids. He searched and patiently watched everyone's fork glide the fresh morsels into their watering mouths. But it had been years since Josh had baked them a cake.

"Nathan, I was talking to you," Josh said.

"Sorry." Nathan's deep voice was barely audible.

"Now, we need to start again. This time properly." Josh rose and clenched the back of his chair. He watched his boys follow suit. Having spent the last twenty-four years teaching high school students, forty-seven year old Josh Henderson had developed a persistent desire for all things proper—he gave instructions, and others followed. Even growing up, his father had taught him that the lessons of manners and proper etiquette must be rehearsed until right. It would only be then that everyone could begin to eat.

Josh sat down, believing his lesson had been sufficiently rehearsed. The boys followed suit. Again, Josh sniffed the air. Mixed with the deep-fried battered shrimp and putrid garbage, there was another sickening odor. Leaning over to look under the table, he examined each boy's socks. Lifting his head, he turned to both, "When was the last time you guys changed your socks?"

Neither of them made eye contact with their father. Hunched over their dishes, they examined their food as though inspecting which bite should enter their mouths next. Their hands went into fast motion. Their shoulders shrugged and just the syllable hum of, "I dunno," sputtered out of their full mouths.

Josh huffed. Rolling the final chicken ball around the flowered Corelle dinner plate and through the sweet and sour sauce, he listened to the non-stop smacking and crunching around him. It would be so different if Margaret had not become ill, he thought to himself, battling to keep his mind from drifting to the stressful events of the day.

Lost in his reverie, he was not aware that the boys had quietly left the table and the room. He stood and stepped away from the abandoned table. He hadn't heard any requests to be excused. The thought to call them back and rehearse more manners weakened his knees as he sucked in a deep breath of disgust.

Taking most of the litter from the table in one load, Josh walked back through the arches that divided the rooms and into the kitchen to throw it all away. Placing both hands on either side of the sink he could feel the crumbs under his flattened palms. With most of his weight resting on the wood grained countertop, he stretched up and winced as a pain stabbed from his lower back and a knot twisted and ripped deeper between his shoulder blades. He glanced out the window.

Perhaps on most nights, Margaret had *not* been present at the dinner table, and the food wasn't ready for supper. Had there been a time? But he'd always made up for her absence.

Josh returned to the sticky table and sat down, muttering into his cup of tea. "I've always made up for her absence." As anticipated, the drink was warm and comforting.

Boys will be boys, he thought, looking for the children they once were in the young men they were now. The open, L-shaped concept made the living room visible from his chair in the dining room.

Watching them, he could see their bodies slumped side-by-side, long legs stretching forth as they peered over their size ten and twelve feet. They were watching "Hockey Night in Canada" on the blasting, sixty-one inch wide television screen. Four mismatched, thin-threaded gray socks hung like elephant ears over the ends of their toes, and the gaping holes at the heels made Josh wonder why they even bothered wearing anything at all.

Don Cherry screamed one insult after another as to who should have taken the penalty. It would be a great night to watch television, but he knew that would never happen. It had been weeks since he'd had a chance to view anything at all. A cereal commercial broke through Cherry's blaring heated argument.

Instantaneously, Nathan snatched the remote from the cluttered coffee table and hid the black wand behind his back and down under the cushions.

"Give me that." Michael clucked his tongue, pushed his lips together into a lemon-sucking pout. He wrestled the body that had grown twice as strong as him over the past year. "You know the Skating Dance Competitions are on the other channel," he demanded again in that discordant little voice, as he nervously tugged on the front spiked cowlick that refused to fall naturally across his narrow forehead. "You promised me."

Nathan smirked, beady eyes narrowed, and he pushed his shoulders back deeper into the worn green fabric. "Not 'til you say, '*uncle.*'"

"NEV-er!" Michael puffed and grabbed Nathan's *Snowmobile* magazine from the stack of sprawled newspapers on the floor, ripping each page as he flipped.

"Why, you …"

"Enough!" Josh screamed. His command easily rose above the commotion. All action stopped. Michael's shoulders stiffened. Nathan lowered his eyes to the brown speckled Berber carpet.

Josh raised his voice higher to compete with the caterwauling voices on the television. "Nathan, give him the remote as you promised, and go take out the garbage. It was supposed to go yesterday."

"Jeez, you always take his side. What about my magazine? Aren't you going to give him shit, too?"

"Hey, watch your mouth." Josh's chair flew back and hit the floor behind him, as he stood erect. Stomping forward, he spoke through gritted teeth, "You may be too big to put across my knee, but now you're old enough to get out of this house and get a job. Next year, you'll need all the money you can get."

Nathan stood, his six foot height towering over Josh by three inches. He stared into the stern face of a tired old man who'd seen and done enough for one day. Nathan lowered his chin and looked away. "You're right, Dad. I'm sorry." He thrust his hand forward to shake on the pledged bond of forgiveness.

Josh glanced up into his son's bright green eyes. His arms opened wide to the seriousness of his invitation. "Too big for a hug from your ol' man?"

The pressure couldn't have felt better when Nathan vise-gripped him into a great big bear hug. A bone cracked in his back. And just before all the air squeezed from every inch of his body, Josh murmured, "Uncle."

"My turn, my turn." Instead of Michael sounding like his fourteen years of age, his voice pleaded like a little boy wanting to go for another ride on the Ferris wheel. He jumped up and down in front of his brother, flapping his arms like a chicken attempting to fly.

"Hey, what's this?" Josh felt the bulge of a package Nathan had just strategically shoved deep into the front pocket of his dress pants.

Nathan winked. A wave of brown hair tossed across his wide forehead. He pointed with the cleft of his square jaw toward the tussled cushions from the chesterfield.

Again, Nathan's cell rang. The hollow noise sounded much like a mini-jackhammer, and the small device hopped at each vibration. Nearing the end of the coffee table, Michael's hand caught the phone in mid-air just before it crashed down from the ledge.

"Nice snag." Nathan ruffled the top of Michael's head before snatching the cell from his grip.

Michael smirked and tipped his chin.

It wasn't until Josh trudged down the long hallway and shut the door to the fourth bedroom he called his den that he pulled the mint green chiffon scarf out from his front pocket.

He pressed the coolness against his cheek. Whiskers snagged the fabric as he brushed it up and down his face. He slowly inhaled Tara's lingering scent of sweet rose petals and wished he could sustain her fragrance forever in his memory. The softness reminded him of the many smooth places he had explored, places he soon discovered were areas where she especially liked to be touched.

Josh replayed the scene in the secret place of his mind. She had moaned her approval, confirming what she needed. Her voice purred forth exactly where she wanted his hands. Cupping her breast in his hand, her huge nipple hardened as he tweaked it with his thumb. His other hand found the nib throbbing while he rhythmically rubbed. Her hot body writhed beneath him, and his name escaped her lips. The warm, dampened results couldn't fool a blind man. She sped to arousal, and the feelings were mutual.

God, how could a man not be turned on? An involuntary sigh escaped Josh's lips just as the phone shrilled on his desk, rudely interrupting his sensuous thoughts.

After tonight's fiasco, he may have blown his promised shoo-in promotion. Would Alex still recommend him to the Board of Directors? He had never seen Tara move so fast when Alex was at the door. Josh curled the scarf around his fist like a tourniquet wrapping around a wounded hand. He released the air trapped in his lungs.

He had no choice. His decision was made.

"Dad," Michael's voice bellowed forth, interrupting Josh's concentration, "the phone's for you." Michael's voice either took on a note of sarcasm or his voice was cracking. Josh wasn't exactly sure which. "It sounds like Ms. Robstead. She wants to talk with you."

Josh grabbed the black handle from its cradle and held his breath. He was about to speak his mind but stopped and listened for her breathing. He wanted desperately to hear the same deep exchange of air he had experienced earlier that night while holding her shivering, naked body in his arms.

Squeezing his eyes shut, he pressed the receiver harder against the side of his head, while flattening the frontal enlargement of his dress pants with the other.

"Okay. Thanks, Mike." Josh let out a deep breath and yelled, "I'll take it in here. You can hang up now."

"Just wanted to make sure you're okay." Tara's voice sounded as smooth and seductive as always.

"Why wouldn't I be okay?" Josh bit down on his molars. His jaw clicked back and forth with each grind.

The nerve of her to openly call him after they had already discussed everything. Hadn't his reasoning been enough to scare her away? This type of scandal could spread through the hallways like a gas leak, a silent threat that could poison Josh's promotion and possibly even kill Tara's teaching position.

The rumors had finally died down since the day Michael came home from school breathless with the hallway gossip that his father and Ms. Robstead were "having a secret love affair." Josh did not want the gossip stirred up again. It was only a matter of time until Tara would be promoted to Vice Principal. More damaging gossip could spoil her chances, along with the convenience of them working together from the same office.

In a town of five thousand, it would take only seconds for the gossip to spread like flames through dry kindling. Hadn't tonight's scare been enough for her to understand and let him go?

"I just wanted to call and tell you that I understand your perspective.

I know your career is a priority in your life. This new position would double your salary and be advantageous for your boys' future. I'd be doing the same thing if I were in your shoes. The last five years of employment income can increase your pension a thousand dollars a month."

"Listen, I've got to go." Josh cleared his throat and bit his lower lip. "This isn't a good time." He blinked back the tears beginning to form in the corners of his eyes. Just tired, he told himself as he tried to coax his brain to switch gears away from the woman who was on the other end.

"Josh," Tara sniffled, "I just want us to continue with our great working relationship and to let you know I'm okay, too."

"Are you sure you're going to be fine?" Josh's jaw relaxed, and his voice purred concern. The ache had fallen from his heart into his gut. Hadn't he observed her as her supervisor and then again in their intimate relationship? For him to try to deflate her mission was like trying to catch a helium balloon that had just left the hemisphere. He shouldn't have to question her strength.

Tara giggled, but it wasn't her usual chuckle. "You know, I'm just amazed we lasted as long as we did. You have your priorities, and I have mine, and neither one of us has been on the same page. It is time I moved on. So, I won't interfere with your life, and that will make both of us winners, right?"

"You're right, Tara. I'm just glad you can now see my side, and I do wish you well in whatever it is you are moving on with." Josh's eyebrows furrowed. His hand with the scarf wiped across his eyes in an attempt to clear his vision.

"You wouldn't happen to have any ideas about who may have tipped Alex off, would you?" Tara sighed. "We've been so careful."

"What are you talking about?"

"I have gone through a list of people who may have reason to see us apart, but I just can't put my finger on it. Who would bring our private encounter to Alex's attention?"

Josh totally ignored her question. His mind was operating as if it were a scratched CD. "How do you plan to move on with your life?"

"We all have to learn to respect each other's new destinations. You always knew what you wanted. Well, now I have discovered mine."

"What are you talking about?" Josh stood from his office chair and combed his hand through his hair as he paced.

Tara snickered, and then her husky voice rasped, "Josh, you just don't worry about me. I think you've got enough to worry about. Well, not any more. Not with me out of the picture. Good luck."

A dial tone buzzed loudly in Josh's ear before he could continue. *Damn that woman!* he cursed under his breath. He slammed the receiver down and struggled to remove the scarf wound around his clenched fist.

Jerking the bottom left drawer open, he chucked the material down and under a pile of one-inch binders before banging the drawer shut.

The phone rang again.

Josh didn't wait for the second ring.

"Are you going to finish what you started?" His voice yelled into the receiver.

A woman's voice cleared with a cough. "Hello. I'm sorry, I must have the wrong number."

"No!" Josh's eyes widened. His heart thumped double-time in his chest and felt like it may come through his ribcage.

"Don't hang up!" For the second time that evening, he heard her voice. "I'm sorry, Alexandra. It's me, Josh." He struggled to catch a full breath as the words caught in his throat. "You have the right number."

✧ ✧ ✧ ✧ ✧

Michael hung up the phone as his father's command yodeled throughout the house and rattled the windows. Perhaps announcing Ms. Robstead's name as a caller had been a bad idea. He slumped back down on the couch and welcomed the heat of his brother's shoulder resting against his. "Sounds like Dad's in a pissy mood again."

Nathan shrugged his shoulders. "What else is new?" he scoffed as his fingers flew over his cell phone keypad.

"You chatting with Nicky again?" Michael peered over his brother's shoulder.

Instantly, Nathan's fist flew in the air and connected hard against his left upper arm. Michael sucked in and caught his breath while waiting for the sharp stab to shoot from his neck and explode the top of his head off. This pound was a good one, and would certainly add to the collection of bruises lining the sides of both arms and legs. As he lifted his arm to avoid any further damage, he wondered if Nathan had any idea what it felt like to be pelted as if standing naked in a hailstorm.

His brother shot him a glance, warning him that a rebuke would result in nothing but a losing battle. But Michael had no plans to submit his body to any more physical pain. He had learned from an early age not to fight back. It was better to rub it off than to tattle to anyone about *his* problems. He had told on Nathan once and had paid a painful price.

He remembered once trying to discuss Nathan's actions with his father, and that had cost him more anguish than the colorful welt itself. He thought he'd never hear the end of Father yelling at him to stop being such a chicken and to fight back like a man.

What did *he* know about being picked on?

Now, if it were Mother, she would know what to do. She would have held him close, bandaged the scrapes, and kissed the tears away. But it wasn't Mother, and never again would he have tears for anyone but her.

Michael's eyes narrowed as he tried to shake the thoughts of returning to school tomorrow. He had shrugged off being slugged once, but the repeated punching of fists was getting more and more difficult to handle.

The idea of meeting up with The Rockan Gang made his body stiffen. They were a bad bunch lately and getting worse by the day, always interested in Michael's whereabouts. But as long as he was careful, he knew he could avoid their ugly faces and being their next punching bag.

"You going to go tell Daddy again?" Nathan's voice slurred with venom as he watched Michael rubbing his shoulder. Michael didn't respond and, instead, slunk down the hallway.

Michael slammed his bedroom door shut, flopped down on his narrow single bed, and stared at the ceiling. The springs groaned. The navy blue and white comforter sank under his hundred and ten pound weight of pure skin and bones. When would his scrawny body turn into the same hard muscle he had observed his brother develop overnight? Or so it seemed.

His hands crossed and wrapped around the top of his head. He used his forearms as pillows that rested on the *Root*-style cushion. Would his toes ever reach the end of the mattress, or would he remain the shortest guy in the class at a height of five feet, five inches? With each passing second, his heart thumped louder in his ears and vibrated his ribcage. Tears threatened to explode behind his closed eyelids.

If only he had someone to talk to. Danny from across the street had a new group of guys he hung around with. More his height and weight, Michael concluded.

"I hate this," Michael whispered under his breath. "Just stop it."

Dangling his head over the side, he peered into the abyss under his bed. It was too dark to see anything. He ferreted around the dirty socks, shirts, and underwear until his hand contacted the rough towel.

At least it hasn't forgotten where it's supposed to be. He grinned, having to stifle a laugh.

A new flutter began to take over as he listened to the welcoming sound of no one on the other side of the oak door. He pulled the weight across the thick shag carpet until the green and pink terrycloth fabric came into view. Carefully, he hauled the parcel up with both hands and blanketed the bundle over his crossed legs. With one hand on the comforter and the other on the towel, he was ready to throw over the covers should the bedroom doorknob turn.

Staring down, he thought of a time when he was too little to go to the big school, so it must have been his fifth birthday party. Danny, his friend from across the street, had gone home. Nathan took off on his new mountain bike to the playground. And Dad, once again, was nowhere to be seen.

It was time for him and his mom to have their special *together* time.

He would never forget how his mother had fetched yet another present wrapped in decorative blue paper. He had no control of his fingers; they couldn't wait to rip the paper. The sound of her giggles over his excitement bubbled and bounced off of each wall, as echoes of complete joy.

He studied the present that now lay in his lap. "You shouldn't have." Michael heard his own voice cut into the quiet of his bedroom. "You mean I can open this now? Right here?" He untangled the towel to expose the treasure.

Kneading the soft fabric, his cheeks burned, and his eyes widened. "Goodie, goodie, you made me one, too." He wrapped the three-foot long pink wool around his neck. "I'll be just as warm as you." His heart had never felt so light.

As if she were still with him at the present moment, he imagined her thin lips pressed into a lopsided grin. She was nothing like Dad.

Not once would she have screamed for him to hang up the phone, no matter how bad things got.

Father must have hated her, too. He must have screamed at her, too, for her to act the way she did, hiding her own parcel. And later, after consuming the bottle's contents, she had staggered to bed. Was Father that dense, not to have participated in her game of "hide and seek"?

Michael pressed the pink softness up to his face and giggled as he did when he was five years old. Sucking in a fortifying breath, he closed his eyes, pretending that her presence was part of the scarf. Her bright red face, soft brown wavy hair, and bright blue eyes searched past his face. His cheeks sunk further into the softness. Her fragrance of daffodils lingered in his nostrils.

Slowly, he lifted the wool fabric away from his face and stared at the weight still nestled in his lap. The transparent bottle was just like the treasure she hid under Father's throne, right under his nose.

Father had no sense as to where to look. She never would have found the need to tip it all the way back if he had only taken the time.

Had Michael not gone into their bedroom that morning, he would not have been the one to find her. No matter how hard he shook her limp body, she just wouldn't wake up. Honestly, he tried to do everything right that morning, but nothing worked, and everything was futile.

His hands shook as he untangled the towel. Quickly, he unscrewed the cap. With all ten fingers wrapped around the twenty-six ounce vodka bottle, he tipped it up and opened his throat. All it took was five swallows last time. The liquid burned down his throat. One, two, three swallows this time should do the trick. The hammering inside his body began to stop.

Could he not just keep tipping the bottle and feeding his body as it screamed to have more? He was no fool. The chug-a-lug would have to wait until he was sure to be alone in the house. Last thing he needed tonight was to have Nathan cuff him on the side of his head or his father to yell at him some more. He'd save the big buzz for later, after his father had gone back to the school and his brother had gone out to visit one of his girlfriends.

Taking a deep breath, he closed his eyes to really feel the fuzz in his head lighten. Everything disappeared. Girlfriends. Who needs them? Who needs anybody? Michael took one more unplanned swig.

From the corner of his eye, he could see his class picture perched under his bedside lamp. Most of the guys got to stand at the back. Everyone had been arranged in neat little rows according to height, grinning toward the photographer. DEERWOOD ELEMENTARY SCHOOL announced the small chalkboard balancing between their hidden shoes. In the first row, front and center, Danny stood grinning into the camera, and next to him was their teacher. Too bad Dad didn't invite her over any more.

The back of his hand crossed his mouth as his lips smacked together. Michael had always liked Ms. Robstead. She had shown him nothing but kindness, and she always enjoyed listening to his stories. She stopped whatever she was doing when he was ready to share, listened attentively as he spoke, and never yelled at him to shut up.

Probably because she would have had a difficult time getting a word in edgewise when she was seeing him, he thought, lifting the bottle up to the blinding hundred-watt bulb shining from the ceiling. He determined the clear liquid content to be about half full. A replacement of his stash would have to be sought in two days, just enough breathing time to find some more money lying around.

His thoughts went back to his father and Ms. Robstead. They actually thought they could keep their affair a secret? Hadn't the entire town of Deerwood known? Father had made some flimsy excuses that she had come over for them to discuss work, or to go over some of the new classes she was given to teach, or he would just admit it felt great to have a woman's touch in the home that often screamed for help.

When she was around, the furniture had been dusted, toilets scrubbed, and never would the garbage have been left at the door. Frankly, Father would never hear of entertaining any company in the home without the three of them racing in a cleanup spree before the arrival. Systematically, each job was assigned and inspected upon completion. A standard of high expectation was set, but the result was well worth it.

Michael never questioned his father, even when Danny had teased him at school about the possibility of having his teacher as his new mommy. Nathan had strongly questioned the reasoning of a grown man to be gallivanting with a coworker—how was he going to handle the situation if they were ever to break up, or even if the reverse happened and they were ever to get married.

When Michael dwelled on the facts, it was just plain sickening, thinking of his teacher bonking her boss; or worse, his father screwing his teacher.

He had to admit, however, that breathing, speaking, and just plain living seemed easier when Ms. Robstead was around. But lately, for some reason, his father had changed into a man on a warpath, and the house looked more like a war zone.

Dad had removed himself from hanging out in the living room and had set up camp in his den. The cave, Michael would call the fourth bedroom, was now set up with a large desk and computer. Though his father explained that he was marking exams or preparing lessons for the next day, Michael doubted that was all he was doing behind the closed door. It was more like he was hiding, although Michael was not sure from what. Whatever it was, it couldn't be worse than what he was going through on the playground.

"It's a good thing Dad's so blind," he whispered to himself and laughed as his heart literally lightened knowing he was as victorious as his mother had been when playing the game. But as quickly as his heart soared, it fell.

His smile died, and he frowned.

"If Dad wasn't so blind, he'd see Ms. Robstead was cool to have around. At least, *she* could make me laugh."

After recapping the bottle and rewrapping the parcel, he pushed everything back under his bed. The Trident package waved as if in a mirage beside the picture frame. His head remained dizzy. Popping the piece of gum into his mouth, he bounced his body on the mattress. Springs caved down and his body sprang up, creaking in rhythm to every chew. His fists shadowboxed the air.

Standing and bouncing on the mattress, Michael hissed out through his clenched front teeth. His head grew even lighter.

A couple of high undercuts smashed his opponent's jaw. The lamp from his end table smashed onto the floor in several pieces.

Spit thrust from between Michael's taut lips, as he twirled around. "Come on, ugly world." His head turned to his classmates and imagined they were screaming spectators lined up in the stands. Even Ms. Robstead's hands waved him forward, coached him on to do battle. She cheered for him to win, confident he could take on the entire world on his own.

"I'll take you on," Michael screamed. But suddenly, his invisible opponent dropkicked him. His laugh caught and died in his throat. Off the bed Michael fell, crashing onto the floor.

Within seconds, his bedroom door flew open. The images of two silhouettes towered over his lifeless body. The ghost of his dead mother beamed over all three. She laughed at the top of her lungs, and Michael joined her. ✦

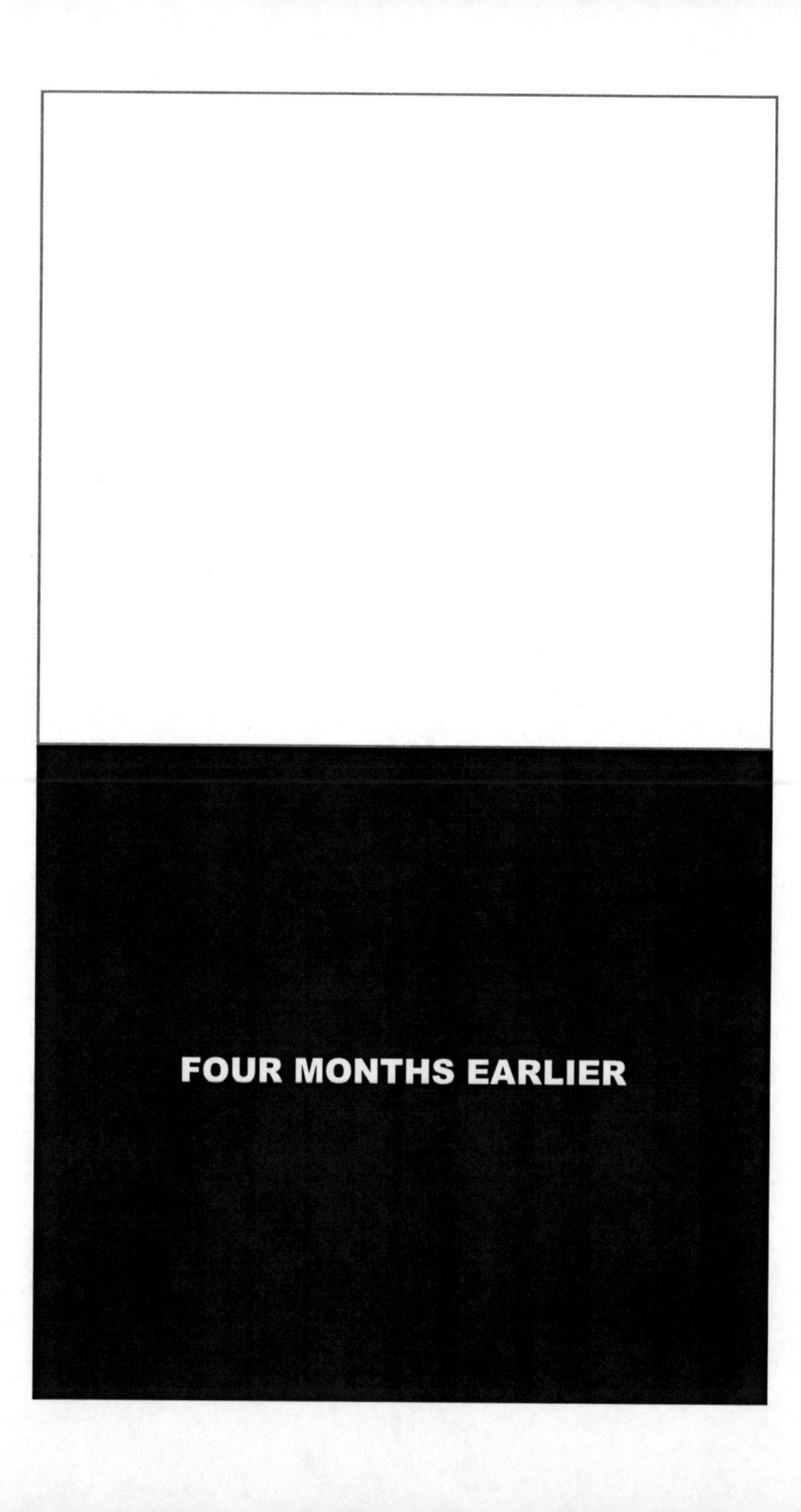

FOUR MONTHS EARLIER

Chapter 3

FOUR MONTHS EARLIER

Two months had passed since Tara and Josh had been caught together in his office. Every time she thought of it, her stomach still churned like she had drunk sour milk.

Tara wrapped her frigid fingers tighter around the hot ceramic cup, willing its warmth to penetrate her flesh and seep deeper into the core of her chilled body. Steam circled up close to her nose in transparent clouds, mixing the aroma of freshly ground coffee beans with *The Hutt's* famous fresh-baked cinnamon buns.

Despite the warmth inside the building, Tara shivered. How could Josh's promotion be more important than their happiness and love for each other? Her deep sigh deflated her lungs. She attempted to breathe, but couldn't.

She still found it difficult to shake the anguish she had felt that fateful night and the look on their boss's face after storming into the office, her eyes flitting from Tara to Josh.

Alex glared at Tara, threatening to fire her on the spot, and then at Josh: "What is it going to be, Joshua?" pointing an accusing finger at Josh's chest while demanding proper protocol in the eyes of the community. With her arms folded in front, foot tapping repetitively on the commercial carpet, she lectured how much she had been doing to guarantee he would be voted as the next Assistant Director. Her mouth nattered as if she was a chipmunk scolding a predator for entering its domain.

Joshua ... Tara had never heard Alex call Josh by his full name. Why now? She had shrugged it off at the time. Now, the question kept emerging from her mind.

Tara's eyes burned with dryness. She set the cup down. Her hands still tingled from the cold. She couldn't shut her mind down from replaying that evening when her worst nightmare became real.

"It's just the way some people handle the grieving process," Tara had heard her best friend console her when she had mentioned this unsettled feeling. She had rehearsed Alex's arrival over and over in her mind and Josh's decision to drop her for his promotion. Her friend had responded as Tara recounted the events, "There's no use dwelling on the past. It's time to move on."

But Tara just couldn't let it go. Her memory went back to that night. Josh had never missed a beat. He answered Alex's question just as he was expected to do—like there was no decision to make, and there was only one answer.

No! Tara had wanted to scream at that moment, but she had caught herself, saving her anger for their heated discussion she knew would take place after Alex had left.

At the time, all Tara could think about was what had happened before Alex's unexpected interruption. Only minutes before, Tara had offered so much of herself in the heat of passion to the man she wanted so badly she could taste it. Not sex. It was pure love.

Never in her life had she relinquished so much and revealed herself so completely in surrendering to the pleasure of her lover. To be totally exposed and to drop all protective boundaries for that wondrous love had been a breathtakingly beautiful dream come true. How could she have let Josh devour her that night, and for what? If she had only known.

Everything, all that Josh had promised, all she had given stopped abruptly, halted by another woman.

Tara slammed her hand down, causing the cup to jump and coffee to slosh over the rim.

For the umpteenth time, she replayed Josh's final words to her after Alex had finally left the school premises: *"It's over, we're through. It's for the best. You need this job just as I need mine."*

His choice and his message were as clear as spring water. Then how come her thoughts were as dark as the black coffee in front of her?

"Mom," Nicole's voice pleaded from the far end of the shop over the three bunches of square tables. She approached her mother's usual corner booth. "Can I have some more money to play another game?"

Tara glanced at the shuffleboard and then reached under the table. Grabbing her purse, she rummaged around the compartment to find just the right amount of change. She shook her head and scooped out a bill.

"Just remember, as soon as you and Steph start to squabble, we're out of here. So don't blow it." Now, if only all her problems could be resolved that easily, without such a high price to pay.

Tara's oldest daughter rolled her big blue eyes and exhaled an audible huff of air just before she snagged her requested loot. "Mom, you say that every time we come here. We're not little anymore."

"Fifteen going on twenty," Tara would vent to her mother whenever they chatted on the telephone about Nicole's newly developed disrespectful behavior. She was the opposite of her sister, two years her junior, who would never have asked for money, and if given any, would have been forever grateful. Nicki, however, consistently swam upstream and complained that it was never enough, incidences were never her fault, and everyone was always against her.

Nicki was not quite a handful but could be. She needed consistent parental monitoring, especially by a single parent trying to teach morals and proper values. Tara knew she would never ask their father to handle that responsibility. Rick had trouble being responsible for himself, let alone his two children.

Tara zipped her purse closed only to find her fingers caught in the zipper. On closer inspection, her nail from the middle finger had ripped and now hung, taunting her teeth to snag and eliminate.

"Damn, cheap purse," Tara cursed under her breath, as she chewed at the numb ends of her fingers.

"You look deep in thought," a cheery voice commented behind her. Kammy Bock gracefully maneuvered her body in front of Tara's booth to figure-eight the table with the dishcloth. With each swipe, her waist-length straight brown hair swayed over her left shoulder and cascaded within inches of the table, even though it had been pinned into a high ponytail. *Why even tie it back?* Tara internally questioned, then shrugged. *Must not be too offensive, never an empty seat in the place.*

"Can I get you something to eat with that coffee, Honey? I promise it'll taste better than what you're feasting on." Her best friend flashed a wide smile and then giggled openly. Using her forearm, she pushed back the stray strands from hanging down into her deep green eyes.

Tara wondered for a moment if Kammy's lashes had grown overnight as her eyes closed and opened, emphasizing the pure white area of her eyes. And how does she get away with grinning so hard without those nasty crow's feet cropping up all over the place? Do ten years and two children morph a woman into being frumpy?

Kammy towered with pencil and pad in hand. Admiring her friend's beauty, Tara noticed that her snug Silver brand jeans rode on her tiny waist, cinched up tight with a black glittered belt. She had chosen to wear a t-shirt with some kind of lettering tucked down under, emphasizing a flat young tummy to go along with her size D-cup breasts. She had a Barbie doll figure and looked fabulous dressed in anything. Just looking at her took Tara's breath away.

"You're too funny." Tara's flat voice spoke nothing of her usual high spirits. She shook her head, "I'll just have the coffee. Not much of an appetite when trying to figure out life these days."

"Well, when you get things figured out, let me know. I could use some answers myself." Kammy tucked the pencil through her hair, exposing a long black gaudy earring, below a row of seven gold hoops.

Ears with jewelry Tara could handle, but facial piercing brought a bad taste to her mouth. *Don't interfere with such beauty.* Tara could remember six years ago, trying to convince her new friend not to get any more piercings. Kammy's father had just died, and her mother decided it was time to travel, leaving Kammy alone and feeling abandoned. Tara enjoyed her new role with Kammy as a pleasant distraction after having left Rick. Soon after their first encounter, what had started out as a mother/daughter relationship changed to a special bond of friendship, more out of necessity for both of them.

"When's your break?" Tara asked while turning to spot her girls, then back up to Kammy.

Kammy scanned over the five heads of customers waiting in a line and past the till toward the tacky open-faced rooster clock on the far wall. "I figure things will die down just after seven." Her head snapped around to the far table as an arm flagged over the nine booths for her attention.

"I can come over after the supper rush." She waved the response, and showed her perfectly straight teeth with a forced smirk.

The fixed tight grin turned back to Tara. Kammy's eyes crossed as she cocked her head to one side. "Hon, looks like you'll be rubbin' my feet tonight."

Tara laughed hard and long, the kind that felt so good. Now her cheeks felt stiff as if she had never lifted the corners of her mouth before. Had it been two months since she had smiled? Sure felt like it.

"I've got to pick the girls up from the rink about nine," Tara answered, flinging her Columbia winter jacket from her shoulders and hanging it on the back of the chair next to her, "but after that, I could sure use some heart to heart."

Lifting her cup for a swallow of coffee, Tara was suddenly stopped by the motion of a coffee pot waving in front of her face. As she extended her hand forward, the cup shook. All remaining contents from the near empty mug splashed up over the edge. She squeezed both her hands even tighter around the cup until all remained still.

"Almost need to put the damn thing down for me to fill it today," Kammy winked knowingly, her finely shaped eyebrows raised higher as she pursed her full glossed lips together to make a straight line. "Looks like we're in for a real treat this evening."

The bells located at the top of the *The Hutt's* entrance door jingled over the radio music. Tara's eyes remained focused on the now full cup of coffee. It was half past four, so there was no need guessing the identity of the customer who had just entered the building.

Marvin Schneider's timing was impeccable. His routine never wavered. She had come to learn that Marvin functioned better on a structured schedule, which was not a surprise since her many challenged fifth grade students needed the same treatment.

A voice sounding much like her own yelled from the shuffleboard table, "Hi, Marvin." Stephanie gave Marvin her best "Queen" wave and a huge genuine smile.

Ignoring everyone and everything, Marvin's face beamed toward the calling voice. His lake-blue eyes twinkled from under the black fake fur hat tucked down over his high forehead. The straps under his double chin quivered as his square jaw hinged from side to side. White frost edged the hat's perimeter, indicating not only the incredibly low temperature outside, but also the distance he had trekked to make it to his place of sanctuary. Without taking off his bulky mismatched black mittens, he snapped his prize possession off his head to reveal speckled grey hair spiked in every direction. No hand smoothed the mess. No need to, for this was Marvin.

"Hello yourself, Stephanie." Marvin smiled, still waving his arm up and down covering the top half of his body. He always smiled from ear to ear.

"The usual, Hon?" Kammy shrilled from behind the counter. Without waiting for a response, she placed a freshly-baked, large chocolate chip cookie and hot milk down in front of his usual chair.

Marvin's bulk was incredible, standing well over six feet tall. Tara watched him attempt to unzip his heavy coat with bound hands. Shaking his head after the third try, he gripped one mitten with his mouth and tore it off. Then using the bare hand that reminded Tara of a catcher's glove, he ripped the other one off.

His face was soaked with a mixture of frost melting down his pitted skin, mucus dripping from both nostrils, and saliva that drooled off his chin in rivulets under the collar of his frayed yellow T-shirt.

Meticulously, he folded his hat and mittens inside the sleeve of his coat that now hung behind his chair.

Tara imagined the work and patience it would take for his mother, at a ripe old age, to care for him, having to harp instructions as if Marvin were a child of four: *better not lose another hat.* And repetitive reminders: *always tuck it in your sleeve, or I'll have to attach the things with strings; wouldn't want to see you get all tangled up.*

"Wipe your chin, Marvin." Kammy flipped a handful of napkins down beside his plate. "You must have really pushed your walk today," she called over her shoulder as she scurried by to serve the next table.

Marvin's eyes crawled up into vacant space. He smiled a toothless grin. "Thank you, Kammy." He crumpled the stack and wiped his entire face as if washing over a bathroom sink.

A minute procedure, Tara noted. And for the next five minutes, she watched him stop and stare into the disheveled white sheets of dampened napkins before snow-plowing the garbage off the table and chucking everything in the bin located right behind him. As if in slow motion, his head lifted, and he called into the air, "I did good today, didn't I, Kammy?"

"You always do good, Honey." She smiled with her lips pressed together while patting the top of his broad shoulders as if he were a dog finishing a magnificent trick. "And you are very welcome." She floated away to yet another customer.

"Well, hi-yo, Taree."

"Hello, Marvin. You made it here," Tara said over the three tables that separated them, "even on this terribly cold day." Smiling into Marvin's face, she sipped at her coffee.

"Yes. Kammy said I did good, Taree. It is very cold today."

"Yes, Marvin, you did good, but now it's my turn to go out and face the cold."

"Where are you going?"

"I have to get my girls to the rink. They skate today."

"Skating is fun. I skate, you know?"

"Do you? That's good." While Tara dressed up to head outside, Marvin's eyes never left her actions. He watched her slip on her navy winter jacket, tug her stocking hat down over her forehead and ears, carefully tuck her thick black bangs up into the wool fabric, and then wrap the body-length scarf up and around her shoulders before donning her matching ski mittens.

Tara's mind drifted to the girls' skating instructor. About four months ago, she had flipped through the *Deerwood Spectator* newspaper and read the article about this new and mysterious man who had moved to Deerwood and became her neighbor.

The writer of the column sounded impressed and honored to have this person as a new addition to the community. He commented that the townsfolk should extend a warm welcome and be appreciative to have a man of such fine caliber professionalism, able and willing to teach their children to figure skate. For the past decade, he had been a dance champion back in the capital city of Regina.

The writer had listed an entire column of credentials and had gone on to reveal such personal information as his single status, his age of twenty-eight, and his personal dream of passing all valuable skills his father had taught him on to the children of the next generation.

He was quoted as saying how thrilled he was to find such a wonderful community where he could continue to work full time and teach what he loved doing the most. The interview had concluded with him expressing his further interests of wanting to join the local fire department and volunteering for several social events. Meeting new people was all part of his agenda.

"Might as well make the young man feel welcome." She could hear Kammy encouraging her to move on with her life and start to see other men. But would Josh change his mind? Would he finally see he would be content with her and that his promotion couldn't bring him the happiness of true love?

In the last two months, however, Josh had made his decision toward his new job quite clear. He had not given her any reason to believe his mind had wavered from his choice.

It was time to move on.

She could be more than hospitable toward this newcomer. Well, she would introduce herself, at least. A tingle of butterflies hit her stomach.

Hadn't Kammy told her that she would someday find a man who was proud to have her at his side? For all these years, it was Josh who had taken advantage of their relationship and was obviously in it just for the sex. What relationship could exist if two people were constantly sneaking around to see each other? Could this man of many talents be the one to replace Josh?

She imagined this new man's strong hand interlocked with hers and visualized him gazing repeatedly into her eyes, both lost in the moment and oblivious to their surroundings …

For a moment, she looks past his shoulder at the locals who stare at them, intensely watching them as the romantic couple. She nods with a huge smile before returning back to his doting attention. They continue to discuss their evening plans for dinner. Yes, an evening drink at the local tavern would be a good idea.

This man would miraculously fulfill her needs, giving her the attention, love, and respect she had always dreamed about. Josh never came close to meeting her expectations. Did he even know what love was? Did she?

The girls had never had a male coach before, a damn good looking one at that. During their last lesson, she had checked him out and physically analyzed him head to toe. He was definitely an interesting addition to this town.

Squeals cut into Tara's thoughts as she blinked and saw both daughters before her, their hands covering their mouths as they stared at her. They were laughing uncontrollably.

Glancing down at herself, Tara realized she must have looked like the abominable snowman. As if in a full body cast, the only thing Tara could move was her eyes. During her deep thoughts, she had wrapped her floor-length scarf around her body as tightly as a cocoon. She looked more like she was heading out to snowmobile for the day than merely taking the brisk walk to her car. With her own two hands, she had tacked herself into a confined predicament she had always avoided like the plague.

"Mom, what are you doing?" Stephanie asked, after she jabbed her sister's side and held her pointer finger to her lips, gesturing silence.

Tara pressed her lips together. The flutter that had been in her stomach shot straight up through her heart and tickled her mind. What started out as a chuckle grew to a giggle and then joined Nicole in uproarious laughter. Only then did Stephanie allow the smirk she had wiped from her face to return. It didn't take long for Marvin to also join in the laughter. From the next table, even Kammy stopped and slapped her thigh with the pad as she flipped her head around.

Tara stood and wobbled around, looking for the world like a penguin. Her arms and legs stiffened and extended wide as if in plaster. Through watery eyes, she saw all of the customers in *The Hutt* turn and beam in her direction. Marvin was laughing so hard he had tears streaming down his face. The exact reaction she was looking for.

"Okay, ladies." Tara tried to stifle the laughter, took in a deep breath, and snorted. Now, as if giving her audience permission, the entire coffee shop of customers broke into laughter.

Tara continued to wobble, eyes widened, and she tipped a half bow around in a semi-circle. She just couldn't stop. It was as if the past two months of seriousness had trapped the freedom to be happy.

There was more to life. And there were more men than Josh Henderson in this town.

"You're making a fool of yourself," Nicole scorned. Her laughter had died, and her solemn face set so rigid it looked as if it may crack.

"Can't a mom laugh?" Tara chuckled.

"Not my mother." Nicole's blue eyes peered down her button nose, her arms folded across her well-defined chest.

Nicole's words and stance pierced through Tara's moment of thrill, stifled what little serenity she scraped from the seriousness of her life. "Now where's this coming from?" Tara's voice lowered with the corners of her mouth.

"Let's just get out of here. Now!" Nicole pushed her chair along the floor and flung it into the table. Scooping her skating bag with one hand, she struggled with her coat with the other. "I don't need this, and I certainly don't need you. In a huff, she exited the building.

Through the window, Tara could see she had already reached the car. Her jacket had whipped open from the wind. She had no hat, scarf, or mittens, but the cold obviously wasn't getting to her.

And again, Tara was left to pick up the pieces.

The mere seconds it took for Nicole to slaughter her with embarrassment was the same length of time it took for Tara's grin to leave her face. The spirit left her as quickly as it had arrived. Why was it permissible for others to have so much fun, but not her?

"Don't listen to her. She's just in one of her moods," Stephanie's smooth voice nurtured forth. She helped her mother untangle the scarf from around the hood of the coat.

"I know, Sweetheart. She's been a little uptight lately. We must not let her mood spoil the fun." Tara placed her mittens back on the table, wishing she could believe the reassuring advice she had just given to her youngest daughter. Retrieving knapsacks, she grabbed Nicole's books she had left. Finally, the table stood naked for their dismissal.

"Bye, Marvin." Stephanie waved in his direction.

"Bye-bye, Taree. Bye-bye Stephanie. And say bye-bye, to Nicolee." Marvin's hand waved. "You have a wonderful day now."

His whole arm continued to flap, never stopping.

"You, too, Marvin." Tara grinned before opening the only exit door. She wondered how long he would continue to wave after they had left.

Winking and waving over at Kammy behind the counter, Tara mouthed, "I'll see you later." All the while, her thoughts had turned and flipped back onto the new skating instructor. She would keep her plans of pursuit as her little secret. Tara spun and floated across the parking lot as she imagined the different ways Devin Tucker could be the answer to all her problems. ✧

NOW

NOW

Perhaps, I don't have the will to fight again.

She re-entered the darkness, feeling more like a mummy ready for her tomb.

In the past, had it not been her passion to prove right and take control of the ammunition that fed the weapon so her opponent would remain in limbo? But had it not been this perspective that brought her to this new place she had heard the nice man call a hospital.

Had she not asked for blankets? Is this not what she wanted? Did she really know? Tara lay immobilized, eyes refusing to open.

She should never have dared to challenge the beliefs and actions of someone so physically strong. Could she not, just for once, comply with someone else and not have to justify the reasoning? No, she just couldn't walk away from defiance. Instead, she had to prove herself right. If only she had not acted against her will, passions, and beliefs. Now she would have to stay here, bound like a mummy.

But I am a fighter. The rush of instant gratification fed the action and gave her the drive she lived for from the past—surviving Rick's harsh verbal attacks had built her to be a strong and independent woman today. The outcome was worth it. Surely, the results would feed her veins and leave her head floating way above her shoulders.

Would she ever crave the chaos again? Wasn't craziness her initial motive to get out of bed every morning? Her heart skipped then took on an extra beat as she recalled her natural abilities: not the need to be the center of attention, but to be the reason for all the action. She loved to stir the pot for nothing.

But she was all of this before *the time* that caused her to now be confined in this stupid hospital. Did she learn nothing from her past relationship with Rick? Again, she had regressed in life's journey, taking her farther back than after she'd left Rick. Now, she could never be herself again. Not with her wrists strapped to the bed and the sheets tucked in until she could scarcely breathe.

There's no comfort in wrapping anyone up. Even my children hated diapers.

Again, Tara argued to herself and then chuckled inside when she thought of her daughters as babies and how they loved to run all over the house totally exposed—free for the pincher claws of the game of "Crab." They hated their bare bottoms being diapered like contents inside a tortilla shell. And when they were newborns in the hospital, the nurses forced their fleeing arms and legs to constrict inside the tightly folded baby blanket. *God, they would get pissed off.*

It had only taken one day to witness their pink skin turn to rosy red and their smooth faces to scrunch up like old leather. She would watch their entire bodies shake violently as the soft cries drastically converted to wails of ear-piercing squeals until she disrobed them.

Terrorized, I say—totally scared to death. She sure showed the staff at Gladstone Central Hospital how to care for infants by freeing their bodies from inside the blankets.

Nothing but happy babies after that.

To be wrapped was confinement; like mother, like daughters.

Tara attempted to lift her hands above the mattress but could only attest to the feel of cold cotton cloths wrapped tightly around her wrists. She was totally immobile and had the inherent desire to cry like a helpless baby.

The need for distractions had become an overwhelming obsession, as with the necessity to keep the voices in her head dormant. Could her will be strong enough to keep them at bay, dormant, a fictitious subconsciousness of the mind? Or would they come alive each time she closed her eyes?

For the first time since being restrained inside the Gladstone Mental Hospital, Tara's eyes fluttered open.

Is anyone around and ready to play? Tara questioned, closed mouthed.

Nothing moved, everything was still.

She listened to the monitors tick like a designated bomb.

She waited patiently for the footsteps, and to see all of the preying vultures come to view her as their specimen. Unable to move her body, her eyes jutted up and down as if searching for a horizon on a rocking ship in the middle of the ocean. The room turned, spinning faster, until her stomach flopped and swished as if she had fallen into a washing machine and the drum was tossing her back and forth.

Suddenly, all sense of direction was lost. With each exchange of air she wheezed, the bile settled. Exhaling, the vomit rose up and gurgled in the base of her throat, the volume of the contents growing each time she breathed. The wall extended. The opening to her throat constricted, closing as her lungs screamed, starving for air. Her windpipe closed, plugged as more vomit fell, piling up on the existing wall.

Tara's dry eyes widened.

She knew the next breath would jar the remnants to fall and build across her throat for total blockage. For a second, she wondered if she had the energy and strength to be sick. Expelling the contents forward could save her, but the natural reflexes of even stretching her tongue wouldn't respond.

Hard soled shoes clunked louder with each step.

Finally, you guys have returned.

"She's choking," Doctor Frances called. His rubber gloved hand guided the cold tube to scratch down her throat. Filtering through the disinfectant smells of the hospital air, a strong odor of soap resided in her olfactory senses, like someone had not quite used enough water to cleanse their hands.

Never had she wanted to know what it would be like to be a choking victim. It had always been a morbid thought, a fear of hers even as a young child.

But here she was, the victim of someone else's madness, awakening after being in a dream-state coma, and then choking to death on her own stomach acids.

I just want to get the hell out. Damn it, I'm not ready to die. I could have chosen to kill myself back in my own bathroom.

Closing her eyes, the wall stopped growing. She sucked in a deep breath of the stale hospital air.

The monitors took on an extra beat. She pictured the metal arm squiggling in exaggerated motions across the page like the motion from the arm of her father's record player after listening to the final song. The papers spat out from the printer, adding to the neatly folded pile on the corked tile.

A door in the stark white wall on the far side of the room opened majestically revealing a camouflaged and insulated entrance door to her room. The air temperature in the room suddenly dropped as it mixed with the pure outside air—a fresh life-filled concoction.

Tara breathed deeply and her nostrils flared as she thought of the doctor's conversation with her visitor.

Don't be telling me I'm here in body but not in mind. I have a brain. Smarter than all of you put together in this stupid place. You can't keep treating me like a caged animal!

The rhythmic strokes of the armed needle branched each line in long swipes covering the entire range, while the heart monitors beeped faster with each raised level of beats.

A commotion stirred at the head of the bed as she heard papers shuffling. She envisioned another set of gloved hands extracting the pile of rubble and examining the results.

"Looks like her conditions are the same as yesterday," another man's deep tone, as smooth as glass, rudely interrupted and overrode Doctor Frances's usual prognoses. This man must be trying kindly to announce his authority to the visitor that had called to pay respects earlier this week.

Great, now we have not one knight but two. Perhaps this is what they meant when they said two heads are better than one.

"Little progress even with higher doses," Mr. Authority belched forth with more force than the administration should give him credit for. Someone an octave above her doc's voice added, "Strange." This man's chords quivered as if astonished, she guessed him to be Doctor Frances's colleague.

Now, what is it they say about three heads? Something about spoiling the stew? There are too many of you guys in here. Get out, I say, get out!

"Her eyes are open. I'll check her pupils." The hum of machines swallowed Mr. Authority's voice. The colleague anxiously extracted the light from his hidden breast pocket and bent forward, clicking the button to produce a light as if he were God himself.

"Tara, can you hear me? Can you speak?"

Before she had a chance to reply, she heard the voice within her head take over. *"We will lead you,"* they called. *"We'll tour you through hell."*

She slid back into the corpse—that damn solidified mummy confined in its tomb. Behind closed lids, she saw blots of vibrant yellow and specks of fire red. The sparkles of colors formed a spray of fireworks, sparking before her, pulsating forward, then receding into the pit of darkness, only to perform again moments later.

Penalty. Too many team members on the ice at the same time. I call the fellow with the least authority to the box. The rest of you will have to play short handed.

Tara's mind drifted to Marvin's smiling face as she thought of how easily he had taken to offered suggestions. Marvin knew when to remain quiet. He was so observant and listened to everything around him.

I want Marvin on my team. The guy with the shaky voice, you're out of here. Haul him off the ice surface before he really screws up.

The colleague leaned his body over Tara, and his warm, sweet peppermint breath feathered her cheek.

Never thought I'd hate the smell of soap and candy.

No light.

Where's that damn bright light? I can't feel his warm hand on my cheek. Nothing! I want to feel his soft touch, like a woman is meant to be touched—slow, soft, and gentle. Nothing quite like the feel of a man's tender touch. Or is it wrong to need a man's touch?

Muscles tightened. She had been so wrong to go after what she wanted. Her body seized into a spasm.

Okay, the decision is mine. I want to die.
You three doctors, go home to your wives and children. Just leave me alone. Wouldn't that make everyone happy?
What dignity do I have left when others are free to fondle and force their own desires upon my lifeless body?
Game's over, boys. Time to go home.

What choice did she have but to remain confined and fondled while being tied down and examined under a microscope? To die should be as simple as to live. Her body settled as a purpose, outlined for her perspective ...

Dying would be easier than living. ✦

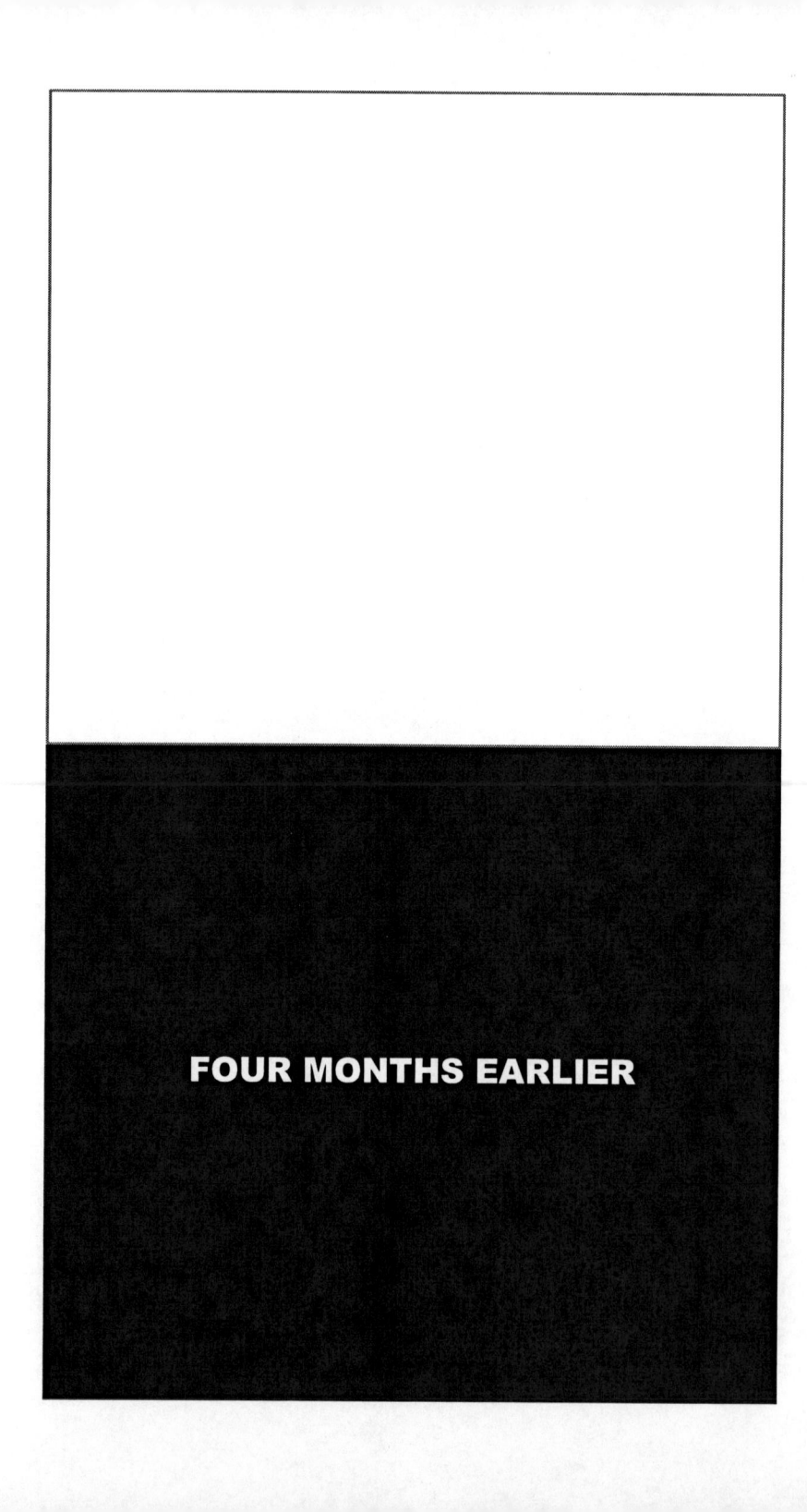

FOUR MONTHS EARLIER

Chapter 4

FOUR MONTHS EARLIER

Devin Tucker slipped his key into the lock, and the knob turned without hesitation. With any luck, he would never have to sneak into his home again. Reminding that bitch to keep the door locked had run its course.

Just thinking of Glenda sent a wave of shivers running up his spine. A cramp pressed into the flank of his groin. He stiffened his forearms to cause clenched fists. Not the kind of body language others would ever witness, especially his students. Not if he had anything to do with it.

The cheap grey linoleum creaked as he tiptoed onto the first set of steps on the split-level landing. Except for the tick of the clock that hung lopsided on the white wall and his own quick breath, the boxed entrance was silent. Alone at last. Not needing to look down, he lowered the steel lunch kit into its place.

Everything has its place, he constantly reminded her. It had been a constant struggle from the time Glenda Schneider had moved in. Finally, he was alone, or so he thought. He had been raised to be right. No unthought-of wrong assumptions. They just never happened, and were not allowed in his vocabulary. His conclusions were based only on the physical evidence. Not a bad motto for a man. Rather observant.

He laughed, careful not to make a sound. The clenched muscles in his fists relaxed, and his jaw clicked open. No sense jumping to conclusions. The need to be rational was essential, just as the need to have a purpose to live.

Can never be too perfect or too careful, his father's words had coached him some ten years ago after he had graduated high school.

Favorable results always worked with careful planning. Again, he laughed silently as he thought of the last woman to overstep her boundaries. Sure taught her a lesson. Getting rid of her had been easy. All it took was organizing the proper sequence of events.

Devin smiled at his own cunning. Had it not been all of his abilities to fine tune that got him the job at the Potash Mine? He now had security and a financially worry-free life, right up to retirement. Life couldn't have been better—perfect, in fact—until she walked into his life.

Bitch! Won't listen. Can't learn. She's just like the others.

Why can't a guy with a decent livelihood find a woman who can support his charming character, appreciate the abundance of attention he is willing to give, and show him the respect he deserves?

Devin scanned the vastness of the main entrance and shrugged. As predicted, princesses never stuck around after their final lesson. What happened to the philosophy, "no pain, no gain"? He lifted his shoulders and whistled a light tune.

Climbing the seven steps up from the main landing, he peered over the empty half wall. Premonition fulfilled. Only dust-bunnies, popcorn kernels, and a tissue mound lay on the Berber carpet where her Chesterfield had been. He grinned, staring at his brown leather chair, the only piece of furniture left in the living room. No more oversized clutter to put up with.

Glenda had insisted the chair would not look good, before she learned her first lesson. He could hear the objectivity in that sneering voice of hers. Such a brave comment to bring forward and present to him, and yet so immature.

Only once in the four months they cohabitated did she dare to voice her opinion, or her lack of interior design expertise, by saying his chair should go out to the dump.

The nerve of that bitch. She couldn't say it was too big and ugly now.

She had caught on quickly that gain came through pain. Only took one backhanded smack to knock her back into place.

Bark, bark, bark, bark.

Devin snapped his head around and steered back down to the main landing. He grabbed the smooth steel knob, ready for Glenda's appearance: *her bloodshot eyes staring into his face, her groveling demeanor as she lowers herself to one knee, and then the series of pleas as her head bows while her shaking hands intertwine above her head.*

Finally, plan of action lesson two: she could repent and own up to her responsibilities.

Yanking the door open to the outside, his breath caught in his throat. A cold gust of snow slapped him hard in the face. He squeezed his eyes together, shuffling back on the landing now wet with melting snow. He grabbed the railing with one hand to sustain his balance on the wet floor. His arm bolted up just in time to shield his face from another gust of the icy wind.

Through his splayed fingers, he stared into the front yard. Naked elm trees waved their empty branches; brown grass lay dormant, as the high wind quickly mixed the white stuff with the mucked leaves.

What's with the sudden change of weather? Didn't the pretty woman announcer on the Weather Channel promise a long autumn continuing into November? Sure, it was usual for the Parkland Region of Central Saskatchewan to be blanketed in snow by the first of November, but he distinctly remembered the chime of her voice and her deepening dimples, as if she should be credited for an extended time of pleasant temperatures. But what did she know? Just another airhead.

Shaking his head, he glanced down into the rusty layer of leaves that was quickly building up from newly fallen snow and then followed the sounds of the terrible commotion Glenda's mutt was making, the animal she cherished and had around twenty-four seven.

A gush of heat traveled up from his inner core and burned his cheeks. Clamping his molars together and squeezing his eyes shut as if to will the visual emptiness away, he stepped back.

Suddenly, he lost his balance.

Devin tripped on more boots and his skate bag left by the doorway. Waves of uncertainty made his head spin. All balance was lost, but not before the dog entangled itself around his legs. One more trip in a tight figure eight around his ankles sent Devin's arms flailing around as if doing a back crawl in the deep end of the pool.

Devin's eyes widened, his mouth made an "O" as a low scream bubbled up from his gut, rose to his throat, and escaped through his open mouth. God, he hated the unexpected terror of total loss of control. A picture flashed before his mind of a drowning victim, activating his instincts to fight for stability. He stretched toward the wooden coat rack, his life raft, but the craft was gone. The room was spinning. Regaining balance was impossible.

Losing control and heading down the stairs was not an option, he resolved. Or was it?

Falling, he crumpled into a ball, but not before his head cracked against the wall. Stair risers stabbed into his spine, and his shoulder felt as though it had been slammed with a baseball bat. His limbs now flailed about as if doing the front crawl in a river, fighting against a strong current. Falling down all eight stairs, he sprawled on the cement floor like a splattered bug on a windshield.

It took a moment until the darkness lifted enough for him to coax his head to lift. He flipped himself over, drew up his knees, and hoisted himself up on all fours by his fists. He begged his body to register anything, but there was nothing. *No physical pain, so nothing to gain.* The mental anguish of surprise had been the worst part.

Crashing on the cement basement floor from that damn dog was not in his plans tonight. That should never have happened. And where the hell were the missing coat rack and the grip entrance mat?

"How dare she take *everything*!"

Detecting a metallic taste in his mouth, he wiped at the warm drool of blood dripping from his bottom lip and then stared at the crimson contents cupped in his palm.

Suddenly, the dog scurried under his belly carriage like a bowling ball of white fur rolling down an alley. Up the steps it fled. Quite a little Shih Tzu, or "little shit" as he liked to call it when Glenda wasn't around.

Devin glared up to where the dog had perched. The dog stared down from the main landing. Its tail wagged, making fun of the whole situation. Being laughed at was not something Devin took lightly.

In a low, slow drawl, "Where's Mommy?" he cajoled.

Shadow thumped the gray-tipped tail like a soldier would manipulate the drumsticks on a snare drum. Black beady eyes peered under long gummy bangs, and its dark snout looked like a wide smile contrasted against its white-furred face. Hoisting itself up on its back haunches, the gray front paws pranced.

The best begging position Devin had seen it do in a while. In fact, up until now, he'd forgotten the damn thing was around.

But it had not always been like that.

That first week, after the dice had been rolled, the mutt had a name and everything. He knew he was out of the starting block when he would pet "her baby," and she had agreed to move in. Advancing around the board was simple. Throwing the odd compliment here and there, he could tell she was pleased. Glenda's head would tilt off-center; she would heave a heavy sigh, gawking as if love struck. And the final roll was so predictable. Just before the finish line, he had enticed her into his bedroom.

Formulated women were so easily pleased. Their sexual encounter was a double thrashing of pure sex. Thank God, she liked it a little rough. He had assured her they would both feel like winners after the game was over. Why, she could barely catch her breath and kept cuddling that mutt as if it was her long lost buddy.

Devin knew she liked it when he had suggested they go back for a replay; she'd said so. He had played the game to perfection. Her face had said it all. She had the whole world: a charismatic man who loved her with all his heart and a mutt that did silly tricks. What more could she want in life? Her leaving was her loss.

Only had to tell her once—get the boundaries set straight before the third lesson had to be enforced. She knew the dog was her package. She was so respectful. Amazing how her listening skills had improved after that first lesson. She proved herself to be such a good sport.

A game was one thing, but competition with a mutt? There was a mutual feeling of hatred between the two. Sure, it growled, but nothing could compare with a few swift kicks when she wasn't around.

See, the mutt was even smarter than she. It knew its place right off the bat. All it took was a few treats to stop its receding lips from curling up when they were all in the same room together. It soon learned, and with total respect.

Now, who's the smart one? A man's sanctuary needs to be respected. The dog has to learn. Enough of being Mr. Nice Guy. Now it was time for the constant battle of forces between the two to be over.

Devin climbed the stairs. The mutt still danced in front of him as if on stage and under the main lights of production.

"Now, that's a good doggie. You stay right there. Where's your Mommy?" The final two stairs seemed steeper than the first eight.

"That's a good girl. You're such a good dog. Begging for a treat, are you? I'll be giving you a *real* treat just as soon as I catch …"

Its tail stopped wagging, its head turned in the opposite direction …

"… you." In the blink of an eye, Devin whisked the air with both arms, then took a nose dive, slamming his face into the Berber carpet with not even a single strand of fur between his clutched fists.

Devin rubbed his nose, nurturing the sting from where the carpet fibers had scraped down his face. Again, both nostrils throbbed. But it wasn't the bloody nose that hurt as he watched the ugly mutt dash down the hallway; the stab of damaged pride was worse.

His heartbeat escalated, pulsing louder inside his ears—a cue to resume with his plan of action. The game he had been taught to win. The trophy he earned as a reward for his victory.

Later, he may have to thank the mutt for setting his priorities in motion. But that wouldn't work; a dead dog can't wag its tail.

It had now dug its own grave, but it would be a hero in the grand finale. What better way to die than for its mistress, and to pay for all wrongs wrought from the four months of existence in this place?

All part of the plan.

Payback time, baby. Not to worry, and so happy to assist in the inevitable destination.

"You have a death wish, do you, Shadow? Come to Daddy, and I'll help you go where you belong." Devin crouched on all fours and peeked under his bed to find nothing. He looked under Glenda's bed. The dog lay plastered against the far wall, frozen, camouflaging itself against its own environment.

"You'll go to a much warmer place than ever before." Devin thought of Glenda's arms around the mutt, how she carried it everywhere like a baby. For the first time that evening, he could feel his face begin to relax, and a grin replaced his pressed lips. The warmth in Glenda's arms would be nothing compared to the hell where he was about to send her mutt.

❖ ❖ ❖ ❖ ❖

Only one more trip back, Glenda Schneider thought to herself as she hoisted the last cardboard box from the hatchback of her SUV Escape.

"Shadow?" She spoke louder, "Shadow? Where are you, girl?" She continued to call out over her shoulder as she scanned the yard in front of her parent's modest two-story home. A cloud of breath charged out from her open lips, and the wind tangled her long, straight mane as it whipped her face. Strands covered her mouth and garbled her speech.

Damn wind. She dropped the cardboard box on the grass, grabbed the handful of hair, twirled it, and then tucked it down deep within her wool jacket so she could resume her mission to get into the house.

Once inside, she set the crate on the floor of the main entrance and bent to unzip her mid-calf black leather boots. For now, she was just thankful she didn't have to come home and do any explaining. Instead, she would resume the role her parents had assigned to her in the first place—house sitter for the jubilant snowbirds. Retirement must be grand. Anything to get out of this hole.

Hadn't she sworn never to return to Deerwood? The place reminded her of a Senior Center. No one was ever in a hurry to go anywhere, and why should they be when they had nowhere to go?

"One of the smallest dots," Glenda remembered telling her out-of-province friend when she flattened the map to show where she had been born and raised.

She had met Rochelle Gardner working the pub on Second Street East located on the perimeter in the city of Regina. "If you ever drive east for about two hours along the Trans Canada to the area known as The Prairie Region and see the Welcome sign and blink, you'll miss it."

The small community consisted of a fire hall, a legion hall, a complex housing both a skating and curling rink, two banks, a Co-op lumber yard with fuel browsers, one grocery store, a post office, three

Chinese restaurants, a privately-owned confectionary store that pumped some no-name fuel, two competing pharmacies, an insurance agency, a three-roomed medical center with a massage parlor connected to a hair salon that sold bathing suits and travel packages, the local tavern located at the base of the old hotel, a tractor dealership that housed enormous combines, sprayers, and other machinery. And there was also *The Hutt* that served coffee, ice cream, and fresh-baked pastries all year round.

In exasperation, Glenda had marveled to Rochelle that she had to travel twenty minutes north on Highway 17 just to hit a clothing store, and it sold only tacky shirts, slacks and, mostly, granny dresses. She guessed the average age they catered to was close to fifty. She had to drive an extra hour and three-quarters from Gladstone into Regina just to find some decent brand-name outfits.

The larger community of Gladstone consisted of all the things Deerwood had, plus a veterinary clinic, a liquor store, a police station and hospital as an amalgamation facility for around a hundred-mile radius.

Glenda and Rochelle had taken the time to scan the map and noted that Deerwood seemed to sit in the middle like the hub of a wheel. The neighboring towns rippled a mere ten miles away and dispersed further onto the next to literally connect hundreds of dots covering the massive area.

Glenda had tried to further explain the expanse of the province by recalling her social studies teacher's lecture on geography. He had told them that the State of Texas could almost fit inside the one province of Saskatchewan. Everything ran in coordinates of due west, east, north, and south, and all the black dots had branched out until a clump had met up with a larger red dot that indicated a city; the largest welt had a star for the capital of Regina, and they counted five other red dots as other minor cities.

At the time, Glenda was not sure of the size of the city where her friend, Rochelle, had come from, so she stretched her tenth grade knowledge to include the fact that forty-six times the population of Regina could fit in New York City. She assumed Regina could be classified as a big town in the eyes of those living in the United States. And so in Glenda's perspective, Deerwood was a tiny shit-hole town.

Glenda reminisced further about her teenage life. On Friday and Saturday nights she would bum rides to one town or another just to get out of her own morgue. But it hadn't taken her long to conclude they were all the same—boring. Each surrounding town mimicked the other towns—a main drag of two paved blocks ending with a stop sign where the drivers cut U-turns to drive back down the same street again.

There was no use pulling off the main drag since the residential areas extended only four puny blocks on either side. There were no traffic lights, like in the big cities.

Instead, if any of the towns reached the milestone population of a thousand, the Mayor insisted on a four-way stop sign to partition the center. The monument itself was enough to warrant handing out the extra balloons on July first to go with the whopping seven-float parade, marking Canada's birthday.

She remembered the first stop sign installed in Deerwood when she had turned seven. And yet, while driving through town this afternoon, she had counted five and concluded that at next summer's celebration, the Mayor would be ecstatic, as this marker looked to be recently installed.

Growing-up, she had listened to her parents boast to their city friends about the joy of raising a family in a small town and how they would never consider living anywhere else in the world. "Everyone knows everyone, and we are always watching out for each other. No roaring traffic around the plentiful fields located on the outskirts of our town. And a single kindergarten to grade twelve school located in the middle of town was filled with wonderful playground equipment so graciously donated by the prosperous Potash Mine."

So, where were her parents today? Glenda questioned in her head as she continued to think of how they would brag about their rich town. How they would give credit to the black topsoil that produced money crops year after year, and the abundance of natural resources just waiting to be hauled out of the ground. Their conversations would end with a relaxed grin on their stupid faces as if they were immersed in a dreamland and had just won a million dollars.

Yet, she had to admit they weren't entirely wrong. Today, while driving from one end of Deerwood to the other in a mere minute and a half, she could see that no one lived in shacks surrounded by run-down yards and sloppy-Joe vehicles. She had known by listening to her father that revenue property never dipped below two hundred thousand dollars in the past year, and she had observed that most of the yards had been manicured to immaculate perfection.

The citizens of Deerwood had more toys than they knew what to do with. It was nothing to see Harleys and motorized golf carts on trailers being pulled behind pull-out, semi-sized motor homes in the summer, and quads and skidoos in the back of their splashy, brand new half-tons in the winter.

But in Glenda's mind, the town had no action to warrant her staying any longer than she had to. So when she tossed the black graduation cap in the air, that afternoon seven years ago, she twirled her gown just knowing her little hatchback would be loaded and ready to leave this God-forsaken place the next day. She vowed never to return.

Boy, had she been wrong! Action was what Glenda sought from the big city of Regina, and trouble was what she had received. Not the kind of thrill she had been looking for. She had been so easily convinced to move back to Deerwood because the situation would be different.

She wasn't living with her parents, so that should have made a big difference. And shacking up with her new acquaintance with his promises of love and attention sure blew that theory right out the window. It had been a big mistake moving back to the place where she swore never to return. How had she been so blind?

Her parents had tried to warn her about her latest fling. A whirlwind passionate love affair, they had called her relationship with the man she thought she loved. She remembered them commenting on Devin's shifty brown eyes, controlled demeanor, and his astute flare for perfection in the fake way.

Yeah, and what did they know, she shrugged off their voiced opinions. Christ, a woman of near twenty-five should be able to make an honest judgment of character. After all, he was a charmer and so wonderfully yummy.

So, here she was, smack dab in the middle of the town where she had been raised, and worse, back into her parent's house she had fled from many years before. Now, she would have to admit defeat.

Again, her parents had been right, and she had been wrong. Wow, would they be happy campers. She could see their nodding heads, crossed arms, foot-tapping in time to her admittance of her total failure as another relationship had backfired.

Perhaps, instead of truth, she could say she had left Devin to become the more responsible daughter they had always dreamed about. Isn't that what they always wanted? She could phone to tell them she had decided to live within the home so she could check to make sure the waterline didn't freeze, the pilot light on the furnace remained ignited, and she would baby their plants so they would stay green and healthy.

What good would the truth do anyway? Isn't life just a submission of constant trials and tribulations, a span of time to learn from one mistake after another? Just like the lively houseplants in the winter—all a fake, really, as compared to the outside frozen ground. Nothing alive, except for the evergreens they had planted in the back yard.

She set the last box down on the kitchen counter and stared out the large back window over the sink. Baby trees, she had repeated her mother's cute phrase for yearlings, no more than a foot tall then. Now, they were towering a good eight feet above the garage roof like a wall of green fabric across the backyard, just like her father had promised. "Mature growth will provide an excellent shelterbelt to protect the house from our strong prairie winds and keep the snow level from reaching its usual height of twelve feet that can accumulate during our winter season," she could hear his lecturing voice drone.

Now, here she was, back in her hometown as her parents' live in—a twenty-five-year-old permanent house sitter, with no cash to pay for her promised responsibility to Marvin. She was alone, irresponsible, and broke again.

Had seven years even passed?

Like a stray dog, it was as if she had dragged herself onto their doorstep once again. Obviously, kicking her out had not served its purpose. But isn't this what her parents wanted: their daughter to come groveling back and admit her mistakes and failures. Admit that she could not live life without their help, and their town was the place she should remain forever?

But she couldn't live here. What if Devin came looking for her? He would know where she had gone, as if she had any choice. He knew where her parents lived, and he would figure it out. He was anything but stupid.

She wondered if he was in his car at this moment, window down, squinting against the sleet, peering around the near-closed dozen stores down Main Street. Pulling up to the only store open past five-thirty and thinking she must be in there. *The Hutt* would give her shelter. He would be fuming while he searched because of *his* lack of finding her.

Or, he would be out on foot, flashlight in hand, combing the bushes and side streets, desperate for her return. His deep concern for her well being—not wanting her to get cold, to be scared, or to feel alone—would soon turn to anger.

Glenda arched her back and stretched. Knowing Devin, he would never react to her escape as she had just imagined. He had not cared then, why would he care now?

More to his *real* character, she imagined him getting home from his usual twelve-hour shift. He would be expecting her to bounce to the door before his beckoning call as if to applaud his grand entrance. And that was just a start. Every night he would tell her his plan.

A little strange, she had thought at first, but acting could be kind of fun. Her only 'A' in high school had been in Drama, and she remembered how much fun it had been to zap out of her own flesh and become someone else completely believable.

The memories of that escapism had washed over her, and she had been convinced that she would enjoy this new role with Devin after all. She could play Wilma and him Fred Flintstone.

But after a while, it got just plain corny. That night, over all the meticulously mapped out, step-by-step expectations of her behavior and actions, she would simply refuse to be his drama queen, and explain how she had grown tired of obliging him and conforming to his hideously designed charade.

It was only yesterday. She had already rehearsed their confrontation a dozen times. She had planned to be upfront with the legitimate reasons for *disobeying his plan of action*. Simple, her acting career was over.

Not.

From that time forward, she knew she was trapped.

Glenda lifted the long-sleeved, wool sweater to reveal a spider web of deep red and purple marks, much the same as the "edgy" tattoo on

Rochelle's back. Except the angry bruising began on the inside of her elbow, wrapped around to her shoulder, and ran down to her wrist.

Life with Devin just wasn't worth the pain. She pinched the turtleneck to ride slightly higher than her chin. She was so thankful that the cold weather gave her the excuse to wear such a piece of clothing, rather than having to apply the tons of cover up she had been used to applying.

It was this morning when she had decided that leaving the psycho was worth more than the ridicule her parents would dish out for her *big* mistake. She had already decided she would have to wait until they returned from their Southern holiday to move forward.

One step at a time, she had heard from somebody, probably her Uncle Josh, another residing citizen of Deerwood who had chosen to remain until *rigor mortis* set in.

Could the Henderson family be so close knit that they couldn't bear leaving the original location where they were born and raised? Was this what the scholars meant when they would comment that roots could grow so deep?

Inseparable, the townsfolk would call the brother and sister team. Glenda's mother used to be very close to Uncle Josh until that day when Glenda found the courage to speak her mind. He had been so obvious in his true feelings toward her brother, Marvin.

And to think that he had lectured about the decency of accepting everyone the way they were. Now, there was a man who never walked the talk. As long as everyone was meeting his expectations, life was grand, and everyone could be part of the happy family.

So Glenda had given him some reasons for disappointments. But was that a plausible reason never to be forgiven? And how could Uncle Josh not accept Marvin? Who couldn't love Marvin?

Glenda shook her thoughts of her uncle from her head. She had other more pertinent problems to worry about. She would have to find another place to live, preferably as far away from Devin as possible.

Or would she be able to leave Deerwood now that things had changed for Marvin?

Marvin would need someone. Perhaps she would have to remain under her parents' roof for the rest of her life. Could life be any worse than venturing out among all the sickos of this world?

"*Where there is one, there are many,*" again, her uncle's voice broke through her thoughts.

After all, wasn't she a lot too old for relying on her mommy and daddy to scare all the boogiemen away? But living with Devin had just proven she was no match for the monster.

"Shadow?" She yelled out the door. It was as if the outside had grown darker before her eyes. The street lamp from across the street did little justice so she flicked the front light on to capture the entire view of the front yard. No ball of bouncing fur or movement over the rustling leaves and whiffs of snow.

Glancing down at her watch, she exhaled loudly. Just past five o'clock. Devin would be home by now. She thought of the final load of items from his duplex: her bed she had purchased with her first check from working the late night shifts at the pub. "The hell with my bed, he can have it."

Her mind momentarily searched for answers. How bad could it be for everyone to live under the same roof? Hell, it would be just like the old times, when everyone was one big happy family. "Yeah, right," the sarcasm frothed from Glenda's lips.

So now, living without Devin's help to pay for Marvin's home care, she would have to go get Marvin and bring him home. *Some changed woman.*

But nothing could change the fact that, at this moment, Glenda knew one thing: being with Devin had been her expensive ticket of living life, a price she wasn't willing to pay anymore.

She wiggled her toes. A shot of instant pain stabbed and coursed through her legs and deep within her thighs. Now, she remembered his fists Charlie-horse deep into the core of her legs. It was like punctuating syllables in each word within a sentence, as each punch spoke of how she was just a bad girl, not worth anything, not good enough.

"Shadow, where are you?" Shutting the front door, her body shook.

Ironically, the 10° F temperature outside seemed warmer than being confined within her parents' dreadfully pale taupe walls.

Following this morning's realization, Glenda had not had much time to think of anything else. She had to pack her things, move them out of his house, and leave before he returned. The negatives for staying with him had begun to outweigh the positives a long time before she had finally found the courage to take the necessary step of moving out. But fear had an amazing hold on her.

Pushing in the doorknob lock, deadbolting, and chaining the front door, she shut the front porch light off. The garage would be a perfect hiding place for her vehicle. Now if she could only find a flashlight.

Traipsing through the vast kitchen to the famous junk drawer, she felt around. *Voilà.* She grabbed the wand and pushed the button forward. A beam of light streamed down low and away from the windows.

She wrapped her coat tighter and headed down the hallway to the thermostat. No way would she keep it down at fifteen if she had to live here. She cranked it up to twenty-two and listened for the hum of the motor to cough up.

After a final check on all the windows and the back door, she walked through the house she knew by heart. Stopping at her brother's room, she examined it with the flashlight. Everything was just the way it had always been before Marvin left.

It had only been a year and a half ago, but the time away was valuable for both him and their parents: a valuable experience of independence for him; and for them, the opportunity to fulfill their dream and travel together for the first time in their lives.

A dream that would be crushed, thanks to her and this new predicament. But what choice did she have? None. She had to leave before it was too late. The signs of his anger were escalating. It was just a matter of time before Devin would have gone too far, exploding and leaving her for dead. So far, blood and bruises had been easy to hide; broken bones and disabled limbs would be more difficult.

Marvin's room was a small but comfortable place to hang out, with his single captain's bed and Gran's quilt draped across the foot.

She entered slowly and glanced at his night table. On top was a rough birdhouse made of pine, a short lamp, and his dinky toys displayed in a circular fashion. His favorite sat in the middle.

She remembered how he would want to share the details of each car. Which one had doors that opened, and his favorite orange sports car that had a trunk that flipped up. How his eyes had shone, taking the wrinkles off his chin. Marvin always had a contagious smile.

Next, she walked into her room.

Mother was so habitual. No use going with the times. Just leave everything the way it was. Glenda recalled how she would scold her mother to get with the present, to quit living in the past. Now, for the first time in her life, she could see her mother's point. Life would be so much easier if time stood still back then. A fantasy thought, but perhaps not totally impossible: to remain a child forever, covered with the comfort and safety of Mommy and Daddy.

Perhaps remaining in the past was impossible, but snubbing out details of the present would not be. For once, it was her turn to have a plan, a no-fail plan. Just to go over the details …

Ring! Ring! Her mother had told her to let all phone messages be answered by the service.

"Shadow," her own voice shrilled in the emptiness. She ran to the kitchen phone hanging on the wall.

"Hello?"

"Hey, you are there." Devin's voice sounded smooth as ice.

Silence.

"Aren't you going to talk to me, Babe?" His voice softened. But it was not the softness of someone who was gentle. More like the sound of a rattler, a snake confident in its ability to strike. The question assaulted her ear like the scent of an unpleasant perfume. Her whole body shook like an earthquake. She went numb.

"No need for you to talk. I do all the talking, remember?"

Though the furnace continued to hum, she felt cold, like the chill of the dreadful winter wind that often settled into her bones after a long winter walk.

"I need you to come home. You belong here. I was as good to you as you were to me. We had a deal. You stay with me, and I keep paying so Marvin can get the proper care at the facility suited for his needs. So, we're going through a rough spot," he continued to ramble, "but all relationships have their ups and downs."

She might as well have been talking to him outside. She bit down on her bottom lip and chewed, teeth rattled into the phone.

"You left Shadow's kennel here, and you know how she loves to go into it when she's nervous. Her cute little body trembles, just like she knows when she's going to get a bath." His malicious laugh gurgled up between his words, and then cackled during a lengthy pause. "As if hiding under the bed works. No fooling us, is there, Babe?"

Glenda lifted the receiver from her pressed ear but suddenly stopped in mid air. *Is that what I think it is ... running water?* She pictured the tub, the drab tub surround, the moist heat rising from the water, and the steam fogging the small room. To think the steamed mirrors had been their romantic way to pass messages of love back and forth.

The receiver clamped back onto her ear. The tub was being filled.

"You missing your baby? No need to worry. She's with me."

Glenda clamped her eyes shut. Her head spun, and she collapsed back against the wall. She stood on rubber legs, feeling as if she were having an out-of-body experience.

Glenda slid down the wall. Every ounce of effort was needed to keep her arm from dropping to her side and letting the receiver fall to the floor. The rest of her body sank like a marionette that was no longer being controlled. Her head fell forward as her neck lost all strength. It was as if her head no longer belonged above her shoulders.

A long, high wail echoed over the rumbling of the water followed by whimpered yelps.

Glenda's heart knocked so fast she couldn't think. No longer cold, she was boiling. Sweat bloomed over her body, and her insides trembled.

"No," she yelled through the receiver. "What do you want from me?"

"It's too late, Baby. I warned you not to fuck with me. You didn't think, again. You never think. Always acting first, then thinking after. Maybe I can't teach you more than I already have."

She could hear the shrill barks of Shadow and the deep rumble of water.

"I knew this crate would come in handy."

Already, Glenda pictured Shadow inside her kennel, scratching and pawing to escape.

"Did you know this crate doesn't float? Works perfect for the mutt, I have to admit, but not worth a damn in water. Never thought of bathing it in this thing, did you? No you wouldn't. Again, you never think."

Tears stung the backs of her eyes. She stifled a sob. "Please, Devin, don't do this. I'm sorry for … for whatever I did wrong."

"See, Glenda, you don't even have the brains to know what you did wrong. I can do better by myself, or perhaps I'll just cast another line. So many ladies would appreciate not only my great charm and good looks, but also my generosity of time and attention."

Glenda's voice escalated as she heard the barking cease. The flow of water stopped. "Oh, my God," she screamed, the wetness on her cheeks ran down and saturated the entire front of her sweater.

His words and knowing Shadow had now been submerged in the full bathtub shot the pain deep into her heart as if she had just been stabbed. "I'm sorry, Shadow. I'm sorry, so sorry."

"You still don't get it. You never knew how good you had it, did you? I would think this is a small price to pay for your stupidity. My lure had been set, and it was all for you, Baby. And this was the thanks I got? It was you who chose not to take the bait. So, now it's you who must pay the price. After all, your life without this mutt will be the sacrificial rescue of your soul. Quite a small price for your repentance, wouldn't you say?"

Shadow barked once. Glenda's ears strained for anything but only got the hollow, annoying signal that the phone connection was dead.

The receiver dropped with a clatter just before Glenda's body crumpled to the floor. ✦

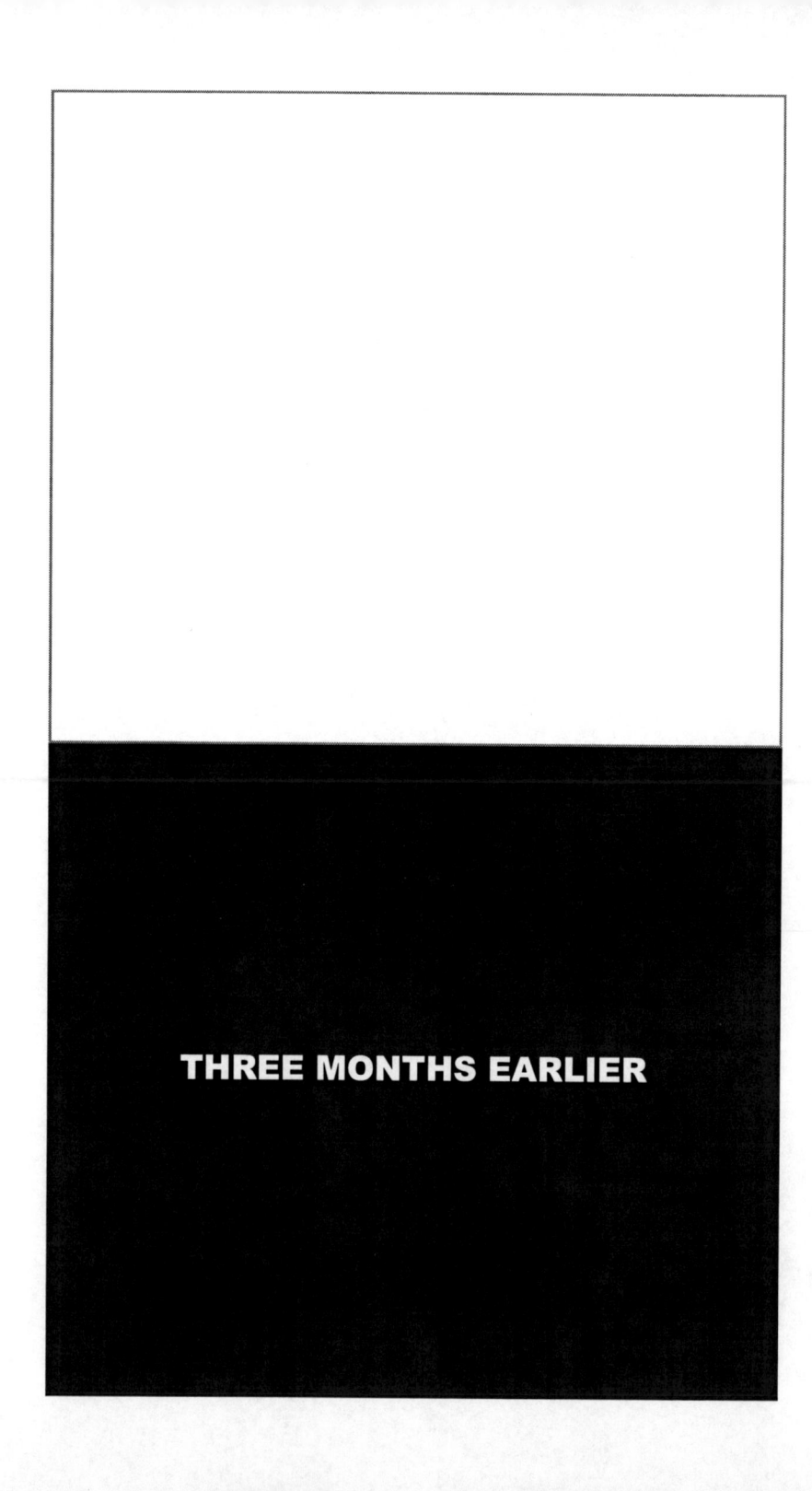

THREE MONTHS EARLIER

Chapter 5

THREE MONTHS EARLIER

It was too quiet for a school hosting three hundred and forty kids. Michael pressed his back against the cool cinderblock wall. His head leaned back. Squeezing his eyes shut, he wished to disappear, simply melt into the crevices of the wall like chewing gum on the bottom of an athletic shoe. But instead, he pictured himself back in his bedroom with the bottle held in the grips of both hands. The vodka burned his throat and lessened the cramps that seemed to gnaw on every muscle.

He opened his eyes. "Never took enough," he whispered as he clenched his fists into tiny balls of fury.

Reaching into his pocket, he extracted the two bundles of twenties he had previously counted. Just enough for a twenty-six ounce bottle and a persistent tip. Michael's heart fluttered as he thought of *his* main man. Finally, someone he could trust.

Now, if only Dad could be more like him.

Again, he peered around the wall, down the dark tunnel hallway to his steel locker. The vacancy of the hallway reminded him of the calm before the storm, or the eye of a tornado his science teacher had taught his class about earlier this year.

He glanced over his shoulder, back toward the main entrance. During the night, someone had hung a banner painted in bold green letters, "Anti-Bullying Day."

He shook his head and resumed his mouse role in a building full of cats. He held his breath as if about to make a twelve foot surface dive. He needed to dart past his father's closed classroom door where Nathan would be trying to stay awake through another one of his boring lectures.

But his legs wouldn't move.

Why his father had assigned him the locker between two classrooms was beyond him.

At least I can't be cornered there. He visualized his locker at the far end of the hall and the three thugs dashing out from behind the bathroom door, taking him by surprise.

He shuddered.

Michael breathed out the air he had been holding. His eyes burned. Planning every second of the day, preparing each move was exhausting. Lately, even sleep seemed unheard of in his vocabulary.

He rubbed the tops of his hard shoulders and winced. If only he could blame the tautness to bulging muscles. He shook his head and sucked in a fortifying breath. His chest rose and puffed out like a full balloon.

Again, he glanced back to the entrance and stared at the sign. Had Nathan been serious when he mentioned Nicole having all her classmates make something in Home Economics as a classroom project for this day?

As Student Council President, Nathan had done quite a bit already to make his final year *fun*—Welcome Week, pep rallies, dress-up spirit days, goofy face painting, shaving heads to raise money for cancer, and now this.

Michael searched his memory for a pre-announcement but found nothing. He hit his head against the wall and clenched his fists down at his side. With his luck, he was probably supposed to wear something to symbolize the event, and now he would be the only one in the school who had forgotten.

Quickly, he dashed out from behind the wall. He reached his locker. Eyes darted over one shoulder, then the other. He dropped his chin.

"Thank you," he whispered under his breath while he cranked open the steel latch. The sound of the screeching metal echoed off each wall, shattering the silence like a clap of thunder on a clear day. His eyes rolled and sweat, beading through the peach-fuzz, nestled above his top lip.

"Home free," his voice bounced back from the inside of his cluttered locker. He grinned and bent down, grabbing the black binder, and tucking it under his arm. Stretching high to reach the top shelf, he snagged the textbook, just as …

Smash! The metal door slammed against him, trapping Michael and his suspended arm against the steel construction of the locker.

A picture flashed for a second, filling his mind:

A guillotine … blade crashes … amputates his arm above the elbow. Opening the locker … dangling worms of veins and arteries … books now saturated in blood …

Excruciating pain shot from his wrist, down his forearm, and throbbed in his right shoulder as his arm disappeared, caught inside as if eaten by a hungry monster. He squeezed his mouth tight, top teeth embedded into his lower lip. The blood pounding through his veins was trapped, and threatened to explode the top of his head off.

"What do you think you're getting, figure skating faggot?" Ben snarled as his eyes blazed like lightning bolts piercing through Michael's own dark brown eyes.

Michael wheezed and swallowed.

"Yo dada goin' a come wunning to da wescue?" Carl added, the spit from his lips spewing into Michael's face causing his eyes to blink back the wash.

Danny, the biggest one of them all, body checked him into the locker, sandwiching his weight, pressing Michael even tighter against the lockers. "What's this?" Danny's hand reached around Michael's head. "Now, ain't this pretty." Lifting his body weight off, he examined the object in his fist, then yanked the pink wool scarf lapped around Michael's neck.

Michael's body twirled like a yoyo. The fabric snaked, burning the tender fibers of his skin. His body morphed into complete numbness.

Michael's eyes darted to the left. A sudden motion from his father's classroom doorway caught his attention … *Nathan*.

Nathan stood hidden. He must be listening to the three knuckleheads' threatening voices. Once again, watching his little brother caught in the trap. But he didn't dare come forward; that only brought big trouble the last time. After that incident, Nathan had lectured Michael about fighting back.

Easy for him to say. And having his father fight Michael's battles had proved futile in the past.

"You a gay boy wearing this pink scarf," Danny boldly stated.

"Pink is only for wimps like you," Ben added.

"You not gonna see smart and stwong men like us wear anything pink like that," Carl continued his mockery.

Michael watched Nathan round the corner, bend at the hips, and hover his lips over the water fountain. He acted as if nothing was out of the ordinary.

All heads lifted. The pent up pressure lessoned as the three backed off. After Nathan had taken a drink, he turned around. There, hanging from around his neck, was a matching scarf, looking identical to the one that remained in Danny's hand.

Michael's heart thumped in his ears. His brother approached. The three thugs glared back at Nathan.

Seconds hung in the air and felt like hours. You could have heard a pin drop.

Danny dropped the scarf at his feet, the scarf his mother had given him just before she died.

"Pick it up!" Nathan ordered, his eyes burning holes through Danny.

Michael glanced at the Rockan Gang, and then back at Nathan. Everything seemed to be moving in slow motion. The entire scenario reminded him of the draw of guns from two cowboys he had watched in a late night western movie. Michael blinked several times. He licked his lips, but the rest of his body refused to move.

"I said, pick the damn scarf up." Nathan's hands fisted. The muscle in his jaw pulsated to the same rhythm as Michael's racing heart.

Ben and Carl took another step back, but not Danny. He remained still, staring back at Nathan.

Nathan turned to walk away, but stopped. He peered over his shoulder. "Go ahead, Michael, pick it up off the floor. Don't want to see Mom's scarf get dirty. If these boys are so insecure and scared to wear whatever they want, I feel sorry for them." He tugged on his own matching scarf around his neck, and flipped the end up over his left shoulder. "After all, it's real men who feel good in their own clothes and don't have to try and skin someone else's."

The bell rang. Michael jumped as if struck.

In fast motion, all the doors to each classroom banged open. Crowds of students pushed out.

Michael's eyes blinked once, then repeatedly. He instinctively rubbed them. His mouth opened wide. He couldn't believe what he was seeing ...

Each and every student had a pink scarf that looked exactly like his. Most had them flung around their necks, but some of the girls had twined them around their pony-tails. Others fastened the neck warmer through their belt loops, and some of the guys had wrapped them around their wrists as sweat bands. All matching: wool, pink, and the exact length as the one laying on the floor inches from Danny's shoe.

A voice boomed forth. For a second, Michael didn't recognize it was his own. "Can I have everyone's attention?" He cleared his throat and tried again. "Attention everyone." Spotting a stool propping a door open, he pulled it out and climbed up on it.

All eyes focused on him.

"Danny boy doesn't feel good enough about himself to wear what he wants."

The crowd sighed and groaned.

"Seems him and his two friends don't want to support us and our mission to stomp out bullying."

Nicole wove herself through the students up to Ben and Carl. From the cardboard box she was hugging, she produced two matching pink scarves and held them before the two Rockan Members. They stood and watched each other as if afraid to make the first move.

"Go ahead." Michael stepped down and marched toward Danny's frozen stance. "Take the scarf and wear it proudly." He bent down to scoop his scarf into his hands so he could press its lingering fragrance from his mother into his face.

As he reached for the scarf, the end of Danny's cowboy boot suddenly smashed into his face. Michael flew back, crashing against the lockers. His nose was like a sieve, blood dripping down and into his mouth. Stars replaced the pitch blackness, and his eyes instantly watered.

Nathan ran to Michael's crumpled form. "I'll get those jerks." He rose, but Michael grabbed his legs. Nathan fell as if he'd been submarine tackled.

Michael crawled to his brother's sprawled out body. "No." He wiped his top lip with the back of his hand, sucking more metallic taste back into his throat. "I need to do this myself."

From the savagely narrow eyes Nathan had worn just seconds ago, his eyes now widened.

Michael stood. The crowd gave Michael room as he staggered toward Danny. Now he stood inches from his face. "Get your fuck'n boot off my scarf." Michael's words spit forth from his clenched teeth.

"Eww, this is a new Mickie boy." Danny tore away from Michael's stare. He searched around the room. The usual chant for a fight did not chorus. There was no fuel to feed the fire. "Come on, everyone, let's hear it: 'Fight! Fight! Fight!'" Danny's voice trailed off in a slow, choppy monotone.

Only silence came from the others.

Mr. Henderson's classroom door opened, and out walked Josh. Nathan held out his arm in front of his father, gesturing for him to stop.

Danny stopped chanting.

Josh's eyes roamed from Michael to Danny and then back to the gathered students who filled the hallway like motionless ants on a log.

The adjacent classroom door opened and out walked Ms. Robstead. She glanced briefly toward Mr. Henderson, and then to the drama that had attracted everyone's attention.

A low drone came from a few students: "Anti-bully. Anti-bully. Anti-bully …" The chants increased in volume as more students joined in: "Anti-bully. Anti-bully. Anti-bully …"

Michael turned, his eyes wandered to his father, and back to Ms. Robstead. Their once tight lips had also formed the word, "Anti-bully." Now the entire student body, including Ms. Robstead and his father, yelled, "Anti-bully. Anti-bully."

Michael kicked the stool closer to Danny and stood on it with his arms held high and wide. He gestured for everyone to stop.

"I just want you to look around." Michael's arm stretched forth and slowly moved across, pointing from one long hallway wall to the other. "See what everyone is wearing? Does what you wear determine who you are?"

A low murmur arose. All heads shook in a "no" gesture. Michael pointed directly at Ben and Carl. Their lowered heads lifted. Everyone turned and stared at the two boys.

"I see we have two new people who have decided to join us to demolish the bullying and make our school a safe place for everyone to be." Ben and Carl stood with a pink scarf over their shoulders, their lips gradually lifted into a half grin.

The crowd cheered.

Michael waited for the hoots and whistles to subside. His voice lowered, and the tears tickled the backs of his eyes. "But what I want everybody to know is that it was my brother who taught me to stand up for myself. It's important to believe in yourself and to feel good about yourself."

His chin dropped, then he lifted his face to the crowd. "The scarf was my mother's. She was a perfect example of someone who tried to stick up for herself, but because she didn't like who she was and someone didn't accept her for the person she was, she didn't get the respect she deserved." Michael found his father's face and glared into his eyes. His heart pounded in his ears, and his fists curled tight. Through clenched teeth, he continued, "She paid a great price in the end." Now the tears fell and mixed with the blood saturating the front of his coat. "But I know she is better off where she is than the other person."

Again, the crowd began to chant, "Anti-bully. Anti-bully. Anti-bully."

Danny stood paralyzed. His head shook from side to side. Quickly, he pushed past the students, down the hallway, and out the exit door of the school.

The entire student body cheered and gathered around Michael. Nathan and two of his friends lifted him high onto their shoulders, bouncing him up and down to the time of the chants. Nicole tossed the original pink scarf up to Michael. He caught it easily with one hand, and smiled. He just couldn't stop grinning. He proudly bow-tied the scarf around his neck, closed his eyes, and silently thanked his mother. ✦

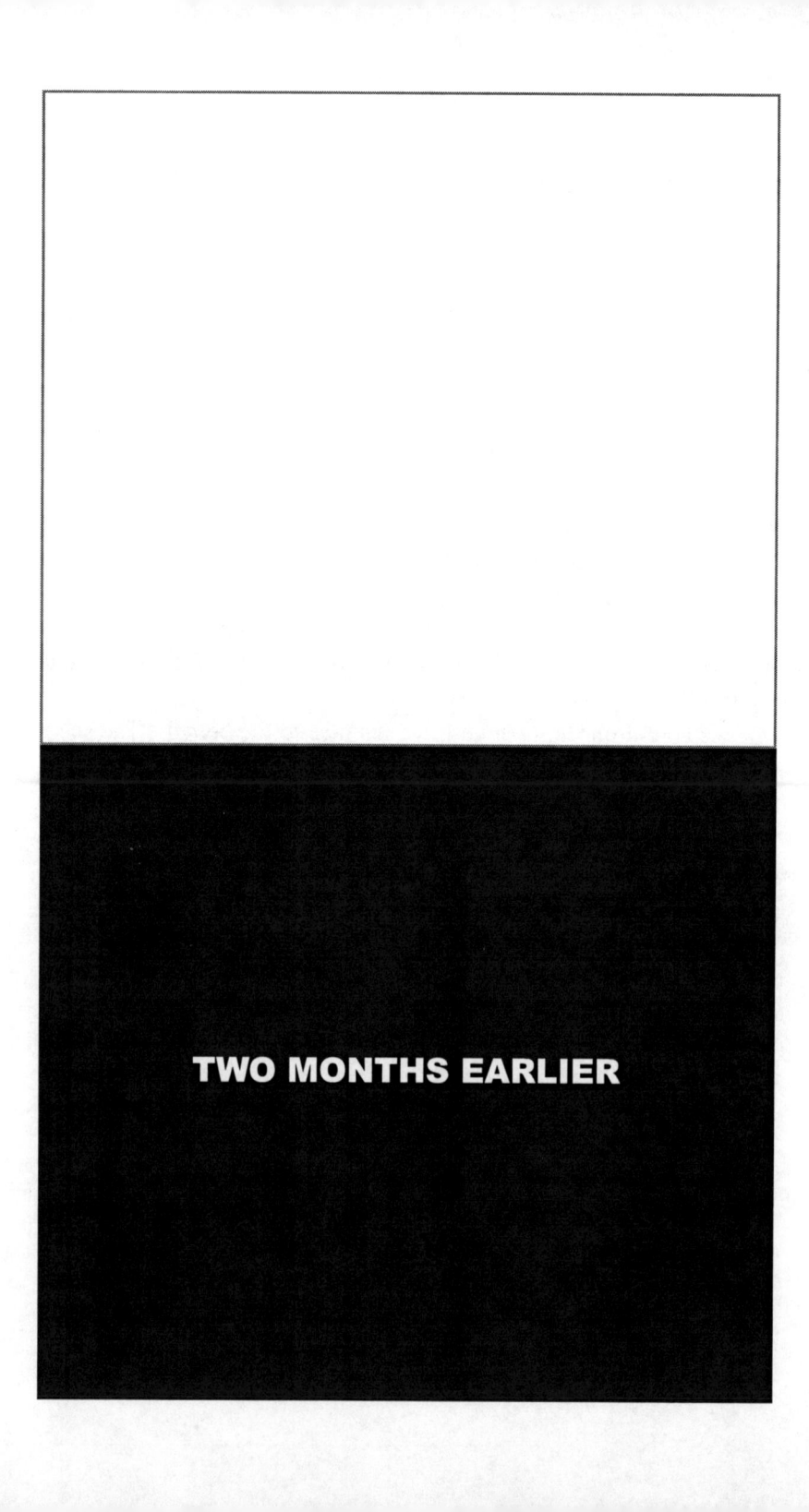

TWO MONTHS EARLIER

Chapter 6

TWO MONTHS EARLIER

Glenda Schneider sat sprawled on the kitchen floor staring into space. She was mesmerized by the hum of the furnace sounding like insects buzzing around her head. The noise reminded her of the nightmare that took place a couple of months back. It felt like yesterday. She fought back the tears that threatened to erupt all over again. That day, as she collapsed in this very same spot, she imagined a swarm of killer bees droning co°nast would dismount after a vault. Snapping the lights on in the kitchen, she tripped on the flashlight, and it spun across the ceramic tile, smashing into the kitchen cupboard toe kick.

Stomping through the empty house, she snapped on all the lights and whipped the curtains wide in each room. Pausing at the top of the stairs, she ran down, passing the humming dryer, until she found what she was looking for.

She stopped at the face of the solid oak glass cabinet and peered in at the uniformly displayed collection of seven guns. A strange vibration quivered up from her legs.

She had no clue what each gun was called or even how to use one, for that matter. But loading, firing, and the purpose of the weapon looked simple enough from what she had watched on cop shows on TV.

Standing on tiptoes, her arms stretched above the oak molding. Her fingers ran along the frame, quickly making contact with the key.

She stared at the assorted guns through the glass and thought of Marvin. She would never forget when they were kids how his face beamed when he had taken her into the basement to show her his secret—the hidden key. She had harshly scolded him never to open the cabinet.

Marvin's smile had dropped, the tears swelled in the corners of his shiny blue eyes as he bawled into his open hands.

"Guns are bad," she had continued to drum, her own eyes wide with the possibility of him not taking her words seriously.

Now, opening the glass door, her hand shook. She reached for the gun with the largest barrel. A shiver slid through her no longer numb body. Lifting the gun from its spot, she sucked in her breath. It was heavier than expected.

Resting one end on the floor, she caressed the shaft of the cold barrel. For the first time in two months, her heart lightened. She enjoyed how the smoothness felt and the feeling of confidence that flowed into her veins.

She pushed the air from her full lungs and swallowed. Closing her eyes, she absorbed the sensation, the tingling, and how her head felt light like a helium balloon. A grin spread slowly on her lips.

So this was what it felt like to feel the power, to be in control.

Devin. Glenda clutched her stomach, feeling his name form a fist and thrust into her gut.

While massaging the cold steel shaft ...

She glared into Devin Tucker's beady brown eyes. Squeezing her eyes shut, she pulled the trigger. An explosive sound blanketed the room. Slowly, she opened her eyes.

"Oops." Her hand cupped over her mouth while she stepped back, dropping the gun at her feet. A gaping hole, the size of her fist, had blasted right through the middle of his body. The once white wall now had smears of crimson streaks and blotches where he had flown back.

"Devin, you make such a mess." She shook her head as if scolding a youngster for having too much fun jumping in mud puddles.

He staggered to his feet and hugged his stomach tight to catch his intestines from swimming out with the bodily fluids. Steam rose into the air. The acrid smell of warm blood permeated the air around him. The deep pool of purple liquid congealed instantly around his shoes.

"Better hold tight. Your guts will soon slither out onto the white cork tile," Glenda said, as if Devin was that careless child who had now spilled his milk.

Directly behind him, the spray of pieces of flesh splattered her wall, the ceiling, and ran down the glass display. Those comforting brown eyes that she had known when they first started dating now looked black and flat like bits of burned skin.

"Why aren't you screaming?" Wasn't he supposed to yell in pain?

Instead, Glenda heard the deafening sound of someone laughing. Devin's look of surprise was enough to know the laughter wasn't coming from his mouth.

"Wait." She scanned the room to affirm that just the two of them were there. "Yes!" She threw her arms over her head and pranced on the spot.

The roar of laughter continued from her mouth.

"Glenee, what's so funny?" Marvin's voice floated down into the basement.

All laughter stopped. Imaginations instantly vanished.

Glancing down, the gun sat cradled in her lap as if she was nursing a baby curled in her arms.

"Just stay where you are," Glenda called up the stairs. She quickly tucked the gun back into its proper compartment, locked the door, and tossed the key up onto the roof of the cabinet. "I'll be right up."

She raced up the steps taking two at a time.

"You have a friend downstairs?" Marvin stood dripping on the mat at the front entrance, his cheeks rosy, his black fake fur hat pulled down nearly covering his eyes. She had no choice but to pull him from Deerwood Care Home and bring him to their parents' house? Without Devin's added income, the funds fell short. But as she suspected, the move was devastating for Marvin. Taking life's turns was no grain of salt for him. It was more like dumping a cereal bowl in his lap.

"Shut the door, Marvin." Her hands rubbed up and down her bare arms. Goose-bumps resided, but the air was not to blame.

"How many times do I have to tell you? When it's this cold outside, the furnace runs constantly. Mom and Dad are going to have a fit when they get their power bill."

"You got a new friend?" Marvin shook off his coat and kicked his boots from each foot. Each one flew off, banging into the oak handrail used to partition the living room.

"No, I don't have a friend downstairs, but I do have someone I want to show you." She thrust deep into her front pocket of her jeans and extracted a crumpled four by six picture and flipped it face down. She couldn't look at his face. His eyes would mock her stupidity of being suckered into his life. How could she be so dumb to trust his lead?

She patted the seat beside her as she slumped on the couch waiting for Marvin to enter.

"You got a picture of your friend?" Marvin practically sat on her knee. He rocked on the nonexistent rocking chair. His eyes, crinkled by his constant grin, never left hers. He looked like he was four years old and about to receive a birthday present.

"Marvin, stop." She clutched his wet thigh and squeezed.

He stopped moving and sat still.

"I've got to show you a picture of a person I never want you to have as a friend. This man is bad."

"Bad boy, bad boy." Again he rocked, but this time, he stared straight ahead. His stern face concentrated on the vacancy before him. Yet, she could tell that he absorbed her words.

"I need you to listen very carefully. His name is Devin Tucker."

"Bad boy, bad boy." Each time he chorused the word "bad," he banged back against the cushion. His rocking increased in momentum with the chant. The entire couch moved.

Glenda sighed. "You remember Shadow?"

"Bad boy, Shadow. Bad boy."

"No. Shadow is not bad. He died, remember?"

Marvin froze and sniffled. "Shadow's gone and never coming home."

Glenda remembered the night she'd first told Marvin about Shadow. He had traced the dog's collar between his thick fingers, and sobbed like a baby. Cradling Marvin in her arms, she had hummed, and patted his back even though she could barely breathe, crushed under his massive weight.

"But I love Shadow," Marvin stated, as if it were the first time he had heard about Shadow's death. He grabbed the tissue Glenda offered and blew his nose. A loud honk with an inhaling snort came from his scrunched face. He turned and hugged Glenda tight.

"I know you love him, Marvin. I loved him, too."

"We going to have a funeral for him, just like we did Goldie?" The drool was now coming off his chin, and he dipped his head forward, rubbing against the wool fabric of her sweater.

Glenda now recalled Goldie, the fish. She had forgotten about the beloved Guppy.

"I'm afraid we can't."

His head cocked up, face serious. "Why not?" A pout formed on his thin chapped lips.

"Because I don't have Shadow to bury."

Marvin's head shook from side to side, faster and faster. He collapsed back onto the brown-striped couch and resumed his rocking back and forth, back and forth, just as if he was sitting in a real rocking chair.

Her voice softened, as soft as she could make it, "I know it's hard to understand." The entire piece of furniture swayed. "I don't get it myself." She placed one arm up and around his shoulders, trying to pressure him to slow his body down.

Her quiet voice suddenly became stern, "I need you to listen to me, Marvin." Finally, his rocking stopped. At the command of her voice, his head turned to hers.

Marvin's look was the same expression he had given her the night she first told him about Shadow. She recalled how she had taken his face in her hands and slowly wiped all the tears still falling from his dusty blue eyes. She had taken another tissue and gently slid it under his nose and across his chin. At that moment, his hands at his side, he had finally closed his damp eyes and waited patiently for her to finish.

She would never forget that evening. After she had finished wiping his face, he opened his eyes and reached for a tissue out of the same box. Taking her face in his hands, he mimicked her actions and slowly wiped the tear from the corner of her matching dusty blue eyes. He grinned so bright he could have lit up the darkest room. Her heart had soared that night, knowing his smile had been saved just for her.

Tears stung the back of her eyes. "Yes, that's right. Shadow's never coming back." Glenda swallowed. Her head grew heavy. "I never want to lose you like I lost Shadow, so I'm going to show you a picture of a man I need you to stay away from."

She flipped the picture over in her lap. She watched Marvin's eyes. Was he paying attention enough to understand and recognize the man who killed Shadow? The same madman who had put her through hell?

"Bad boy, bad boy." His finger stabbed hard against the photo resting on Glenda's thigh. Without looking down, she imagined each stab punching Devin's face.

"Okay, that's enough." She moved her now bruised leg away from his and crumpled Devin's picture into a ball. "Garbage. This man is nothing but garbage. You hear me, Marvin? You must never go near this man." She rose and stomped into the kitchen, opened the cupboard door under the sink, and threw the picture away. "Devin Tucker is bad. A real bad boy," Marvin repeated as he crushed the fabric beside him.

"Okay, that's enough." Her muscles tightened as she stood watching her dear brother chant, rock, and throw side punches into the cushions. She had told him enough to make her point. Soon, there would be nothing left of the couch. She knew from experience that Marvin could be like a pussycat on the inside, but he could react like a lion on the outside.

"Get your stuff back on. We need to get out of here for a while."

Glenda waited for Marvin in the SUV. She squinted down at the face of her tiny watch. The usual five minutes to get ready to leave the house was a fifteen-minute production with Marvin. She shivered in time to the idling vehicle as it sputtered and coughed in the -4° F temperature.

Waiting in the dark, she willed the front door to open and the light to spill over the four-foot snow banks as the bulk of a giant emerged and plunged through the deep snow in her direction. Sidewalks were unheard of in Marvin's perspective. The more obstacles, the better he liked it.

"Where are we going?" Marvin asked. The Ford rocked when the two hundred fifty pound man yanked the door closed. He pushed up his big black raccoon hat with the bulk of his mittens and peered under, studying Glenda's face.

"Just get your belt on." She sounded like a drill sergeant.

He didn't move.

Her voice softened. "We are going to visit our uncle and cousins. It will be fun, trust me." She reached across the gearshift and patted Marvin's leg and then glanced into his happy face. She grinned back, although her heart wasn't smiling. She had been dreading this necessary trip for weeks.

In front of her uncle's home, Glenda threw the SUV into park. Just seeing his house brought back a lot of ugly memories. Her Uncle Josh would never listen to her mother's pleas in her defense.

Glenda recalled the last visit from her uncle. That night, her bags were packed, and she was ready to be shipped off. *Shipped off to market*, she couldn't help thinking. Never had she heard a sister yell at a brother the way her mother scolded Uncle Josh's actions.

"Glenda's only a child," her mother yelled at him. "Yes, I'm ready to hear the truth and accept suggestions, but suspending her the last time didn't do any good. What makes you think sending her away will?"

Glenda could only hear her mother's high pitch, as her uncle's voice was too low and soft. Her mother continued, "All kids experiment. It's just that some get caught and others don't."

There had been further discussion until her mother's voice grew just as soft as his. But Glenda was able to pick up the gist, "Josh, it's not easy raising teenagers. Someday you will have your own to deal with, and then you'll see."

That was the last time she had seen her uncle and her mother in the same room together. And Marvin had been instructed never to go to his uncle's place again.

"Here, let me help you take that off." Glenda took off her black gloves and stretched over her seatbelt to Marvin's head. "I thought I told you to take it all off as soon as we got in the SUV? Now you're going to be soaking wet."

"I can do it myself!" Marvin's voice shouted over his muffled pink scarf.

"Okay, okay." Her arms flew up over her head as if she was a citizen held up at gunpoint in a bank. "I'm just trying to help." She sneered and stared back at Marvin, watching him wrestle with his bulk. "And where'd you get that?" She pointed at his obvious mismatched scarf.

He paused, stationary, for a good minute.

"Nick." He lifted his chin with a smile that could warm an icicle. "Nicki gave it to me."

"Nicki who?"

"Taree's little girl. She wants everyone who is special to wear it."

Special, my ass, Glenda thought to herself. Probably a kid trying to poke fun at him for not knowing any better. Why else would someone pass off a pink neck warmer? She had no idea who Taree was or the actual significance of the scarf, and she knew it would be too many questions for Marvin to answer, even on a good day.

Turning, she shrugged and looked toward Uncle Josh's front door. She had rehearsed a thousand times how she would enter, what she would say, and when would be the best time.

"Now, you stay here. I'm going to talk with Uncle Josh. I will leave the truck running to keep you warm, but don't touch anything. Do you hear me, Marvin?"

Marvin nodded. Again his body rocked as he rehearsed her orders. Stopping, he turned back to her and responded, "I won't touch anything, Glenee. I will do good." Then back to his rocking and chanting.

She shut the door and trekked down the sidewalk that wound its way from the street to the front of the house.

Through the darkness, a light shone above the entrance door and another one over the double detached doorway of the garage. She concentrated with each step. Her arms were held wide as if she were walking along a balance beam while she maneuvered around the deceiving depths of the snowdrifts.

It had been seven years since she had entered her uncle's home and over a year before that since she had even spoken to the man.

In her eyes, he was a highly respectable principal, and she could never measure up to his standards. That day, when she was nearly finished with grade eleven, he had told her he was genuinely concerned and wanted to help. But hadn't he just finished yelling at her out in the hallway and calling her and the gang a bunch of lowlifes?

The day she quit school, she had sat in his office across from his big bald desk and glared at him—his actions, voice, and mannerisms—as he dialed. The thumping in her ears had been so loud she could barely hear the "heart to heart" conversation between him and her mother.

Something about his little niece that had turned wild overnight and being unsure of how far she would go before there was no return. More about his deep distress for her well-being, while noting the rockslide of grades, the several absentee slips, and the record of several observations of her belligerent behavior with the homeroom teacher. And it didn't help for him to find the stash in her locker. A little weed never hurt anybody, she remembered trying to explain to her father that evening while at a collaborate affair. They had arranged for her to be sent to St. Mary's Catholic School, just outside of Regina.

She had thrown her things into a suitcase while her parents stood in the doorway of her bedroom trying to explain the logic in their decision. The words: "zap the devil," "voodoo the devil," and more about "bringing in the angels" had fallen on her shoulders like white crap from a pigeon.

Wouldn't life for them be a hell of a lot easier with her out of the picture? And now, Uncle Josh's words echoed in her head as he had told her parents to *send her away.* Yes, his voice of wisdom: *out of sight and out of mind.*

But here she was, back in body to pay a visit to the uncle who had her shipped away. And bringing Marvin was going to be an even bigger deal—the biggest test of all time.

A year after Uncle Josh had passed sentence on her, she came back for Aunty Margaret's funeral. It had been the last time she had entered this home. Entering his home, she now wondered where her Uncle Josh was hiding among all the roaming black zombies. Was he scared to come out and listen to all she had pent up inside and admit he had been wrong to send her away?

She had been ready to give him a "heart to heart," as he called a conversation between caring individuals. Would it kill him to meet face to face with her in the same room?

Now if Aunty Margaret were still alive, she would set him straight. In fact, she would have told all the people in her house to either smack a smile on their droopy faces or get out. And she would have told her husband to quit hiding and face his own demons.

Aunty Margaret had known what it was like to make a few wrong turns, but she accepted herself as who she was, not what everyone else wanted her to be. It wasn't her that had the problems, it was everyone around her. "Normalcy," she had held up her glass in a toast, "is a setting on the temperature control inside one's home." And she would cackle. But not Uncle Joshua. His face would remain stern. He would never think *that* was funny. Would he be happy now that his wife was out of sight forever?

Glenda plunged through snow up to her knees as the depth increased the closer she got to the house. She paused just before she rang the doorbell, and glanced back to her vehicle. Marvin's body rocked back and forth in the passenger seat. Taking a deep breath, she turned back to the door, stretched, and pushed the buzzer.

Desperate, Glenda had thought to herself as she waited for a response on the other side of the door. She must be desperate to ask Uncle Josh to watch Marvin for her while she went to work at the hospital. But what choice did she have when much of the janitorial work had to be done after hours? With her parents out of town, she knew of nowhere else to turn. Since leaving Devin, her income had been cut in half, so she could no longer afford to keep Marvin at the Deerwood Lodge.

Muffled sounds of running steps from inside hit her ears as she exhaled a deep breath. Remembering the day of Aunty Margaret's funeral, she had watched the two motherless boys squirm on the floral couch between the shoulders of respectable mourners. After receiving permission, they ran from the living room, their expressions showing their relief at having fulfilled the customary duty. But where was their father? Shouldn't he have had his arms around both children, wrapping their hearts in comfort?

She listened to the running footsteps on the other side of the door. Just knowing she would not have to face Uncle Josh in the next few seconds helped a little. Perhaps time was needed for her to drum up her next stage of courage.

Marvin had loved his home at Deerwood Lodge, and the care he received was perfect. But all of it cost money, financing she no longer had … the pay-off was getting just too dangerous. Glenda shivered as she remembered Devin's moods becoming darker and more violent. Having the double income just wasn't worth it. She would find another way for her share in providing the proper care for Marvin. Her parents paid half, but she had insisted on paying for the other half. It just made her feel better.

It was something like a trade-off for being such a handful while growing up. It was the least she could do; at least it felt so in her heart. And finding this job as a custodial worker at the Fairview Central Hospital was just the beginning. With one more job like that one, she would soon be back on her feet. Marvin would be able to go back living in his comfortable home, and she could get out of this shit-hole town. All would just take time, time she didn't seem to have right now.

The door opened. Glenda stared straight across at the brown-haired boy she guessed to be around sixteen years of age as the acne told no lie. He appeared to stand guard behind the open door of her uncle's house, pretending to be brave toward an unannounced visitor, or intruder, as she could fathom his thoughts registering within his thick head. The young man's standoffish expression regarded Glenda with a mixture of fear and uncertainty.

"Well, well, well, a little Marvin." Glenda waved, smiled, but then noted his eyes were brown instead of blue, lacking the spark she was used to seeing. "I'm Glenda, and I have come to see your father. Is he home?"

The boy stepped back and tilted his head. He stared at the guest who had come unannounced to his front doorstep. "He ... he's in the garage, I think. You want me to go get him?"

Glenda responded mostly with her hands, "No, no, I'll just go get him myself. That's okay."

The boy glanced past her shoulders in the direction of the road. His face scrunched as he asked, "Why is your interior light on and your passenger door open?"

Glenda twirled around and gasped, "Oh, my God, now where did he go?" She ran back to her vehicle, glancing over one shoulder then the other. She scanned inside for any sign of his clothing. Thankfully, he had the sense to put everything back on, but where would he go?

"What's the matter? Your dog get out or something?" The boy, fully dressed for a winter carnival, stood gawking inside the vehicle and spoke over her shoulder.

"No!" She shook her head. "Not my dog, my brother."

"I can help you find him." The boy's words rushed out of his mouth. Glenda had no time to argue or explain. She had to find him soon.

Marvin could make great distance with little time, and with this being a new part of town and an unfamiliar neighborhood, he could be just about anywhere by now. He could get lost, scared, and he may even freeze to death. God, why couldn't she just be a little bit more responsible? How difficult could it be to care for a younger brother?

"I will need your help. I'm not familiar with this side of town so I'm not sure where he'd go." Glenda paced in front of the lights of her vehicle, flapping her arms like wings.

"Well, I'll need a little more to go on, like, what does he look like? And what does he like to play with? It sure is cold for a little boy to be running around." He followed her motion.

Glenda stopped in her tracks. She stared evenly into the boy's face that matched Marvin's. "No, you don't understand. He's not a little boy." Using her hands she lifted them as high as she could reach over her head to gesture his size, "He is a huge man," her voice lowered an octave, "but with a little boy's mind."

"Okay, I get it." The boy quickly responded as he took an abrupt turn in the opposite direction and began to plod up the street. "What's his name?" He called back over his shoulder, jogging in a fast pace.

Glenda followed her helper. "Marvin. He goes by the name Marvin." She tried to think of something, anything that may distinguish him from anyone else that may be wandering around town in the dark, in the middle of winter with no place to go. She continued, "He is a huge man, wearing a big black coat, a pink wrap-around neck warmer, and a black silly-looking raccoon hat."

Michael stopped and waited for her to catch-up. "Did you say he would be wearing a pink neck warmer?" His eyes had changed from dull to a shine. She tried to read them, but couldn't.

"Yes, a pink scarf." Glenda huffed. "Where are we going?"

"Kids. Lots of kids. He would be going where he would hear kids playing. I know cause we used to have a dog, and every time he would leave the house and we'd have to search for him, our dog would be where there were a lot of kids. Being a Wednesday night, there's only one place in town where everyone goes to hang out." He gestured for her to follow as he resumed his fast pace for two solid blocks.

Glenda's jog slowed down to a walk. And then she stopped in her tracks. Right in front of her was the last place she wanted to be. She could not go inside the skating rink. He would be there. She could never face Devin Tucker again.

✧ ✧ ✧ ✧ ✧

The chatter of voices and laughter floated down the street. A hockey team was unloading from a chartered bus at the door of the skating rink. A feat that looked effortless, as Michael watched the kids trudge their thirty-pound bag along the snow and ice like they had just picked up their luggage from the plane terminal. This would be the place where Marvin would head, but there was no sign of him anywhere.

"Perhaps he went inside. Come on, let's go in and check out the place," Michael said just before he reached the group of hockey players. Turning, he saw that Marvin's sister's face had gone from crimson red from the nippy wind to snow white. She remained solid in her stance. "You go in and look for him."

"Looks like you've seen a ghost. Are you all right?" Michael asked.

"I'm fine. I'm fine. You just do me this big favor and go in, will you? You have to find Marvin. He'll be scared out of his mind not knowing where he is and all."

Michael whipped off his mitt and felt inside his pocket. The bundle of money remained exactly where he had stuffed it the night before. Perhaps his luck was changing. He could now round up Devin, who had promised him a nice package.

Michael's throat constricted and his lips tightened. It was the first time since this whole venture with this lady that he had even thought about the booze.

Hadn't the fact that he could help this woman find her brother left a much better taste in his mouth? Just as his jaw relaxed, his throat opened to allow a full breath of air to find his much depleted lungs.

Like a flip of a coin. Heads—if he had a chance to be with Devin alone, he would grab the bottle while inside. Tails—if he found Marvin, he would leave the booze and decide it was a sign, he should quit before it's too late. He would hate to get caught … his father would kill him.

Just as his fate was near met three months ago. A good thing he was smart enough to shove the bottle under the bed before he got carried away jumping on the bed and boxing all the bad guys away. He would never forget the look of concern on the faces of his father and brother. How stupid could he be?

"I'll go in for you. Just stay right here, and I'll be right back."

The woman's shoulders instantly dropped as she leaned her body up against the steel framed building to wait.

"Hey, he's nowhere inside." Michael's said as he returned from his trek into the building.

"What are we going to do now?" Her voice escalated.

Michael shifted the strap to the other shoulder. "Follow me. We'll go back to my house and start to make some calls. I know everyone in town."

The woman's eyes glanced down, and her head cranked around Michael's body. "What's with the bag?"

"Just my skates. Let's go," Michael responded, hoping the bottles of vodka didn't clink together, bust, and spill all over.

✧ ✧ ✧ ✧ ✧

Josh held his breath and used his entire weight as a force to push open the heavy garage door. Only after he flicked on the lights and looked around the inside of his domain was he able to push out the contained air from his expanded lungs.

He could have chosen the office, but he had decided that tonight he needed to busy his hands. He wanted to produce something of substance, unlike the distorted fragments of senseless reasoning bouncing in his skull. He would awaken the dormant muse, pull the creativity from hibernation, and produce something that would be conclusive, unlike his many unanswered questions.

Seven years was a long time to sleep. Had he not mourned enough? How much time would be acceptable to snap out of the grieving widower state? Josh wished he could take a community poll just to witness everyone's head nod in affirmation that it was time he lived life the way he wanted, rather than the way everyone expected him to behave.

He thought back to Alex's confrontation. Was it fair for him to

present himself as such a spectacle, stuffing his own happiness aside?
It surely wasn't fair for Tara. He just couldn't get her off his mind. It had been three months since they had officially called things off between them. A good move, he remembered thinking soon after they had separated. He had also thought the pangs of loneliness were sure to subside and leave completely as time went by. But no, it seemed the more time he spent apart from her, the more he had to admit to himself that he really missed her.

He glanced around his shop. The inside of the double heated garage was just as he remembered. A perfect place of refuge to bask in the joys of shaping rough oak into a finished product using his own collected tools and his own two hands.

Five feet off the cement floor, tattered boxes splashed the north wall. From the northeast corner, bikes hung upside down from the ceiling. Dark mahogany kitchen cabinets he had rescued from the dump twenty years before framed the other corner and ran down along the south wall. With his truck parked outside on the driveway, there was enough room for him to pull all his saws out from under the blankets.

Like hockey cards to a boy, an excessive amount of hand tools lined the peg wall in front of him. Margaret had accused that his expensive collection of tools and his enjoyment of woodworking robbed the family of precious time spent together. He remembered he had argued back that his time in the garage was his deserved time out away from chaos. It did not mean that he didn't enjoy playing with his boys and conversing with his wife.

He stood in his working triangle. His table saws and jigsaws were his working collection of tools. They lined around him while a portable heater, glowing red with emitted heat, hummed next to his working area. A fifteen-by-eight-foot table sat atop his heavy-duty sawhorses he had designed to hold the majority of the weight. All of which he had pulled from the adjacent wall to sit foremost and center in his domain. It was a woodworker's palace.

Heading to the far end, he lowered himself onto an upside-down five-gallon plastic pail and continued to ponder his dilemma: how was he going to hoist this cumbersome sheet through his table saw? Not wanting to interrupt his precious time and nurtured isolation, he wasn't about to call upon one of his sons from the house. He rose to search for another board he could use. He rummaged though a pile of scrap lumber.

Unlike the large board that could be cut into many pieces, Josh could not cut his life into any more pieces. Tara had no logic to her ideas. Between work and being a full-time father, there just didn't seem to be anything left. No time even for himself ... until now. With her out of the picture and his boys busy with their own lives, he could come to his garage and work. The idea had seemed so logical. Time for his own hobbies would be good for him. It would allow him time to sort some of the chaos that seemed to be bouncing within his head.

He found a larger chunk of wood and enjoyed the zing and smell of burning wood as it moved through the saw. Most of the cuts had been completed from his small sheet of rough plywood and two-by-four studs. The pieces were neatly propped up against the only bare wall. One more piece was necessary to begin the project. But again, there was the dilemma of how he would hoist such a large piece up and through his saw.

Couldn't Tara see how confusing their relationship would be on the children, how their intimacy would raise community speculation and hinder his chance at promotion? He had worked tremendously hard to climb the ladder and be at the top of his wage scale. What was so wrong with having their little secret and keeping things just the way they were? He had even tried to reason how her job could be jeopardized if they had continued their affair and been caught.

Yet, she had sounded like she didn't care. That evening phone call after their abrupt interruption from Alex, all Tara could think about was to find blame as to who would have called Alexandra to interrupt their time together, or more, their intimate passion that had never been so good. Could she not see it was just a matter of time before they got caught?

Josh stopped his fishing for a board and brought forth a long slender stud that he knew would add to his project at a later time.

It did seem way too coincidental for Alexandra to show up after school hours instead of her usual communication by phone.

But Tara had to realize the decision was necessary. He had to choose his job over her. Could she not see how his ultimate goal in life was so important to him? To complete his teaching years as Assistant Director and to capitalize on the full-pension benefits was a smart way to think.

He needed to be able to provide for his kids and their secondary education. Who has time for love anyway? Josh first pictured Tara pleading her stand, and then his mind drifted back to his wife. Margaret, sitting across the kitchen table with the drunken stupor expression to which he had grown accustomed, had pleaded for more—more time with him, more attention for their children, and more love. But how could he give more when he had given everything he had?

The second twelve-by-twelve thin rough plywood sheet balanced on the floor against the wall. The sheet was so tall it practically touched the ceiling. Thoughts of fetching Nat or Mike from the house would solve his problem.

The steel insulated door banged open.

Josh sprang to his feet. He would have preferred to flee rather than fight, but there was only one way out of the garage, and the intruder now blocked the entire door.

There before him was a Sasquatch of a man. "What do you want from me?" Josh's words flew out of his mouth.

Marvin's bulky mitt grabbed hold of his raccoon hat and swiped it easily off his head. A smile grew on his face. This man looked around, his shoulders hunched to his ears as he looked to be sucking the remnants of sawdust lingering in the air.

"You Uncle Josh?"

Taking a step toward the stranger, Josh saw the shadows clear. Within his view, was a face he had not seen in over seven years shining back into his own. Memories of this man being the last one who actually worked in his private space became clear—the times when he would take Marvin out to his garage and, together, they would build birdhouses. Marvin would take such pride doing each stage. The process had been just as much fun as the product. Had the destination of life somehow overshadowed the journey?

"Marvin, is that you?" Josh asked, as he stepped closer and watched the man's arms extend wide. In the next sheer moment, Marvin grabbed him, his body wrapped tightly, hugged until breathless.

Marvin released his hold and gently set him back down on the cement floor. His coat was off in a matter of seconds. He already found a hammer. Peering inside the cigarette tin filled with nuts and bolts and stationed on the window frame, he shook it. "Where's a nail?"

Josh shook his head as the miracle of answered prayer stood before him. "I need you, Marvin. You want to give me a hand with this board?" He turned to the lumber and heard the hammer drop with the container. Marvin's feet clomped behind him.

No further words needed to be exchanged. It was as if he had never left his side. Marvin hoisted the huge plywood over his head like it was a large sheet of writing paper and set it down at the exact angle for the blade on the table saw. Tara's face flashed momentarily through Josh's mind as the zing of the saw finished the final cut. It was as if everything made sense.

As Marvin helped hold two sticks of two-by-fours together, Josh's heart ached. It was like something fragile had now broken inside, and the pieces were like glass lodged in his gut. Memories of when he had cut ties with the family came into focus.

He remembered when Alex had warned him of the necessity to live by her standards. She advised that his wife's death would pay him greater respect from the community as long as he cut out the baggage, kept his nose clean, and had all his ducks lined in a row.

Josh thought of how he had chosen to protect his reputation over Tara. And then there was Glenda. He had made such rash comments to his sister about a quick fix to her problem with a crazy teen. He had so readily agreed to cut family ties as a reason for neglecting Marvin, who had become attached to his hip. Had Alex led him astray? Had he allowed his own professional goals to get in the way of everything important in his life? He had to admit it was true. Now, he had taken on the role of a stern principal just to gain standing for his purpose of gaining authority. Had he really agreed to give up on his priorities in life to gain the respect of Alexandra Conway?

Shame sliced Josh from the inside.

✧ ✧ ✧ ✧ ✧

Uncle Josh's house looked as intimidating as the first time Glenda had approached it earlier that evening. She had barely been able to keep up with this boy she had already figured must be Michael. From what she could recall from the kids' pictures cropped inside the Christmas cards they had received every year, this boy wasn't Nathan. If anything like herself, Michael's geeky looks would turn from an ugly duckling to a swan in no time. She remembered that stage of awkwardness and how she had never been asked out once all through high school, and then, boom, single life was filled with one guy after another. Making up for lost time, she had told herself.

"In there." Michael stood panting, pointing below the light to the single insulated door on the garage. His voice dropped down to barely an audible decibel. "I hear voices in there." He turned and opened the back door of a gigantic truck and discarded his skate bag.

Glenda fought for air while waiting for him to return to her side. "Well, what are you waiting for?" Michael asked.

"You go in. It's your garage and your dad, so you go in." Glenda lowered her voice, hoping it would work for him to make the first move.

Michael's face turned back to the door, but he made no motion to open it.

Brushing by him, Glenda cut in front. "Ah, step aside. What are you scared of?" She turned the knob and body slammed the door open.

The bright light from inside the building was enough to blind a person. It took Glenda three or four strong blinks to adjust.

"Marvin! You know better …"

"Hi, Glenee, look what I made you?" Marvin held up framing of an unfinished birdhouse and then swung it inches from her nose. "I did good, didn't I, Glenee?"

Her hand brushed aside the frame. She stepped to the side. She would acknowledge Marvin's achievements in a moment, but right now, she just had to see the man who had told her she wasn't good enough and had split her family apart. She first had to tell this man what she had been feeling all these years. She would listen to him forgive her, and then she could ask him to help her with Marvin.

"Dad, I'm sorry for bothering you," Michael's voice squeaked from behind. He looked as if he was hiding from the boogieman.

Josh Henderson emerged from behind a sheet of plywood. He looked a lot smaller than she remembered, and his grin and brown twinkling eyes were unrecognizable. "Son, it's okay. You did good."

"See, everyone is good," Marvin said. He bent down and shook the young man's hand. "My name is Marvin. You want to go inside and play dinky toys?"

For the first time since she had met her cousin, his mouth drew up on the corners and a smile covered his face.

Glancing from Marvin to Michael, if it hadn't been for the size their seven year age difference made and the color of their eyes, they could have been mistaken for twins.

"Yeah, I'd like that." Michael took Marvin's coat from the hook and held it out. Quickly, the door closed behind them.

Glenda sucked in a huge gulp of air. All previous thoughts about her reasons for making contact with her uncle vanished. Instead, she was ready to pelt Uncle Josh with everything she had, a tongue-lashing she had been saving for seven years. He was going to hear everything she had in her heart and on her mind, whether he wanted to hear it or not. ✦

NOW

Chapter 7

NOW

Gladstone Central Hospital
Mental Health Division
Gladstone, Saskatchewan

*W*hy *do they have to cinch these straps so tight?* Tara lengthened her fingers, then squeezed them into a ball. *Lift, I tell you. Move.* She attempted to raise her arm off the bed, but found it impossible.

I know, this bed is more like a platform, and I'm Frankenstein. So when's the mad scientist going to arrive and tilt me up and down. Her body stiffened as if strapped to a teeter-totter and waiting for a ride.

Not Frankenstein. I can be the Incredible Hulk and spring from the table. Her stomach muscles tightened, wanting to explode out from under the sheets. *If they'd just let me go, I'd be fine. Who's in charge here anyway? Can't I get some service around here? Good hired help is so difficult to find, and they expect to be making a fortune. No more quality anymore. Just wham, bam, thank you, ma'am.*

The creaky door sliced the silence in the room. *Ah, I was to give that damn door a name. I forgot. Nothing new with this mind of mine. Used to be so smart all the time. Now I have a memory like an elephant. An elephant kept in a cage. An elephant kept in a cage, tied up.*

The sound of the hard-soled shoes echoed louder with each step. *Busy place, this zoo. Just throw me some hay, and maybe, only if you're lucky, I'll do some tricks for you.*

"Any change in her condition?" Doctor Frances's voice asked.

She heard the snap of a pen. *No, it must be the snap of his light.*

"Negative. But it only took half the time to stabilize her after the last seizure." The deep voice replied.

Seizure, what seizure? When did I have a seizure?

"What's the protocol for visitors in this part of the ward?" the deep voice questioned while shuffling papers she assumed would be from the chart board. No doubt, this person examined the posted information and stats.

She imagined Doctor Frances glancing over the shoulder of the man with the deep voice while instructing: "Many factors have to be considered. Regardless of the patient's condition, we make the final call, so we have to consider all the variables. Each patient responds differently to their visitors. It may be beneficial, but sometimes it can be detrimental to their mental state. We will have to closely monitor her as each person enters this room."

More shuffling of paper and then the scrape and scratch she concluded to be his signature on the bottom line of the final page.

"According to her chart, there appears to be no genetic history of depression in her family. Probably why she hasn't been closely monitored in the past," the deep voice added.

"She appears to be totally unresponsive right now, but the more positive talk around her, the better," the deep voice added. If we can apply psychotherapy and eliminate stress, she may even respond."

"I will let you take responsibility for that decision. I'm just here to show you around and introduce you to the patients who are at high risk on this floor. I have seen your credentials, and I trust you can make that call yourself. But if you do feel you need a second opinion, just buzz my pager. I'll be around," Doctor Frances said.

Doc Frances is spread pretty thin, you know. Something like the way I like my peanut butter on toast.

"I will leave you with one recommendation: keep it to one visitor at a time." Doctor Frances added in a far off voice as if he was on the other side of the room. "Unless she becomes fully conscious, I don't need to be paged. All I can say is she better become stable within the next twenty-four hours. With every minute she stays in a state of semi-consciousness, it reduces the chance of any medication ever taking proper affect. Our goal is for her to resume life as a productive citizen in society, not a terminal patient in a hospital."

Stable, I thought this was a zoo, not a barn. I know, I'll call this my stall, and all I need now is a manger. Yes, the bright star is above my stable and all the shepherds have come to bear gifts. If I can have any say, it is this: I call upon the drummer boy. I always liked that carol. "Pa-rum-pa-pum-pum." I got the tune, but the words ... damn, just aren't there.

"Don't touch anything. Just visit like you said," the deep voice announced to her next visitor.

"Yeah, I hear you," a girl's soft whisper affirmed his instructions.

The hard-soled shoes became distantly faint. The door opened with a creak and banged shut.

Am I alone? Hello, is anyone here? Tara questioned in her head.

"Mom, can you hear me?"

Nicole, is that you?

"Mommy, I miss you so much," Stephanie howled. Her sobbing stopped. "I mean, I ..." she sniffled, "I want you to wake up so we can go home together."

Oh, baby, I love you.

"Mom, don't worry. I've arranged for us to be taken to school and stuff until you get better." Nicole's voice was strong.

Come, give me a hug. I need to feel you.

"I love ... I love you, Mommy," Stephanie stammered.

"I'm sorry, Mom," Nicole said. "I feel ..." her voice cracked. "This is all my fault," she cried.

"What Nicole is trying to say is, from now on, we're going to help you more," Stephanie stated boldly. "We can carry our own skating bags and make our own lunches and stuff."

"We ..." Nicole sniffled into an audible sigh. "I need you. I'm sorry. I promise never to be mean to you again."

Okay, time for me to get out of here.

The creaky door opened. "It's time," the colleague's voice announced.

Time. Time? Time to let me out of here! ✧

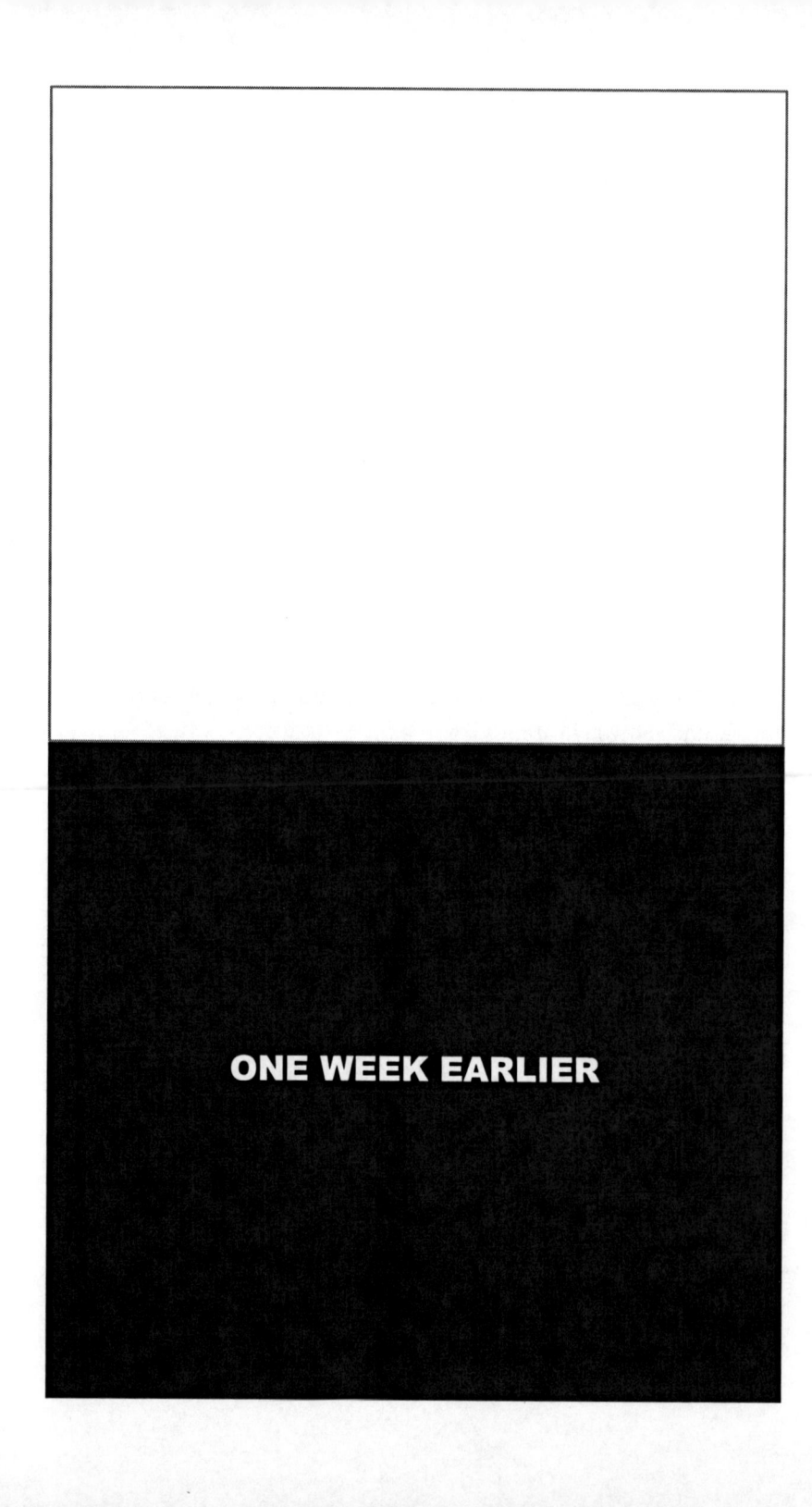

ONE WEEK EARLIER

ONE WEEK EARLIER

In five easy strides, Devin skated smoothly in front of Tara. She caught his swift movement but remained motionless. She sat peering over the scuffed wooden hockey boards, trying desperately to focus only on her children.

She glimpsed nervously over her shoulder and then back across the far end of the ice surface into the crowd of teenagers who had congregated in a huddle. Her heart raced. She pretended not to notice his form a few feet in front of her.

She should never have come out onto the ice surface. She could have continued to watch from inside the waiting room. But this evening, she had taken the notion to comply with Kammy's encouragement. She had decided it was time to come out of her shell and live a little.

Over the last few weeks of watching Devin, Tara had found him interesting. The more she observed, the more she recognized many of the same teaching techniques she used in the classroom. He taught his students with such enthusiasm, used games for them to exploit their energy and advance their skill. Never did his students wander away from his class looking lost and bored. They stuck to him like a band-aide. He played along, leading the group through each drill.

She could relate not only with how her students responded to her as a teacher, but also, how she used to connect with Josh as a co-worker. Over the past few months, however, the bond she had with Josh lost cohesiveness. No matter how hard she tried to attach to the man she loved, she knew there was nothing left.

Since then, she had been very careful to keep their relationship strictly professional, a conduct between principal and teacher, although many times it had been difficult not to delve back into their usual flirtatious selves. She forbade herself to fall back into that deep hole. She kept away from his office and refused to be sucked back into the arousal of sexual chemistry they both emitted every time they were in the same room.

They had two years of unforgettable sex, but Tara wanted more. She needed a man who would give her the time and attention she deserved. Respect, she had confided in Kammy, is one of the best qualities a man could show a woman. She had told Kammy that she wanted a man to share her life, travel together, and to go walking hand in hand down the streets. She didn't need a man who feared someone seeing them together, who made her feel she had to look over her shoulder every second.

From the moment she said good-bye to Josh, she decided it was time to implement a huge change in her life. Her own needs and desires needed to be at the forefront.

Kammy had congratulated Tara. She witnessed Tara taking more time for herself. Tara was finally doing more of what she *wanted* to do rather than what she *had* to do. Tara had stopped tutoring and now filled this time by showing a greater interest in her daughters' lives.

She attended their skating lessons. It was not particularly time consuming in Tara's perspective, as the hour seemed to speed by.

She was giving her support, she had told her girls, to monitor their progression in extra-curricular activities. Furthering her own interests and involving herself in some of her own hobbies was an added benefit.

Tara glanced down at her hands folded in her lap. She remembered the other night when Nicole had approached her on the subject of her changed behavior. Nicole was wondering why her mother's usual evening activities of marking papers had turned into time spent in a skating arena. Where had this new desire come from?

She reassured her that it was healthy for adults to explore other avenues of interests and to change their routines. Tara continued to explain the best quality time a parent could spend was with her family, and, in the past, she had spent too many hours working overtime.

Tara vowed to leave the school by four every day. She even stopped bringing work home so she could focus more on her daughters' activities.

Since she and Josh had stopped seeing each other, Tara changed her regular schedule. Less time spent at school meant there was less chance of encountering Josh. More time at the rink meant a greater chance of expanding her interests.

Tara squeezed her numb hands. Moisture penetrated the fabric inside her wool gloves.

Devin skated closer. Coming right for her … he spun around and jumped professionally into a flying sit-spin. His form poised to perfection.

Gracefully, he widened his arms, landing on one foot for a finale she was sure would have scored him high points if judged by someone other than herself. She knew very little about figure skating, but what she saw looked flawless.

Next thing she knew, she stood and clapped. Her face lightened with a smile.

Devin gave a small bow and glanced up into Tara's eyes. "Hi." He shook off his mitt, extended his arm above his head. He reached for her hand as if giving honors to a Majesty Queen. His eyes never left hers.

"You can come closer. I won't bite." A huge grin cropped most of his round face as a dimple on his left cheek deepened. The black curly strands flipped to one side across his short forehead and tucked behind both ears, exposing a diamond stud that sparkled from his left earlobe. His appearance reminded Tara of a city boy. Even his clothes said chic designed. She had never seen a young man wear apparel in such a grand style in the town of Deerwood, from the black-coated figure skates, past the snug pocket-hipped pants, right to his collared shirt pressed under the fitted jacket. She noted he wasn't overly muscular but had more of a lean sports physique that gave him the grace on ice that she had watched during many lessons before.

Tara hesitated momentarily before stepping down from the second bleacher. She extended her hand down to the man she had been studying for the past couple of months.

Her findings were nothing of a surprise. She had learned he was originally from Regina, his job had him transferred to Deerwood, he had no family around, and he took his extra job very seriously. The kids testified to his politeness and expertise that filled them with the attention, respect and knowledge any young teenager craved from an adult.

Tara had heard rumors of a live-in girlfriend but later found out that things never worked out. She hadn't caught the name of the young woman, but doubted she would know her. His girlfriend had come with Devin to Deerwood from a city a hundred and twenty miles away.

So here he was, a single man in a town with literally only a handful of single women. And as luck would have it, here Tara was, ready for a man looking for a single woman.

"Hi," Tara's voice trembled, wondering if her voice sounded hollow to him over the empty stands. She extended her bare hand down, and then stumbled forward.

Devin held her hand a little longer than expected.

The air sweltered from immediate attraction.

Tara shivered under his touch. The softness matched his smooth figures on the ice; firm and sure, yet sensual and appealing. The warmth radiated up from her palm and melted her heart within seconds. She stood hypnotically in his trance, enjoying the feel of this man's touch.

A group of his students whizzed by and whistled in acknowledgment of their private meeting. She pulled away as if her hand had touched a hot element. Nicole and Stephanie stole a sideways glance as they skated by.

Devin chuckled and shrugged his shoulders. "You a little jumpy?"

Now, she wished he would ask for her hand back. The cold air from the rink's temperatures nipped at the ends of her fingers and spanked her hand. As an excuse to look away from his stare, she glanced down hoping to hide her burning cheeks.

She replaced her mitten back on her hand. It was very difficult to look away from his intense brown eyes, but more than necessary before he could see her make a fool of herself. She was no school-aged girl with a crush on a boy in her class, but to be honest, that was exactly how she felt.

Now, she was tongue-tied. *Speak, say something*, the voice in her head shouted. "Ah, nice to meet you. I'm Nicole and Stephanie's mom."

Devin laughed easily, while plopping his jaw onto his open palms.

He rested his elbows on the boards and kept staring into Tara's eyes. "Yes, I know who you are. You're also my neighbor. I'm just so surprised it's taken this long for us to meet. Why, with a beautiful woman within reach, what in the world would keep us from getting together?"

Tara collapsed down on the benches. Her legs just wouldn't hold her anymore. "You want us to get together?" She asked the question for two reasons. One, she wasn't even sure what had been said in the past few minutes. And two, she couldn't believe he was asking her out on a date. Could he not see she was a complete decade older than him? What could he possibly see interesting in her?

"Yeah." He rose, stood solid as if he were standing on a large-based block, rather than over the two thin blades screwed at the bottom of his shoes. "I can bring over the beverage if you want to make supper. It's been a long time since I had some homemade grub."

"I would love to cook for you." Tara smiled. It had been ages since she cooked for a man, and she knew right away her special spaghetti would be the highlight on the menu. The timing was perfect. Her girls planned to be off visiting their father for the weekend.

Tara's mind instantly filled with the details of the meal. "Friday," Tara blurted out. "How 'bout this Friday at seven?"

Heavy boots clomped toward the ice surface from the changing rooms located under the bleachers. Any second her daughters would round the corner and be in front of her, tugging her arms to leave the building. And worse, they would see her talking with Devin.

Devin's face lit up. "You're the best. I will count the hours 'til we meet again." He skated away.

She followed his form. He approached one of his students from the other end of the building. Tara took a big gulp and released the air slowly through her mouth. *Too good to be true.* She shook her head and rehearsed his words, then hers, just so everything could really sink in.

"Mom, will you carry this for me?" Nicole pleaded as she plopped down the pink canvas skating bag and her knapsack from school.

"Who's that with your skating teacher?" Tara stared out past her daughters' heads, her jaw pointing in Devin's direction.

Simultaneously, their heads snapped around, and Stephanie was the first to respond. "You know who that is. That's Michael. Michael

Henderson." She turned back to Nicole and pushed her forward. "He skipped lessons tonight, so he's probably had to go and report a whopper excuse, but I'd imagine most of his reasons are about used up by now."

"I didn't know he took figure skating lessons?" Tara bent down to retrieve Nicole's bags and flung the weight over her right shoulder. Now she was sure to look like a hiker, all packed-up and ready for a long haul. The bulk of the one skating bag, a knapsack, and her huge black purse were enough to fill her back. "Here." She stuck out her hand. "I might as well carry yours as well."

Stephanie took one look at her mother and shook her head. "It's okay, Mom. I've got this." She smiled, and led the way down the wooden planks of the bleachers.

"So how long has Michael been taking lessons?" Tara asked.

"Forever. Where have you been?" Nicole mumbled down at her feet, then called over her shoulder, "Doesn't do much for his character though. He's been having a tough time at the school with the Rockan Gang. They've taken to calling him 'faggot' and the skating teacher his bed partner."

Tara stopped. "That's ridiculous. Does his father know about this?" her voice had raised a full octave.

"How would I know?" Nicole responded and waved for her mother to continue following them down the planks, toward the exit door.

"I saw the pack of vultures lined up outside Mr. Henderson's office the other day." Stephanie shrugged. "But I'm not sure why they were being hauled in there this time."

"They have been getting cozy," Nicole said.

"Who and what are you talking about?" Tara asked.

"Michael and Devin. I keep getting the feeling there's something going on. Like they're keeping a secret or something." Nicole shook wildly in an overemphasized gesture, as if to fling off a swarm of ants that had landed on her body.

"Oh, you're just being silly," Tara responded, as she glanced back over her shoulder thinking she may wave at Devin if she was to catch his eye. But instead, she could see he was still in a heated discussion with Michael. Their bodies were close together, eyes welded. Devin's one hand rested on Michael's shoulder. Periodically, both would side glance over each others' shoulders and then back to each other. Michael had struggled with fetching something from his front pocket and was now placing the wad in Devin's hands. After Devin deposited the bulk into his front pocket, he pointed toward the dressing room doors. Michael raced away.

Devin was not gay; he was ethical, respected by his students. He would never take advantage of his position. Hadn't he just asked her out on a date?

The sound of the word 'date' rang uncomfortably in Tara's head. She felt butterflies flittering around in her stomach. She stopped. Instead of their wings tickling her insides, the insects had grown heavy, and their legs turned into long toes with sharp claws.

Tara grabbed her middle as a sharp pain stabbed into her side.

Now the insect flitted inside her guts. They were like angry flies caught on the inside of a windowpane, spreading from her stomach up into her head. The deadly varmints multiplied in numbers.

Tara's hands flew to her head, squeezing the sides as if the pressure could force the demons out. She fell to the planks on her knees and doubled over, dropping her baggage.

Stephanie stopped. She glanced back to her line of followers. "Mom, are you okay?" She pushed past her sister who had halted in her tracks but kept muttering, as if talking to her feet.

Stephanie's arm wrapped around her mother's hunched shoulders.

Tara's eyes crawled up her youngest daughter's body. She smiled. "Just give me a second. I need to catch my breath." With her stance wide, she rubbed through the ski jacket, pressing one fist of the mitten firmly into her stomach, while the other hand remained on her head.

Hadn't she remembered to take her meds today? It had been a while since she had gone for an annual physical, but it had been on her list of "changes" she had made for herself. A promise she had made to Kammy who had expressed her worries in confidence. Tara had told Kammy she was as healthy as an ox and should not worry.

After her brief lecture, Tara had taken the time to view her items of self-care. The last time she had a physical, she recalled discussing symptoms of dizziness, headaches that felt like severe hangovers, and memory loss that had occurred during her divorce. Stress, the doctor had diagnosed, with a quick remedy of rest and relaxation. He prescribed a strong sedative in the form of a sleeping pill and a daily antidepressant. And he was right. A few nights of deep, restful sleep; a great holiday away; and a daily pill had been all that was needed to turn all negative symptoms into remission.

She had been feeling well until recently, since she and Josh had agreed to go their separate ways. She noticed these symptoms had been getting worse again.

Lately, she had been forgetting details and was lagging behind her top students. The new curriculums were becoming more and more difficult to understand and incorporate into her daily lessons. And the other day, she had even had to use her register to scan for the names of her students who had been with her most of the year.

Time to go back for some different pills, she had thought to herself and shrugged the warning signs away. Perhaps a shared holiday with a companion was the prescription. Like an apple a day, a good man would keep the doctor away.

Tara grinned through clenched teeth. Her mind flew to Devin. She imagined them walking arm in arm down the beaches of some place hot. Miraculously, her pain was subsiding with each new thought.

By the time she was able to catch her breath, Tara had noticed even Nicole's worried eyes staring back into her own.

Tara leaned back, nestled back in the solid arms of … "Oh, my God." Tara stood straight. "I'm sorry. I didn't mean for you to …"

"Here." Devin hugged Tara's back as if she were suspended in a hanging hammock. "It's okay," he coaxed in a soft voice. "Just relax." He supported her weight as she collapsed into a lying position, and cradled her head in his lap. She allowed her muscles to relax. "Just breathe deeply," Devin instructed with a smooth tone.

Tara closed her eyes taking in a deep breath of fresh air. She imagined a shield of solid armor lifting her before the daggers of ill thoughts, the sharp knives trying to penetrate her mind.

The physical signs were now screaming at her to think positive, happy thoughts. She imagined the spears ricocheting off the steel armor. She exhaled slowly through her nose, using the same method she had learned during yoga class.

Her thoughts returned to the pile of bent arrows strewn at her feet.

Her past: it was senseless to keep thinking of Josh. She couldn't change him to become the man she needed in her life. Her future: it was ridiculous to keep thinking of Devin and their first date. She couldn't determine his thoughts and feelings toward her.

It was absolutely crazy to keep worrying about anything that could go wrong or that may be unacceptable in the eyes of others. She was determined to put herself first and not worry about the opinions of others. Easier said then done.

Breathing rhythmically, she envisioned herself sweeping the mess around her shoes into a huge dustpan and throwing everything away in the garbage bin. Tara's eyes opened. She grinned up at the three heads with their worried expressions.

"I'm fine now." Tara groaned and tried to sit up. She welcomed Devin's assistance. His body molded behind her. She wanted to tip her chin, tilt her head back into the curve of his neck just to feel what it would be like to listen to his deep breathing, the pounding of his heart beneath his jacket. Tara shook her head and cleared her throat, abolishing the sexual thoughts from her mind. "I just need a little help standing."

Devin's arms came up under her armpits. He slowly hoisted her up onto her feet. The girls had cleared the way. They stood speechless, watching the entire performance. At that moment, Tara shut her eyes and savored the experience and her feelings. Hadn't it felt wonderful to know she could let go and allow someone else to control the situation?

Suddenly, Devin scooped Tara into his arms. He carried her inside the waiting room. Her eyes remained closed. She wrapped her arms around his neck, burying her face into his broad chest. The fragrance of spice aftershave hit her nostrils. She swallowed the air as if starving.

Carefully, he laid her down on the padded theatre seats that lined the glass partition of the facility.

Tara smiled up into his mischievous grin. "Thank you." She knew she didn't have to say anymore. But was all of this really necessary? Had she really needed to be carried?

Yes, she could hear Kammy respond to Tara's multiple questions on the protocol for proper behavior when in the presence of a charismatic man for the first time, and not just any guy, but a hot young man who obviously found her attractive enough to call her "beautiful." ✦

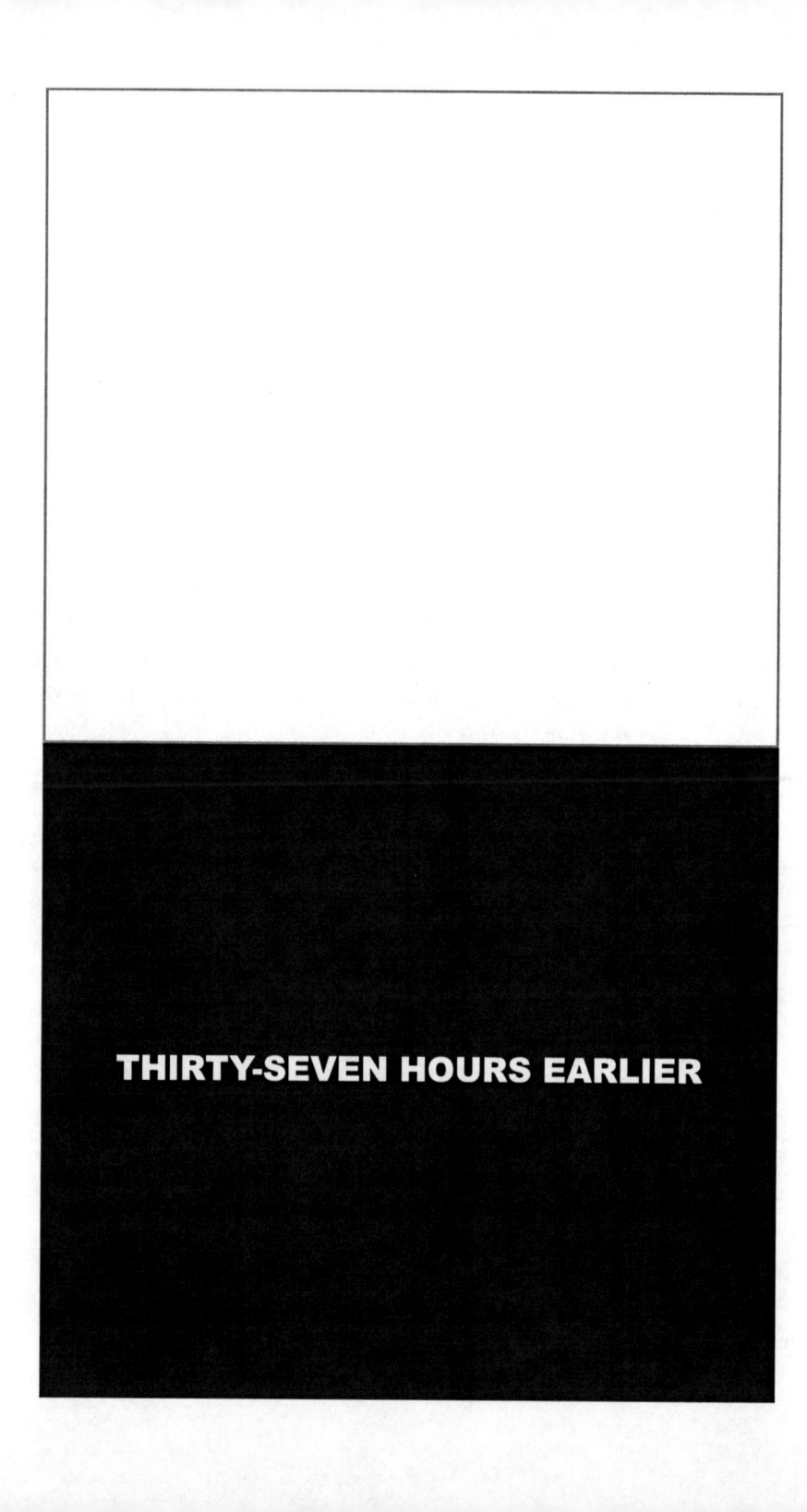

THIRTY-SEVEN HOURS EARLIER

Chapter 8

THIRTY-SEVEN HOURS EARLIER

Tara quickly decided after arriving at *The Hutt* during a Friday lunch hour that she should know better than to submit herself to such confusion. The warm, stuffy air in no way reflected the freezing temperature outside. Could the chatter of all the customers create this much stifling heat? Yet, in spite of the chaos, she needed to escape her house. It was imperative to defeat the madness echoing in her brain.

As she sat in her usual booth waiting for Kammy to return with her order, she had time to think. In less than seven hours, she would be conversing with Devin in her home. He was a charismatic man whom she had studied over the past couple of months, pursued, and more than caught his attention. A flutter in her stomach turned sharp. She sucked in a breath, and then released it slowly to extinguish the razor blades ripping her insides. She had a bad case of nerves, or so she convinced herself.

She had fled her home earlier in hopes that *The Hutt* would divert her thoughts, and she could focus on others rather than herself. It had been a crazy morning. She went home from school after trying to avoid any contact with Josh all day but found herself starved for fresh air in her small duplex. The walls felt as if they were closing in on her.

Tara shrugged off her jacket and looked around. It was packed.

There wasn't a free seat in the place.

Why isn't the commotion working? Her pulse continued to throb in her head. She rubbed her temples.

The aroma of fresh donuts and coffee beans permeated her nostrils. The day wasn't a complete write off. She grinned, taking a deep breath.

Her mind drifted off to this morning before work. Devin's unannounced visit was such a nice surprise. He's so smart, introducing Nicole and Stephanie to his pride and joy by having his little dog come bouncing into the duplex. What a great idea.

Tara rested her chin on her open palms just as she heard the bell above the entrance door. *Josh?*

Her spirits shifted to anxiety. Her head snapped up for a glimpse of his face, but she was sadly mistaken. Instead, Bob Taylor strutted through the door and made a beeline right to his wife. He never took a second glance anywhere else but remained focused on her face. She beamed when she saw him, and Tara noticed that she followed every move he made. He reached her in a matter of seconds, looking as though nothing in this world mattered but her. Bending across the table, he kissed her lightly on her upturned cheek.

Josh would never arrive unannounced, so why did she bother looking up to see if it was *him* coming through the door? Her heart sank. Why was she still dreaming of him in her life?

If only the knowledge that Michael had gained could somehow rub off on Josh. Tara thought back to the anti-bullying rally in the hallway. Michael had been so brave to face the Rockan Gang. Now, why couldn't Josh face Alex the same way? Could Josh not cut and paste himself onto the same page as everyone else? Could he not see that being bullied provided nothing for his morale, and he would be the loser in the end?

But he refused to change, didn't want to learn or get help. More importantly, Josh refused to admit his chosen path was wrong. It wasn't the promotion that would bring him happiness. It was the people around him.

If only she could have made him see this. He had so much love inside, but he had a lot of trouble showing it.

His choice—his loss. Tara squeezed her mittens hard. She glanced down to where her knuckles had turned white. She could kill the person who had called Alexandra that night.

Tara glanced over the three round tables to Marvin's usual spot. He sat rhythmically stirring his hot milk. The laces from his untied heavy bush boots lay limp, soaking up the melted snow. Just below his man-boobs, she noticed an added spot of food greased within the folds of his yellow sweater. She couldn't help wondering what it was like to live in Marvin's world. Over the lunch hour ruckus, his low voice sang a familiar nursery rhyme, *Pop Goes the Weasel*. And for just a second, she was tempted to join him.

Abruptly, the humming stopped. "Why are you looking at me, Taree?" Marvin's deep voice floated over the hum of conversations as if he was the only other person in the room. The sound hit Tara's ears in full impact. Although clear, his words were slower than usual today.

Tara's head snapped away, and then slowly, she turned back to Marvin. "I'm just thinking. I mean, I'm just thinking how much I like your hat, Marvin."

"You like my hat?" His whiskered cheeks grew round as his moist lips curled up into one of the widest grins she had ever seen.

Tara smiled back and repeated, "Yes, I like your hat."

"I like your hat, too, Taree." His bright eyes danced into hers.

"Well, thank you Marvin." Her gaze dropped down to her coffee cup as if examining the contents.

She looked around the congested room. No one was alone. Everyone had someone else. Each of the twenty or so expressions looked as though they were either sharing their most ultimate secrets or discussing the dreams of their lives coming true. Bob Taylor and his wife were oblivious to the world around them.

Having no one across her table never bothered Tara before, so why now? She had never really felt like she belonged or could handle most conversations for fear of saying too much. Except with Josh. With him, she never held anything back. She spoke her mind, and exposed her heart. And look what that got her ...

"What is wrong, Taree? You don't like your hat?"

"No, Marvin." Tara pressed her lips together. She willed the corners of her mouth to curl up.

The bells tinkled above the entrance door.

Tara followed Marvin's eyes. A gust of winter wind penetrated through her purple wool sweater. The clean smell of crisp country air mixed with the tantalizing aroma of fresh baked bread was like nature's remedy for carrying away all illness. Instantly, her head felt light, clear, and her headache disappeared.

A young woman Tara guessed to be around Kammy's age came through the door. Did this stranger not want to be accepted by the small community of Deerwood? Tara closely studied her body language but found her difficult to read.

This young woman's eyes looked downward, as if examining the ugly speckled gray tiles. She obviously did not know that the protocol when entering a room, walking down the sidewalk, or meeting anyone in a small town was to make eye contact as the tenuous exchange of proper greeting, whether coming or going. But she had no intention of glancing up to meet any of the curious eyes in this building.

Instead, she skittered to the back of the food order line, slightly shifting the heavy black scarf around her open v-neck that exposed a turtleneck that rode high onto her chin. Her face remained hidden as if she was a Muslim woman. She quickly whipped off her matching mittens, rubbed her hands together, and then blew hard into her closed fists.

Repetitiously on the spot, she raised up and down in her Thinsulate black boots, not caring about the snow turning to mud beneath her stance. She pulled her matching stocking cap farther down on her heavily creased forehead.

"Glenee!" Marvin's deep voice boomed. His chair screeched across the gray tile, the back wobbling on two legs as he pushed back and up from his perch.

The lady's head snapped toward Marvin's voice. Quickly, she pulled the scarf down and the hat up. Her face lit up as if seeing a long lost friend for the first time. She ran over to Marvin's table, eyes never leaving his face. Her shoulders lifted with her palms up, as she extended herself into a wide stance. She looked as if she was ready to scoop up her own lost child.

"Marvin, I'm so glad I ran into you here." She wrapped her long arms halfway around his back, squeezing hard enough to cause indents to press into his wool sweater.

Tara openly sighed while she watched the stranger collapse in a chair across from Marvin.

"Could I bother you for a refill?" Tara called to Kammy as she held her cup up and over the Artisan Gelato glass display counter to where Kammy stood.

Kammy's body spun like a ballerina, coffee butler in hand. She expertly filled Tara's cup to the brim. "How you doing today, Hon? Been thinking about you." She twirled back to set the coffee butler down on the cluttered cupboard behind her. She resumed her stance in front of Tara.

"I'm great."

Kammy's eyes squinted, perfectly etched eyebrows lifted and her lips parted.

"Okay, okay, I'm fine." Tara glanced down to find a stray napkin. "So I'm kind of having a bad day." Her fingers tucked the napkin into her fist and then tried to smooth it back to its original form, as if designing a new craft from recycled paper. "Everyone has bad days." She stopped fiddling and glanced up.

There was a brief pause as Tara watched Kammy's brows etch even higher. She stood immobile waiting for Tara to spill her guts.

"Josh told me that he really needs to talk with me, but frankly, I just don't want to hear it." She folded the napkin and lined up its corners. "We both agreed to stop seeing each other, and it's time for us to move on with our lives. I just want him to leave me alone, so I can start over." Tara bit her quivering bottom lip. She needed to stop the persistent question on her mind: how do you say good-bye to someone you love more than life itself?

"Hon, sounds to me like he's not wanting to let you go, and he wants both sex with you and his promotion." Kammy's free hand reached for Tara's anxious hands. "But are you really ready to let him go?" Kammy covered both of Tara's hands and gently squeezed until the anxious motion subsided.

"Well, maybe Josh does have something important to discuss. I mean, he did seem excited, and there was a gleam in his eyes he hasn't had for ages. He said something about a new self-discovery. We didn't have any private time to get into it. I just could feel myself getting suckered back under his spell." She folded the napkin flat again. "I just don't like it."

"Sounds to me you answered my question. You don't need Josh. Just get out there and have some fun. You deserve it, girl." Kammy patted her hand and smiled.

Tara grinned. "I'm through with wasting time. It's just too valuable, and I do deserve to have a life." She raised her mug as if toasting before a large audience. "Tonight is the beginning of my new life—without Josh." She took a sip.

"Now you got my curiosity. Hon, what you got planned?"

Tara leaned over the counter. "How does a cozy, intimate dinner with a charming young man who's full of energy and not afraid to be seen with me out in public sound?" Tara stood straight and winked.

"How lucky can you get? Sounds like I need one of those. Are there any clones?"

"Lucky? Try pure talent from someone who knows how to snag a stray fish from the sea."

Kammy giggled and began to wipe the counter. "Well, Hon, last time I checked, there wasn't a hell of a lot of water in the basin of this huge metropolis. Honey, I know you better than anyone else; when it comes to you wanting something, you don't even need a barbed hook. Now, who is this marlin?"

"That, my darling," Tara chuckled and flipped the back of her hand out over the counter as if she was swatting away mosquitoes, "I will share with you after the weekend." Now, it was Tara's turn to pat Kammy's hand around the dishcloth.

Kammy stopped wiping and stomped her foot. "Oh, come on, you can't do this to me." A scowl replaced the grin, and a huge pout formed all over her face.

Tara laughed. "We have to have something to chat about after the weekend." She leaned over the counter and cupped her hand around her mouth as if she was about to tell a secret.

Kammy leaned forward, turned her head, and tucked a lost stray hair behind her left ear to meet her best friend's gesture.

While bending over the counter, Tara whispered, "Who is that lady sitting across from Marvin? She looks familiar, but I just can't place her." She glanced over her shoulder and snuck a peek at the woman and Marvin who were deeply immersed into a serious discussion.

Marvin had lost his lopsided grin. His eyes remained down, staring at his massive hands folded in his lap. His usual relaxed body was replaced with hunched shoulders.

The lady had a scowl of pure anger. Her fingers clenched as if soon she would use her fist as a gavel on the top of the bare table.

A quick shiver ran up Tara's spine. She sensed trouble. But what did she know about judging a person's character on sight, or from actually getting to know someone? She had been wrong about so many people in her past. A snapshot picture of Rick and Josh snapped into her mind. Tara shook her head.

Kammy rose and searched past Tara's head to Marvin's table. But her eyes didn't stop there. Suddenly, they became wide.

"Josh just pulled up."

"What?"

"Don't look back, he'll see you."

"Now this is stupid. I want to see."

"No, just wait. That woman with Marvin looks like she knows him. She's waving through the window at him." A short honk and then the bells chimed above the door.

Tara turned to view the parking lot through the massive full faced windows. With Josh's vehicle window down, she could see his handsome face turned up to the woman who was standing beside his car.

Tara had seen that look on Josh's face before: caring, loving, and full of passion. He opened his door and stood with arms out wide. The woman crushed into his body, and his arms instantly wrapped around her.

"Oh, my God," the words pushed out through Tara's open fingers as her hand flew up to her mouth. This morning's breakfast flipped over in her stomach like pancakes on a grill. She couldn't breathe. Tears streamed down her cheeks. Her vision clouded with moisture and a sudden darkness.

Kammy rushed around the counter. She grabbed Tara's waist. "Sit down, Honey. Come and sit down." She led her to the nearest empty chair and table.

"How could the bastard?" Tara wiped the corners of her eyes with the napkin she had squeezed inside her fist. Her head bowed and shook back and forth.

Kammy's arm wrapped around Tara's shoulders, her hands pressed deep on her upper arms. "You deserve so much better," she whispered into her ear.

Tara blew her nose and sat straight. She struggled out of Kammy's tight hold.

"I guess that was my ticket to freedom." She sniffled as the darkness faded and brought on the light from within her head.

Tara grabbed her coat and flung it on. She hurled herself out the door.

In the parking lot, she trudged past the spot where she had just witnessed two lovers embrace. Snow pelted her entire body, but instead of cold, her cheeks burned as if licked by flames.

Tonight, I'll make sure the spaghetti sauce has a special zing. ✧

NOW

NOW

Gladstone Central Hospital
Mental Health Division
Gladstone, Saskatchewan

All that marked the passage of time for Tara were the events—visitors coming and going, doctors rushing through the door, sirens blaring, and Stephanie and Nicole fleeing her hospital room.

Girls, come back. Come back and play for me.

Quick footsteps squeaked louder, closer, and suddenly stopped. Rapid breathing matched the sudden bustle in the room.

The ruckus stopped, and the monitors resumed their steady rhythm.

The next visitor was new. It was a woman for sure. Her perfume sweetened the stale hospital air.

The cool sheet pressed farther under Tara's shoulders as this person continued to stuff the fabric down and around her body.

Might as well be comforting a corpse.

So the girls left, and now before me is an angel. Yes, I have an angel who comes to bear gifts.

"Honey, you have to wake up. You can snap out of this one," the woman commanded between sniffles. She snorted then blew her nose. "The game's over, and we're waiting for you to wake up."

But I like to play the game. What else is there for me? He took everything away.

"The waiting room is packed. Everyone wants to see you—your students, teachers, lots of people I haven't seen in ages."

Are you not listening to me? He broke me completely. I have nothing else to give.

"Hon, I need you to come have tea with me. We can work something out. If you need some place to stay, you and the girls can come live with me."

I know. I know. I get ten points for guessing the angel.

Kammy, right?

Oh, Kammy. Do I have a lot to tell you. But first, can you tell these bozos to let me go. Look, they have me strapped in here like a wild animal. I can't even move to scratch my nose. And that damn machine. I need some quiet around here. How's a person supposed to sleep? And one more request: the door. Can you bring some oil the next time you come? Someone really needs to fix that door.

"I'll do anything for you. All you have to do is wake up and ask."

My head is pounding. Ah, it's like the worst hangover ever. When is whatever they've got pumping through my veins ever going to work?

"I know if you were awake right now, you'd be telling me everything. I'm ready to listen."

I told you everything already, but it doesn't solve the problem. There is no solution. The cops said there's nothing left to do. Why am I the prisoner?

The sound of chair legs dragged along the tiled floor, and something crashed. *Now, that does nothing for my head.*

"I need to make a confession."

What?

Again, the cool cotton sheets tucked and now molded even tighter to Tara's body.

Enough with the blankets! I hate being tucked in. Just give my body a little freedom here. I'm finding it hard to breathe as it is. Now back to this confession. What do you need to tell me?

"I'll come back to see you again. I want you to be awake though,"

her voice quivered.
What aren't you telling me? It's Marvin, right? He didn't make it.
"I'm worried about you. This is not like you to just lie there and let someone take power over you." She sounded louder by the second. "You are strong for everyone else. It's time you got strong for yourself."
Let's not talk about me right now. Words are easy to say. I'm to be strong. Sure. And where am I supposed to find strength? I have nothing more to give.
"There's a waiting room full of people praying for you. They are trying to feed you strength. Josh hasn't gone home since you were admitted. I'm worried about him."
Why worry about him? He's out of the picture. Am I missing something here? What about Marvin?
"Hon, it's time you learned to let those who love you help."
Don't do this to me. You know I don't like to focus on myself. Let's get back to Josh. What's wrong?
What about Nicole and Stephanie? Where are my girls? Who's taking care of them? Wasn't there something you wanted to tell me?
"I have to go now. I love you, girlfriend."
Wait, don't go. I need to know more. What about my girls? Please tell me he doesn't have them. I fought so hard to have them. Tell me I haven't lost them again.
The monitors beeped in closer frequency.
He killed Marvin, didn't he?
The squeaky door opened and closed several times. Suddenly, the fresh soap smell took over Kammy's favorite lilac fragrance. Something cold pressed into Tara's cheek. She smelled the strong odor of surgical plastic. The top of her one cheek was pulled down as her eyelid was forced up.
"Pupils are normal. She seems to be coming to," Doctor Frances said. "Tell the others to go home. She can't have any more visitors today. Prognosis looks good. She's beginning to stabilize."
Hey, Doc, I need something for my head.
"She'll need a good twenty-four hours of rest and solitude just to be sure."
It feels like it's going to explode off my shoulders. ✦

THIRTY-FIVE HOURS EARLIER

Chapter 9

THIRTY-FIVE HOURS EARLIER

Leaving Deerwood on Highway 8 South, Josh drove in silence. Jackson's Cemetery was the most logical place to take his two passengers on this Friday afternoon. He couldn't remember the last time he had taken any time away from work, and certainty not for the reason of visiting his wife's grave.

After turning west down the back grid, the engine interrupted the badgering questions in Josh's head and awakened Michael from the back seat.

"I don't get it. Why do we need to come here?" Michael crossed his arms over his coat and snuggled his nose down into the pink wool scarf. "Why didn't Nathan have to come? His leg jiggled as if attached to a vibrator. "Wouldn't Marvin want to be with us?"

"Someone had to stay back with Marvin. There's no way I would have Marvin come out here. He would never understand." Glenda exchanged the mail in her hands while donning her black mittens. "I wish we could have gone into Gladstone first, so we could have picked up some flowers. And I could have mailed this." She squinted at the gleam of the sun glistening off the pure white snowdrifts.

Flipping the visor down, she glanced over her shoulder. "I bet you've got a lot more questions." She pressed her shoulders back into the leather bucket seats. "I know I did when I was your age." She tossed the postcard down into the console and reached to turn down the heater fan. "But I was too smart to listen."

"This is stupid. You want to go, you go, but I'm staying in the truck." Michael's voice rose far above the rev of the engine.

Next to the only access gate, Josh put the truck into neutral. The steel-linked fence wrapped around the cemetery, housing around fifty graves. The partitioned area was mostly bare. Except for the tops of each tombstone, a blanket of snow covered the flat prairie landscape.

Josh squinted across the vast area toward the far corner. A lonely oak tree towered in the eastern corner. A ten-foot hedge of thick dormant lilacs traced the entire perimeter.

Josh turned to the backseat and saw pure fear in his son's eyes. He wanted to ignore Michael's expression, to turn back and pretend his son wasn't scared. He wished Michael was smiling and laughing instead, hating to see anyone in such agony. But he wasn't laughing, and it was time to change the way he had been handling his family and his life.

He thought of his past and how he had usually turned away and got busy doing something else to avoid the stressful situations. It wasn't until Glenda told her story and opened up her true feelings that Josh discovered how extremely important it was to be sensitive. He realized how much influence he had on others as she expressed her poor self-image that had formed from a situation that happened so very long ago.

Making amends had never been in Josh's vocabulary until Glenda's visit. She had been the second person that night he had turned to and asked for forgiveness, and it felt right. Damn good, in fact. The look on Marvin's face just before he was crushed into his body, and then Glenda's sideways glances of uncertainty until the sparkle entered her eyes and her mouth lifted into a grin.

This was just the start of a life he had always dreamed about—to really be there for the people he loved. He remembered sitting down in his office later that night and making a list of all persons he had harmed. He knew he had to activate and reach out.

"I'm sorry." Josh licked his dry lips and stared deep into his son's brown eyes. Michael shrugged, dipping his chin. "We'll just clear your mother's plot, say what's on our hearts, and head back into town."

Opening the door, Josh stepped out into the deep snow that was up to the running boards. Michael just sat and shivered.

He looked so small and frail, not the bold young man he had witnessed just that afternoon who stood tall and led an entire school on a rampage to conquer bullies and make the school environment a safer place to learn.

"Come." Josh extended his hand.

Michael stopped shaking, his brows furrowed. "You expect me to just forget the past and jump into your arms as if nothing ever happened?" He closed his eyes and clenched his jaws so tight it creased his chin as he drew back. "You were never there for me when I needed you."

He pushed past his father and trudged in the snow toward the towering tree. He yelled over his shoulder. "Where were you?" His arms gestured wide as if trying to cover the vast area.

Josh dropped his head into his hands. His shoulders sagged, and his chest tightened. He was scarcely able to take a breath.

An arm wrapped and squeezed around his shoulders. He glanced straight across into Glenda's glistening brown eyes. And there, for just a second, he saw it ... Margaret's expression of approval. It was the look she would give him after he had done something worthy. She acted on pure pride.

He quickly wiped the tear trickling down his cheek with the back of his sleeve. "Let's go." Josh broke free from Glenda's grasp.

"No." She grabbed his arm, and he stopped. "Let me go and talk to him first."

His heart thumped in his ears. His breath came in short bursts of gray clouds. He pressed his lips together and clenched down hard.

"Please." She tipped her chin down, and looked up. "Just give me a few minutes, and I'll wave you over."

Taking a deep breath, his knees weakened. Josh nodded his head and got back into the truck. He watched Glenda long stride, as if jumping hurdles during a track and field day, to match the footprints of his youngest son.

Josh dropped his head. His eyes floated toward Glenda's meticulous handwriting. Picking up the single postcard, he glanced up. She had already covered half the distance toward Michael. While keeping his hand under the surface of the dashboard, he placed his glasses on his face and read:

> Dear Rochelle,
>
> As you can see by this postcard, I'm now in Deerwood, Saskatchewan. It took me a long time to get here, and I'm not sure how long I will be staying.
>
> During the day, I work as a janitor at a hospital in Gladstone, a town twenty minutes from Deerwood. I have no social life to speak of, so I've decided to accept an offer from my uncle to work as a custodial worker at a school right in Deerwood. It will be kind of tough work and difficult to juggle, but with double income, I will soon be able to have enough money so Marvin can go back to his Care Home.
>
> Working two jobs will be exhausting, but it'll keep me busy. Most important, it'll keep my mind off of him.
>
> Love,
> Glenda

Josh's face hardened. He slid his frames from his nose and stuck them back into the breast pocket of his shirt. The least he could do is help her out. Watching Marvin while she worked wouldn't be a chore. He thought of how Marvin had been a great help out in the garage and how he'd bonded to Michael right away.

"You don't have to work so hard," he had told her, remembering their discussion about her persistence to earn a double income to house Marvin. "I can help pay," he had insisted. But she wouldn't hear of the logic. She wanted to take the responsibility herself.

Josh shook his head while thinking that she sure had grown up in the past seven years. But who was this guy she was referring to? Had he missed something she had said? There was no one in her life living in Deerwood. Well, at least he had never seen her with anyone but her brother.

Perhaps he could help her get back together with this special man.

A shimmer caught the corner of his eye. Josh peered down the only road leading up to the cemetery. A red, four-door Chrysler was fast approaching his truck. He slammed his palm into the steering wheel. Had she followed him out of town?

The car stopped directly behind his vehicle, and the door opened. Alexandra trudged through the deep snow and approached the driver's side. Josh opened the door and stepped out.

"Hey, what brings you to this neck of the woods?" Josh pasted a smile on his face.

Today, she was wearing the long mink coat he had given his wife for their second Christmas together. Just a month before Margaret died, as if she had been planning her death, she began subtly dispersing all of her valuables to friends and family until most of her jewelry was gone from its case. Trinkets disappeared from the cabinet. Fine china was given away to her brother's wife. And, nonchalantly, she had given her favorite jacket to her sister.

Had he known at the time, he would have been furious. But it was just another secret he wasn't privy to, or perhaps he chose not to see.

All Josh could remember was Margaret saying that she was so glad she had a twin who wore the same size clothing because nothing would go to waste. Could he not have picked up on the clues before the time? How much more frank could she have been to tell him she wasn't planning on living, and dying had been more of what she had in mind.

"I tried to stop you at the corner, but you must not have seen me." She tucked the dark collar up over her face. Her long eyelashes blinked as if willing away the tears that could wash away the heavy makeup. The air chilled the skin, but it was not cold enough to make her cheeks that red. He had noticed lately how she plastered the stuff on.

"It must be important to come all this way."

"I have great news." She smiled, yet her grin was nothing like Margaret's. For identical twins, Josh could see nothing similar in their appearance. Margaret's facial features had been soft, her stance and motions delicate and graceful.

Alexandra was tough. She was a woman hardwired in a man's position of pure strength. Her profession was her family, and she ran a tough ship. The school always came in under budget, the public applauded her decision making, and the teachers trusted her administration abilities. This last year had been the toughest with the cutbacks, but as she had predicted, all had worked well in the end.

Josh noticed the staff had worked as a team with little more working hours than anyone had been used to in the past. With four more months left in the school year, everyone at the last staff meeting had cheered with the confidence that the end was in sight. No one felt they had failed toward their goals of educating every individual.

Thanks to Tara. She had been the leader. He watched her encourage their coworkers, stand by him all the way, and accept whatever was handed to her.

"Here I thought you and I were thinking along the same lines." Josh scowled. "When was the last time you spent some time with your sister?"

Alex's bright red lips flattened. She looked as if she was about to say something but stopped.

"What's the great news? I could use some about now?" Josh kicked the snow, trying not to think of Tara. He watched it stick to the toe of his black boot.

Alex's face beamed. "There's been an unofficial announcement in the office. Since I was the one who nominated and fought for your new position, the local and division bodies thought it most appropriate to hold a signing of a new contract. There will be a celebration for you at my choice of location." Her arms went out wide. "I would like to invite you to my home for a dinner party set for tomorrow night."

Josh's heart sank. He went back to making scuff marks in the snow.

Alex's body bounced as if dancing a jig on the spot. "Didn't you hear me? This is exactly what we've been planning for over a year." Her hands hugged her hips, and her head tilted to the side. "What's wrong with you?"

"You know," he said, glancing up, "I don't think this is the place or the time to be sharing this kind of information with me."

"Listen, if you don't want this job, just keep it up," she huffed. "I've bent over backwards making sure your name remained at the top of the list." Her voice rose, and Josh glanced over the hood of the truck in the direction of Glenda and Michael. Both were down on their hands and knees clearing off the snow from Margaret's plot, much like two children building a castle in the sand. Neither one looked up in his direction.

Josh tugged at the thick fur of her sleeve. "Will you shush? All I need is for the two of them to hear you."

Alex ripped her arm away. "You sure have been acting strange lately," she said through clenched teeth.

And then her voice softened. "Listen, you're right." She shook her head. "I'm sorry. I shouldn't have come out here. I should have just called you after I phoned the school and they said you'd taken off for the afternoon."

Josh looked up.

"Family has always been a priority for you, Josh. Just think, after you sign the official contract of Assistant Director tomorrow night, your boys will be set for life." She stepped closer. He could smell the odor of heavily scented baby powder deodorant and her breath of Juicy Fruit as she rolled the small wad of gum back with the curl of her tongue.

He swallowed and stepped back.

Again, she stepped forward. "Don't blow it this time, Josh," she whispered, her sharp words slicing the air as if cutting through tough plastic.

Alexandra glanced in the direction of Margaret's headstone. "She would be proud of you." She brought her head close to his. "And this will be a win-win for everyone. Trust me," she smirked.

Josh watched the red dot disappear down the road with the swirling torrent of snow. Alex was right. The signing of this promotion would have made Margaret happy. She had always thought their children should have the best opportunity possible for their future dreams.

But advancing in his career wouldn't make all his past mistakes go away. How could Alexandra say everyone would win?

Was all the talk around the staffroom right when they gossiped about Alex's true motive for creating a new position? The teachers whispered their assumptions, insisting she was looking for an easy way out—someone to carry her load. One employee he overheard spoke about how thrilled Alexandra would be after advancing Josh to Assistant Director so her job would become easier. *Such a selfish bitch*, he had heard the teacher continue with another colleague. *She just wants to pursue other interests and hobbies she's never had the chance to do.*

Was this the reason why, all of a sudden, he got the feeling that only he could fit the bill? Would these extra hours she was planning for him to work really benefit his family if he was never going to be home? Perhaps Tara was right.

Josh flung open the back door and spotted the shovel partially hidden. Hoisting Michael's heavy skating bag up onto the seat at eye level, he heard something clang and smash. He reached for the zipper and tugged it back.

"What're you doin'?" Michael's voice boomed directly behind him.

Josh jumped. He quickly lifted his hands as if held up at gunpoint. His heart thumped loudly in his ears. Turning, he took a deep breath. His ribs felt as if they were squeezed inside a press.

"If you respect my property, you won't open that bag." Michael pronounced each syllable with clear and strong emphasis.

"Son, I think we need to talk." Nothing but hatred was written on Michael's face.

"If you back away, we have nothing to talk about."

"I can't do this any more." Josh's voice softened. "It's time we both faced what we have been ignoring."

"I don't know what you're talking about. Just walk away, Dad. You're," he swallowed, "so good at that." A sob caught in Michael's throat. "Just turn around and pre … pretend nothing."

Michael's eyes glistened. His bottom lip quivered and then pressed tight. For the second time that afternoon, Josh opened his arms for him.

Michael stepped back. "Why do you always do this?" Anger returned to his face, but his eyes softened. "If only you would have been there, none of this would be happening." He shook his head and then stared down at his boots. A sob escaped before his chin lifted. His wild eyes made contact.

Glaring into his father's eyes, Michael charged into his father's body. His arms flailed wildly, punching air until one fist struck Josh's chin.

Josh's head flew back, knocking sense into his thoughts. The muscles in Josh's forearms strengthened. He caught Michael's second fist, set to fly with the next punch, and pinned his arms around his body, hugging him tightly.

"You made mom drink." His son wheezed, the words pressed out from his mouth. "You killed her. You should have woke her up. You should have been there," he cried while struggling to break free.

The force was amazingly strong. Michael's body kept bucking as if he was riding on a bull from the Calgary Stampede, but Josh's arms remained in a tight hug. Finally, he settled.

Michael's breathing was labored. "I couldn't wake her up." He gulped air, choked as if drowning in his own spit. "No matter how hard I tried, she just wouldn't open her eyes." The tears flowed from Michael's eyes, down his face.

Josh swallowed hard. His face burned from the wetness frozen on his cheeks. "It's okay, son. It's okay. I'm here now." His body shook. Together they crumpled to the ground. "I'm not going anywhere," he cooed.

Snow penetrated through his pants. His butt and legs were soaked, but none of that mattered. He would remain motionless for as long as it took. His mouth pressed up against the side of Michael's head. Arms were still wrapped, pinned around his body. And his legs acted as a twist-tie, straddled and woven over Michael's. Michael's wet hair, plastered with sweat, stuck to his cheek.

Josh closed his eyes and sucked in a big breath. He smelled the familiar scent of his own child as if he was back in time. He held the baby, towel drying him fresh out of the tub. A lullaby came to Josh's memory from somewhere ... no words, just the tune of a wordless melody. Josh rocked Michael as if he was still this baby.

"I'm sorry, Michael." He swallowed the lump in his throat. I'm so sorry." The tears trickled down his cheeks, mixing with Michael's sweat and hair. Michael's body relaxed as if in a trance. Josh released the grip around Michael's upper body. He lifted his legs, setting Michael's trapped legs free.

Suddenly, Michael's body twirled. His arms moved as if he was now a true wrestler. Josh winced, unsure of where the next blow would hit.

But, instead, Michael swung his arms around Josh's body, engulfing him with a suffocating hug. His arms, legs, his entire body couldn't have melted closer.

In the middle of a prairie winter, covered in snow, Michael and Josh held each other in nurturing love. Never had Josh's body burned with such relief. ✦

THIRTY-FOUR HOURS EARLIER

Chapter 10

THIRTY-FOUR HOURS EARLIER

Josh groaned as he stretched for Michael's hand to hoist him from the snow bank. His muscles ached, but his heart had never felt so light and free.

"Here, I'll get your back." Josh turned, and Michael swiped the sticky snow from his father's coat and down the legs of his pants.

"We need to do this, son." Josh spoke softly over his shoulder, then turned around.

"I know. It's just so hard." Michael looked down and sniffled, wiping his nose with the back of his sleeve.

"Come. Glenda's waiting for us."

The few seconds it took to trudge from the truck to Margaret's gravesite was worthwhile time to Josh. He rehearsed his words and cleared his thoughts. He would need to be gentle and honest with the two people he had lost in his past but had been fortunate enough to regain in the present.

"I thought you were going to bring the shovel." Glenda asked. She stood tall over the only cleared headstone in the cemetery.

"Looks like you kids did a good enough job." Josh grinned. He folded his hands in a pyramid and then let them drop together in front of his body.

With Michael and Glenda on either side of him, they stared down over Margaret's plot.

"I still don't see why we had to come here?" Michael tugged his scarf up over his nose.

"I want you kids to read the message." Josh pointed to his wife's headstone and read aloud the message he'd memorized:

> Loving friends and family, weep not for me
> To take me home to be at rest
> How happy, happy I shall be
> God loved her more, and He thought best.

Josh's mind drifted to the past—the memories he had shoved down into his heart, vowing never to reveal. He pictured his life with Margaret contained in a large box. The day's events held inside, sealed and hidden. Now was the time for the past to be opened, exposed, and handled with care.

The inscription on the grave stone had guided Josh. The message was her way of guiding him in the right direction, giving him permission to open the flaps. Josh thought about that morning. Now that the box was open, everything that had happened became as clear as a pane of glass.

Michael yells ... Josh pushes his bedroom door open ... A scream catches in his throat ... his son on the floor ... his wife laying beside him ... Michael sobbing ... Josh fighting to pull him off his mother's lifeless body.

Josh had yelled, scolded Michael as if he was being disciplined for a malicious act. "Leave. Go back to your room. Stay there!"

Had he returned to his son's room to console him as the hysterical screams from his son rose from behind the closed bedroom door? Josh's chin dropped. His shoulders sagged.

"I'm sorry I wasn't there for you that morning when you tried to wake her." He worked his jaw, clutching his hands.

"Wake her?" Michael's voice rose louder than before. He turned to his father. "Dad, when are you going to be able to say the words?"

Josh squeezed his eyes closed, swallowing hard.

"She's dead. Mom's dead. Just say it."

Josh opened his eyes and turned toward Glenda. She stood tall, eyes wide, motionless as if frozen to the spot. "What do you think of the message she left us?" He asked Glenda as if Michael was nowhere in sight.

"Dad, will you get out of your classroom for once," Michael said.

"Don't interrupt," Josh scowled at Michael. "I was speaking to Glenda."

Glenda's eyes never left his. She pursed her lips, licked them, and then stepped closer. Her arm wrapped around his waist. "Uncle Josh …"

He pulled away.

"Aunty Margaret … she's dead."

Staring down at her grave, Josh shook his head. "I should have seen the signs. I should have been there to stop her. If only I could have made her stop drinking."

Michael cleared his throat. "You can't make anyone stop. She was sick. She needed to want to quit."

Josh turned to Michael, placing both hands on his shoulders. He recognized the pain in his eyes, felt the rigid form. "I want to help you, Michael." Tears stung the corners of his eyes. "Your mother is …" He cleared his throat. "Your mother is dead, and it's time we moved on." He gently shook Michael, breaking his wide, strong stance. "I'm here for you, but it is you who has to make the choice. Are you ready for help?"

Michael collapsed into Josh's arms. He wept as his body shook.

Josh's one arm extended wide. Glenda hesitated for just a moment before falling into the double mold.

"As for you, young lady, don't you worry about Marvin, we'll take care of him." Josh hugged her tightly. "Perhaps I can even help you get back with your special man."

Immediately, Glenda broke free. She pushed herself back. Her eyes narrowed. "What're you talking about?"

"Your postcard. I know I shouldn't have read it while I was waiting in the truck." Josh released Michael and watched him wipe his wet face with the back of his sleeve. He turned back to Glenda. "You sounded so heartbroken, and yet you never mentioned you had a boyfriend."

"Boyfriend?" Her voice shook as she kicked the snow. "Trust me, he's no boyfriend."

"Sorry. I shouldn't have been so nosy." Josh glanced down, then back up. "But I care about you, so I want to help you if I can."

"I just gotta get enough money saved up so Marvin can go back to his Care Home." She stood tall, throwing her dark mane of hair over her shoulders. "Then I can get the hell out of here." Her abrasive tone shook with her hands as she reached up to push back her stocking cap. "As far away from *him* as possible."

"Who are you talking about?" Michael questioned.

"Just never mind." Glenda charged back to the truck.

Josh watched the truck rock with the slamming of the door. He turned back to Michael. "We need to ... I need to say good-bye to your mother. You were a bigger man than me. You were able to say good-bye a long time ago. I also need to face some facts before it's too late. I can't watch you drink yourself to death. I don't want to lose you, too."

"I'm not going to die," Michael scoffed.

"I believe you may have a drinking problem, son." Josh dropped his chin, waiting for Michael's response. His mind raced back to that night when Michael lay dazed at the foot of his bed, oblivious to his surroundings, a crooked smile pasted on his face and staring at the ceiling. His reaction time seemed to be in slow motion, delayed, until he finally snapped to attention the moment he and Nathan came forward. Josh remembered how he had crashed back against the wall like a scared wild animal. His back was pressed against the wall, screaming for everyone to stay back, ordering distance between him and anyone who threatened to come near.

Michael said nothing. Josh glanced back up to Michael's face. He looked as if he'd been slapped.

Finally, the weight of the words hit him. "Listen." Michael whipped off his mitten and had his finger pointed inches from his father's nose. "You're a little late for a rescue mission." He shoved the mitten back on and shook his fist in the air. "Just stay out of my life."

"I won't stay out of your life." Josh glared back at his son. "I love you. I won't lose you like I lost your mother." Josh's voice softened. "What about the booze in your bag?"

"It's not mine!" Michael quickly answered. He turned down the same path Glenda had taken a few minutes before. "Just stay out of it."

"Whose is it?" Josh called, following Michael's trail.

"None of your business," Michael spoke over his shoulder. "Don't worry, I'll get rid of it."

Josh could barely match the long strides in front of him. "Hey, don't talk to me like that."

Michael stopped and turned. "How do you want me to talk to you?" He glared. "You can sure dish it out, but you can't take it."

Heat rose into Josh's cheeks, and his hands became wet with sweat. "I'm your father, and you better start showing me respect."

"Respect? You want *me* to show *you* respect?" Michael turned and resumed the short distance to the truck, speaking just above a whisper, "I learned from the best."

Glenda had started the truck. The warm air hit Josh like a gale wind. Had anything been resolved from this planned visit to Margaret's grave? He knew he must work on accepting his wife's death. He had made himself clear with Glenda about helping her with Marvin. He had told Michael he was sorry for not being with him that morning he found his mother. But had Michael believed his remorse? Michael was so angry and defiant, and the possibility of him following in his mother's footsteps was a sure bet. Michael had inherited her gene as an alcoholic. Josh reached for the knob and turned down the heater fan.

"Again, I want to apologize to both of you," Josh said as he glanced up at the rear view mirror and saw Michael's head bowed. He turned his head and saw Glenda's eyes fixed on the open field out the side window.

"Glenda, I'm sorry for my past behavior. I should never have stuck my nose into your mother's affairs by suggesting they ignore your rebellious time as a teenager. Sending you away was not the answer. I would never want someone to insist that I send my boys away. I was wrong. I hope you can forgive me."

Glenda's head turned, her eyes sparkled with wetness. "You did what you thought was best at the time." She released a heavy sigh. "I forgive you." She grinned, tight lipped.

"Michael ..."

"Dad, can't we wait and talk about this when we get home." His eyes flew to Glenda and then back to his father's. "If you respect me, I need you to give me some time."

Josh didn't say anything. His stomach flipped.

During the drive back to Deerwood, Josh tried to reason his thoughts. Where was that happy balance between being there for someone you love and letting them go?

His heart ached as his mind flashed back to Tara. She had never left his side through the good and the bad. The entire time, no matter what news he dished out to his employees, her words were full of encouragement and praise. She would even cheer in her funny kind of way, coaching him that whatever he had done was the best.

Hadn't Glenda echoed the same words, just minutes ago?

Isn't Michael asking him to let him go, just as he had asked Tara a few months ago? Had she felt the same feelings he was having right now?

"I'll give you the weekend, and then we'll have to sit down and have a serious talk." Through the rearview mirror, Josh watched Michael's shoulders drop while his head nodded.

There was a welcome silence inside the cab on the drive home.

Josh had come up with a plan but would need some guidance. He glanced across to Glenda. She had just put her headset over her ears and shut her eyes to listen to her music.

If only he could talk to someone about Michael. There was only one person he knew he could confide in and trust. It seemed Tara had purposely avoided him all morning. She didn't answer his calls and told him quite frankly that she didn't want anything to do with him or his life again.

His plan would work, he was sure. Now if only he could run everything by Tara. She would know what to do.

He stretched to turn up the volume on the radio, humming to his own tunes. ✦

THIRTY HOURS EARLIER

Chapter 11

THIRTY HOURS EARLIER

Soon Tara would be in total darkness. The tiny one-person kitchen in the duplex was quickly losing natural light. Tara flipped the small, eye-level switch on the mismatched range hood.

She continued to make circular motions in the spaghetti sauce with a large wooden spoon as if stirring a brew in a caldron. Her eyes burned from dryness as she stood staring at the swirling mixture of red. She breathed into her nostrils the tantalizing aroma of fresh simmering tomatoes, celery, onions, fried hamburger meat, and a variety of Italian spices. Her stomach growled.

While she stirred, she hummed the familiar soft rock tunes coming from her CD stacker that was plugged in on the counter. Her bare toes tapped to the exact beat of the song.

On the next burner sat the largest pot with a lid that she could find in the back of the deep cupboard. The water was near boiling, and she welcomed the moist air that warmed her naked arms. Steam escaped from the corners until a sudden sizzle and the repetitious bouncing of the lid interrupted her thoughts. She jumped and quickly lifted the lid. As if angry, the water rolled and spit over the sides, splashing onto the red-hot element. Turning both elements off, she wiped her hands on her apron and sauntered toward the side window. She peered around the closed blind over the table set for two.

The same light that had been peeking through the center slits of his curtains earlier was now casting its glow across the front yard. Still, for the past hour, there had been no action or sign of Devin himself.

She glanced over her shoulder and up at the clock hanging above the sink to read five minutes after seven. Had they not agreed that dinner would be at seven this Friday? Had she imagined the entire scene of Devin asking her out on a date, picking her up in his strong arms, and whisking her away just after he had called her beautiful?

Her stomach flipped and sagged as if pulled down by a heavy weight.

He would be here any second. Her mind pulled into positive gear, steering her back to their first encounter. How comforting his arms had felt around her deflated body. She had slowly opened her eyes to stare into the gorgeous eyes of ... Josh.

Josh? Could she just stop thinking about *him* and get with the present? She charged back to the stove and flipped the burner under her sauce pan to ignite. She gripped the stirring spoon tighter. Her heart slowed as she huffed. Yet, Josh wouldn't think of being late for anything.

A gentle nudge poked through the bottom of her pant cuff. In a fright, Tara trembled and looked down. A pure white ball of fur sat at her feet wagging its tail. Black beady eyes peered up under its white bangs and over its short black-tipped nose.

Tara bent down and picked the dog up into her arms. She cradled it as if it were a baby. Its snout reached up under her chin and licked her neck. "You are so cute." She giggled and rubbed its belly while its head turned from side to side, sprawling its undercarriage to expose more stomach.

"So, you're Shadow. Why haven't I seen you before?" Tara would have let the girls take the dog to their father's house for the weekend, but she knew Rick would have nothing to do with it. "You probably miss your daddy. He'll be here pretty soon." Shadow wiggled and lapped her chin again with her rough tongue. "That tickles," she laughed, setting her down. Shadow pranced up on her haunches, begging for more.

"Now, no more," she attempted to scold, but her voice sounded light. Shadow's tail wagged harder, and she flipped over onto her back just as the telephone rang.

In the few seconds it took Tara to pick up the phone on its third ring, she had thought of each possible caller and their possible reasons for trying to connect with her.

Devin: "Sorry, but I made a huge mistake. I'm not interested in meeting with you."

The girls: "Dad has other plans for the weekend, so we're coming home early."

Josh: "I'm sorry about being such an ass. Can we start over."

Yeah, right, Tara snorted.

She let out her breath after she heard Kammy's voice begin to chirp on the other end. "Don't blame me for wanting to check up on you. The way you ripped out of the shop, I thought you may have killed someone by now."

"Yeah, some day I'll learn how to control this temper of mine." Tara giggled while collapsing on the worn couch. She scrunched a throw pillow into her arms, squeezing it to her stomach.

"So, when are you coming over for tea? I kind of thought you'd have a lot more free time now so we could hang out."

"I want to see you soon, but I've got plans for this evening." Tara exchanged the receiver from one ear to the other.

"Yes, so you've said. Now you have my curiosity going. What plans have you got?"

"I need my life to move on. Josh obviously isn't interested in me." Tara swallowed hard. "I need separation so I can learn more about myself."

"Are you forgetting who you're talking to?"

"Okay, what I really need is a man who'll give me the time of day, one I can call my own, and who will be proud to be seen with me." She wrapped the long chord around her big toe and jiggled the cord. "Josh isn't right for me, and I don't need him." She pulled the curl straight, stretching the line an extra foot away from her body. "I'm ready to date." Releasing the cord, she let the white wire snap back into its curled state.

"You sound like you know what you're talking about, but," Kammy paused and her usual rattling slowed as if she was having difficulty finding the right words, "dating someone else is something you never mentioned before."

"Yes, dating." Tara squeezed the pillow into her body. She had concluded that dating Devin would be the perfect solution to remove Josh from her obsessive thoughts. Devin would bring excitement to her life beyond her tenuous position of being Ms. Robstead—the hard-working, unmarried teacher at Deerwood School who had sneaked around with her boss because she was madly in love with the man who had more important priorities in life than her. Wasn't it true that he would rather be caught dead than to be seen as a public spectacle by her side?

"Tell me more," Kammy's voice gained speed.

"There's someone here who's kind of interesting." Tara skipped over to the window and tipped the blind to its side. She peered across to her neighbor's house. Nothing had changed. "I'm having dinner with him tonight." *Unless he really isn't interested.*

"You don't surprise me, girl. I've seen the way guys look you over. They spot you in the restaurant and stare as if you're a go-go girl. They drool and have to lap their tongues back into their gaping mouths. They practically follow you around like a puppy dog."

"Oh, stop now." Tara laughed and tossed the pillow onto the matching chair. "You know, I would love to keep chatting, but I better go. He's due to arrive any minute."

The butterflies tickled inside her stomach, and her heart felt light as if suspended up into the ceiling. "Call me tomorrow, and I'll fill you in."

"Be sure to rehearse all the details, Honey. I could use a little more excitement in my life."

After hanging up the phone, Tara entered the half bath on the main level. She flipped on the light and turned on the tap. Washing her hands, she glanced up into the medicine cabinet mirror.

Her eyes looked cloudy, not quite blood shot but more yellow than white. The week had been long and difficult, and now everything that had happened over the past few months was beginning to take a visual toll on her face. The medication prescribed had helped her sleep a full ten hours last night, and her muscles thanked her in the morning. But today's events had set her back.

She thought of that pretty young woman who danced from *The Hutt* out into Josh's arms. Tara's face blurred as the tears hovered over the rim. She ripped off a chunk of toilet paper and blew her nose.

Josh had no problem letting her go and continuing with his new life.

Why couldn't she just forget about him? Dabbing the corners of her eyes, careful not to interrupt the detailed makeup Tara had meticulously reapplied after she had come home from school, she added a new coat of frosted pink lipstick to her full lips. Smacking her mouth closed, she ground her lips back and forth. Opening her mouth, she smiled into the mirror as if in front of a camera. The reflection exposed bright shining straight teeth.

"Beautiful, eh, Devin?" She shook her head and tried again with a soft smile. She watched how her eyes took on a new sparkle and the creases around her lids followed the lines up into her perfectly etched brows.

"Fake it 'til you make it, right, Josh?"

The door bell rang. Her stomach turned. "Oh, God, he's here."

Shadow barked furiously. Tara whipped off the apron from around her tiny waste and flipped down the pointed collar from her cotton blouse. Tucking the fabric firmly down into her tight jeans, she glanced back into the mirror for one final inspection. Her straight black hair glistened. She quickly flipped it down and around her ears in a manicured bob. From the outside, she looked like a million dollars, but on the inside, she felt like a dish rag.

"Coming," she yelled from the bathroom. "It's okay, Shadow, Daddy's here." The dog barked in time to Tara's marching steps to the top of the stairs.

"Come in, come in." She smiled. "Close the door quick, or we'll be able to make snowmen in here." She greeted Devin with a light voice.

Shadow growled and took off down the stairs from the landing, down into the bottom level. "Here I thought she'd be all over you. Shadow hasn't seen you all day."

Devin shrugged. He reached down his side like a dancer and gracefully removed his boots. His thick, jet-black hair fell forward. She shook her head trying not to notice his hands and the athletic physique in his performance.

He peered through his dark locks, while deep-brown eyes softened. His smooth face rounded from the wide grin that sent dimples to embed deeply in both cheeks. Extending his hidden arm from behind his back, he produced the promised addition to the meal.

"I thought this would go better with our evening than wine, being it's so cold outside. Sorry for the mix-up tonight. I'm running a tad late."

Taking the bottle from his hand, she smiled, "No problem. The unforeseen happens sometimes." She turned the dark bottle with both hands. "It is so cold, I couldn't agree with you more." She read the label: *Baileys*—seventeen percent proof.

"A perfect choice of beverage. You are so perceptive." She stood tall.

Brushing the snow from his pants, he lowered his cuffs from his jeans and a pile dumped out onto the floor mat. "I guess I should have walked around our driveways instead of cutting through the snowdrifts. I didn't think it would be that deep. God, we've had a lot of snow this winter." He cantered up the steps, taking two at a time. "Do you really think I'm perceptive?" He cocked his head sideways.

She had never seen a man with such smooth actions. He gingerly lifted onto his socked toes until he reached the top of the main level.

"Hello?" He waved his hand in front of her face.

She stepped back and blinked. "Oh, yes, I think you are very perceptive, especially for a guy." She headed for the kitchen where she took down two crystal glasses. After adding ice cubes, she poured in the thick, creamy liqueur.

"You seem to be very in tune with your surroundings, and I deem myself a natural when it comes to reading someone's personality and body language." She handed him the glass, trying to avoid those dark ruminating eyes.

"Oh, you can make yourself comfortable in the living room." Her arms spanned wide, nearly spilling the freshly poured contents. "I'll be there in a minute." She twirled around back toward the kitchen. "I just have to turn on the stove and let this sauce simmer. Please put some lights on. It's dreadfully dark for this time of the day." Her eyes rolled up as she rushed away.

"I hope you're hungry," she called over her shoulder. His eyes roamed about the room as he examined her furnishings. His lips pursed and forced air propelling out of his full cheeks as if he had been holding his breath.

"I'm famished." He called back and sat on the couch. "You have a nice place here."

"Yeah, it's just like your home," she replied as she entered the living room, laughing at the comparison.

He chuckled. "I mean your furniture is awesome." His head jerked to the side, causing his dark locks to lift higher.

"Are you kidding? This is all my mom's stuff. When I left Rick, I left everything with him. So, here I am, like a kid just out of high school scrounging off my mom. I had most of the bedrooms remodeled, so the next step will be the upstairs."

"I take it Rick was your husband?"

Tara sat on the adjacent chair and nodded. Setting her glass down on a coaster in front of her, she lifted her chin. "It's been seven years."

"That's a long time."

"And what about you?"

"Nothing serious. Haven't had anyone enter my life that has caught my serious attention until I noticed you." He winked and lifted his glass in a toast. "Let's celebrate tonight for us; getting to know each other. Never know if things will click or not." He stretched across and clinked her crystal with his own. He tipped the glass and swallowed half the contents in one gulp.

Tara stood, unsure if it was a feeble attempt to avoid his piercing brown eyes or to relieve the flutter cramping her stomach. Since Devin had entered her home, she felt as if she was a teenager with a crush on a boy who was sitting next to her in the classroom. Was the attraction mutual? Was this the way a single woman of thirty-five felt when dating a stranger for the first time?

"What are you thinking?" The question flew out of her mouth, too late to stop stupidity. She sat back down in the same spot and took a huge swallow. The creamy liquid instantly warmed her mouth and slid down her throat in a smooth motion.

Devin shook his head as if to wake up from a trance. "Two things, actually. First, I couldn't help but smell your supper and think to myself that no matter how good it tastes, it's not as damn yummy as you. And second, I was just thinking how cool it is that all of this stuff matches my stuff."

Tara dropped her chin for fear of sudden disappointment and to hide the scowl smeared across her face. Again, she lifted her glass, this time welcoming the burn and hoping to stifle the thoughts that kept surfacing nearly every second.

Blending homes had never entered her mind with anyone except with Josh. She had dreamed of that possibility, a time when her girls and Josh's boys would mix into a united family.

In the past, during the odd social staff function that involved families, she had taken extra time to observe how the children got along and whether or not they mixed comfortably.

Tara was always impressed.

She watched the way Nicole chatted with Nathan. Best friends, her daughter had mentioned at one time as her fingers flew over the keypad of the laptop while connecting back and forth in text fashion. When Tara had asked about her daughter's feelings toward this boy, she scowled and practically spit on the ground before saying she saw him only as a brother. He was too good of a friend ...

The two younger children got along but weren't as close. They had little in common and had more of a tolerant relationship. They guarded each other's privacy in a respectful fashion.

Tara had dreamed of the six of them under one roof. They would have meals together, discussing schoolwork and new social outings, just like the *"Brady Bunch"*—one big happy blended family. But this dream dissolved as quickly as salt in hot water.

Could she even think of her and Devin living together? Regardless of her vociferous internal protest, she found herself strangely thrilled by the scenario of her and Devin under the same roof.

She took another sip and the ice cubes hit her front teeth. Her eyes grew wide.

Devin picked up on the cue a little too quickly. "Can I pour you another drink? Looks like we are both thirsty, sucking them back and practically licking our glasses clean. See, we have a lot in common."

Tara nodded. She nearly chuckled out loud as she realized it had been years since she had heard such jargon. She was not usually someone who sucked back booze. Coffee maybe, but drinking for the affect of alcohol dropped from her life right after she graduated from college. At that time, she prided herself in being a grown-up, able to take responsibilities and be in control of whatever she set her mind to.

Never had she wished to go back to those days when the focus was on parties involving way too much booze. It was a shame that Rick never came through that era. He had always been a kid who never wanted to grow up. Perhaps he was right when they signed the final divorce papers. Perhaps it was she who had changed and not Rick.

As she waited for Devin to return from refilling their classes, her head tipped back. For the first time that day, the knots in her neck stretched and finally disappeared. All of her muscles relaxed, and her head lightened. Even Josh faded from her mind. Now she wondered whether she should dismiss Devin back to his home or follow through with her own desire to throw herself into his arms.

As the evening wore on, Devin's ideas became the best she ever heard. She could feel herself hanging onto every word as he encouraged her to take a risk, dare to live a little, not to worry about her job, forget Josh and his obvious blindness. He did not appreciated that he had let go of a good woman, and he would be the one to suffer in the end.

On first impressions, Devin was very good looking, but like a fine wine, he became better looking as the evening wore on. By eleven o'clock that night, he had become deadly hot and sexy. Constant compliments rushed out of his perfect mouth about her appearance, abilities, and the awesome dinner they had eaten late. She couldn't stop smiling.

She squinted at the hands on the clock, trying to focus on the numbers. "Does that say two o'clock?" Her words slurred, brows furrowed, and the straightened arm swayed sideways until the pointing finger was nowhere close to the clock.

"Yeah, it's late." He rose off the couch.

"No, don't go yet. Da night is young." She stood, teetered, and then fell into his arms. "Just like you." Her finger stabbed his chest as he supported her entire weight.

"Come on. I'll take you to bed." His voice deepened. His strength was like a warrior ready to lead his troops into battle. He dropped his sword and shield before lifting her easily into his arms.

As if in a replay from earlier that week, she snuggled her nose under his chin and wrapped her arms around his thick neck. She felt the rhythm of each footstep as he descended down the stairs into her bedroom.

"Don't forget your stuff." Her head snapped up. The room spun out of control, forcing her to settle back down onto his chest. "You may need it later," she mumbled.

Her eyelids felt as if they had been glued shut. In unison, the beating of his heart matched perfectly with each breath she took. Her mind delved onto him. Devin had given her the best night in her life. And no one else had ever said she was yummy before.

"And not just yummy either, but *damned* yummy," she said. The words were intended to remain in her mind, but they sputtered out of her mouth as she felt the cool cotton sheets press up against the heat of her cheek. She giggled mischievously into the gorgeous dark eyes of the great knight who had come to her rescue. ✦

FIFTEEN HOURS EARLIER

Chapter 12

FIFTEEN HOURS EARLIER

Tara's head felt glued to the pillow. Her eyes refused to open to the morning sun beaming through the slits of the horizontal blinds.

Blinking back to darkness, she became totally lost in her perception of time and place. Her surreal sense that she was floating around the room was immediately followed by the anticipation of the sudden impact when she would hit the ground. A tidal wave of anxiety sparked through her body as she attempted to decipher last night's events. She retraced every step, praying she had not done anything stupid.

Turning her head and peeking through her sore lids, she let out a heavy sigh. Thank God the bed was empty beside her. The strewn covers gave no clue to the events of the previous evening, and searching her memory proved futile.

Tara squeezed her eyes shut and plowed her face into the pillow. Berating herself, she slammed her fists into the mattress on both sides of her head.

"Stupid!" Her tongue remained stuck to the roof of her mouth causing the word to sound garbled even to her own ears. Whipping the pillow out and throwing it on the floor, she banged her face into the solid mattress. Her head ached from the movement.

Gathering the blanket around her naked breasts, she teetered to the bathroom and stuck her head under the tap. The water flowed full blast past her lips. She sucked most into her parched mouth.

The room spun as she fought to raise the toilet seat. Bending over, she puked up everything in her stomach and then dry heaved. Still trying to remember last night's events, she hoped the worst possible scenario flushed with the remnants in her belly.

In the bright kitchen, she cinched the cloth belt of her housecoat around her waist and stretched to reach the coffee filters. The clanging of dishes magnified like church bells in her head. The pounding of drums racked with each pulse throughout her body. Her body felt stiff and her muscles shook, as if she had washed a dozen windows from the top rung of a twelve-foot ladder.

"Good morning," a deep voice spoke just behind her ear.

Tara jumped, clutching her chest.

"You idiot!" Not sure if the scolding was for him or if her words were meant for herself.

Devin held out his arms showing his palms. He looked like a soldier surrendering to the enemy.

"What are you trying to do, scare me to death?" She stood staring boldly into Devin's bewildered face. Her heart raced as if stuck in her ears. Blood rushed into her face, igniting her cheeks.

He stepped back. "Whoa, girl, I didn't mean to startle you." His head bent down as if scolded like a small child. "I'm really truly sorry."

She swallowed and took in a deep breath as she turned back to the coffee machine.

"I know you didn't mean to scare me, but don't you *ever* do that again." She spit the words from her mouth. She hoped he couldn't see her legs shaking from under the terrycloth robe.

"See, that's why we hooked up so well, Tara. We communicate so easily. We don't hold anything back. We can be ourselves. When was the last time you could really be yourself?" He pulled out the chair from the table. "Here, you sit. I'll make that for you." He slid around her body, very close. His scent, fresh and clean, immediately filled her nostrils. It was a tantalizing odor of pure masculinity.

Leaning back against the chair, she took a long, deep breath, now wondering why she felt so deflated. She hid her trembling hands that she had always considered graceful and capable but now seemed clumsy and lost. Hadn't this been what she always wanted—a man she could wake up with who would make her morning coffee, chat about the prospective daily events, plan outings, or lounge around the house together?

She pressed her lips together and forced the corners up. Standing, she walked over behind his back. She reached for his arm that was draped into the coffee tin.

"I'm sorry." She gently touched his thick forearm and combed the thin, soft, dark hair through her fingers. "I'm not used to having an overnight guest." Her mind fished for details, but everything was still in such a fog.

He stopped digging and stood tall in front of her. His brown eyes softened, while his dimples deepened. "I didn't stay over." He chuckled and turned back to the counter. "Now you made me lose count. How many scoops did I already put in?"

She breathed a sigh of relief.

Coffee had never tasted better. How could she complain? She sat across the table from a gorgeous man she had allowed into her home, a gentleman who had treated her with complete respect and was taking such good care of her. He listened to all she had pent up inside for the last few months. Tara suspected she repeated the same information from last night. But nonetheless, he listened attentively and agreed with everything she said. How could she have spoken so harshly to a man as caring as Devin? Wasn't she the one who spent the last two years sneaking around with her boss? She was the one who needed to be scolded for sticking with a man who obviously never cared about her or saw the importance of her needs.

Had Josh ever listened? Tara thought of how easily Josh dismissed her for another woman.

Now it was her turn to do the happy dance. By chance, she had snagged the ideal man and the only eligible single guy in town. He was like a genie in a bottle, a complete stranger who miraculously appeared as if it was time for her dreams to come true. Devin was more than willing to grant her any wish her heart desired, even if it meant the dreaded "C" word—commitment. He was searching for the same. Nothing could be better.

"So if you didn't stay over, how did you end up in my kitchen this morning?" Tara tucked a loose strand of hair behind her ear.

"I forgot Shadow." He sipped at his coffee and watched the dark liquid sit in the cup. "I thought I'd sneak in and get her without waking you." He tipped the cup back in the same manner as the glass last night. He glanced up before dragging his tongue over his moist lips.

Tara nodded her head, keeping her gaze pinned at the cup and away from Devin's handsome smirk, trying desperately not to invite him downstairs to help her dress down for the day. "If you'll excuse me, I must get ready for the day."

"Sure. I'll just see myself out." He pulled back from the table.

"No," her voice rushed. "I mean, please don't leave yet." She stepped closer to his sculpted body.

His eyes crinkled, full lips lifted into a smirk. With his right hand, he watched the tips of his fingers slowly trace the contours of her face.

Her eyes closed as she welcomed the touch. Starting at her forehead, his hand moved down her cheek, chin, and neck. Goose bumps rose over her entire body. She slowly sucked in a fortifying breath.

Stopping just short of the opening of her robe, he gently fanned back up. Her knees weakened. She waited for his strong arms to catch her from falling.

Holding her close, he wrapped his arms around her shaking body. He whispered in her ear, "I'll be ..."

Suddenly, the main entrance door burst open. Josh stood at the bottom of the stairs. His eyes widened with a look of sheer shock.

Tara pushed Devin away just as her belt slid to the floor. Tara gasped as her robe fell open exposing her aroused breasts. Quickly, she wrapped herself tight and held her breath.

"What the hell is going on here?" Josh's voice boomed. She had seen the expression on his face before. It was worry, pure anger, and thickly covered with disgust. She felt like a teenager caught making out with her boyfriend.

A shriek rose in her throat.

"Josh." Her one hand splayed across her chest, the other cupped her mouth. "What are you doing here?" She stared down into Josh's hard, glaring, brown eyes. They matched his thick, dark, glistening curls. His shoulders looked as if they might explode from his jacket, like the transformation of *The Incredible Hulk* character. She imagined his perfectly pressed dress pants and matching shiny oxfords ripping to shreds as his muscles tripled in size.

"Who's this?" Josh shouted, ignoring Tara's question.

Her head turned back to Devin. She saw his soft brown eyes and the diamond stud sparkling from his left ear. His lean body was clothed in tight-fitting, faded denims. His oversized hoodie and bare feet ... he was just plain yummy all around.

"Josh, this is Devin Tucker. Devin, Josh Henderson."

"Hey," said Devin, raising his hand and giving a thumbs-up.

Even with the motion inches from her, Josh's eyes never wavered off of Tara. Her morning appearance would have indicated she must have just crawled out of bed, and not alone.

Heat rose to Tara's skin. Her throat tightened as she suddenly realized it was the first time Josh had ever seen her like this. Before today, she had always pictured their first morning together as being totally different. She imagined them waking with matching tousled hair, mischievous grins, and shiny gleams in both their eyes after a wild night of lovemaking. Then they would dive back under the covers for a replay before they both dressed for work and got the kids up for school. What had just happened was nothing like what she had pictured.

Just for a second, Josh glared at Devin. Turning, he walked out and slammed the door shut.

Tara peered around the heavy living room drapes. She watched him slide up into his truck beside his new woman from the restaurant.

Was he planning a formal introduction or what? The blood shot down a few degrees and now felt like ice surging through Tara's veins. Her hands became clammy and stiffened into fists at her sides. Her throat constricted, and her eyes welled with tears. All emotions twisted in her chest.

"Everything okay, Tara?" Devin asked from behind her. His voice sounded soft and comforting, yet he made no advance to comfort her until she signaled her wishes.

She turned, her shoulders slumping forward. Her chin dropped. "Could be better."

He nodded, stepping only inches from where she stood. He opened his arms. "You don't have to live life alone. I'm here for you."

She fell into his embrace, putting her wet face against his chest as he held her tight.

"I'm the perceptive one, remember? You can trust me," he said, and pulled away with his hands remaining on her shoulders. A serious expression blanketed his entire face.

Her muscles tightened, and she glanced away. She broke free of his hold. There was too much happening all at once. It was too fast, too soon, while at the same time, Devin's presence felt right. Her headache took on a new severity. She thought of Kammy's advice. It was time for her to move on and find someone special in her life. She deserved to be proudly shown to the community of Deerwood, not as a trophy or a productive employee, but as a wonderful, sexy woman, a team partner. Devin could be that type of man. She saw him introducing her to his students, picking her up after school, taking her out to dinner—hands intertwined over the table as they gazed into each other's eyes, oblivious to their surroundings.

"Do you want me to leave you alone?" His soft voice broke through her swirling thoughts.

"No," she spoke quicker than anticipated. She glanced up, smiling. "I'd like you to stay for the weekend," she whispered into his ear. ✧

NOW

NOW!

Gladstone Central Hospital
Mental Health Division
Gladstone, Saskatchewan

As if in an elevator shaft, the light quickly faded as she descended below the surface.

Dank air covered Tara's body, emptying any reserved inner peace, sucking the little warmth from her body. She had read that hell was hot and full of fire.

Where's the blinding brightness, the licking flames? I want to feel the burn. She fell down into the farthest depths of her soul. All was dark and cold. *Is this what it's like being buried alive?*

Her face twitched as the metallic smell of trapped minerals tickled her nose.

I'm going to sneeze.

Perhaps an explosion would clear her head, put everything in proper perspective, awake her from this state of total confinement. Instead, the top to her coffin closed. Now, she couldn't breathe.

I told you I want to live. She fought to wiggle her arms free, but the sides were too close, the lid too tight. *Let me out of here!*

Through the transparent walls, the ground blurred like a motion picture set in fast-forward. Instead of the scene elongating, layers of soil and mud eventually ran together, the kind of sensation that forced your eyes shut, or dizziness would take over. Rocked with motion, she felt sick to her stomach.

Cold, frosty air rose, chilling whatever exposed skin was available. She fell faster. Her bare toes froze as her sheet puffed out like a parachute.

She recalled the times as a little girl when she was sent to spend summer vacations at her grandparents' old farmhouse. In the beginning, the visits were forced by her parents, but she quickly came to crave her times there. They became much more to her than just visits with her grandparents.

Never would she ever admit the truth. She would feel free to share the expected responses: describing freshly baked gingerbread cookies in the warm kitchen heated solely by the wood stove, and the do's and don'ts of her grandparents' peculiarities and expectations. But little did they know—Gram and Gramp's place had something better than all the love any family could ever share ...

She remembered listening for the heater fan to kick on as her signal. She would pitter-patter to the corner of the room and stand over the metal grates. Her body tingled as total transformation began to take place.

Overcome by a state of bliss, the little girl vanished. Her frilly nightgown transformed into a beautiful Cinderella gown, causing her to feel like a fairy princess in a fictional story. As her toes magically lifted off the floor, her body floated higher and higher until her princess tiara touched the whitewashed ceiling.

She cherished this feeling. As long as she remained over the rush of air, all worries disappeared, voices diminished to silence. Peace at last.

It was only a game, really, but who would win, her or the heat?

The heat liked to disturb her fleeting moments of serenity. Flames licked around each leg and burned the tender skin around her toes, scarring the bottoms of her tiny, delicate feet. Intuition yelled for her to step off to the side, but if she listened, the results would be disastrous. The glorious fantasy would dissipate. Falling from the ceiling, she would crash down to the cold wooden floor. A crumpled heap of rubbish was how she would feel. The pretty dress would be gone. She hated that feeling. There was only one solution: to remain standing on the register. It was well worth the reward. If she beat the heat and stood long enough, the pain subsided into glorious numbness.

Now, lying on the hospital bed, she prayed for the same numbness, as the air wrapped around her body like water streaming from a shower. She remembered how the burn lasted only a few seconds before she would feel nothing at all.

Blankets, I need blankets. I keep on asking, but no one is listening. Why couldn't people be more like Marvin? He would give anyone the shirt off his back, that man. And at least he listens.

She accelerated farther down. A high pitch, sounding like rubber belts being thread through a pulley at high speed, came from under her coffin.

You can let me off any time.

As if on command, the whir slowed, much like a subway car coming to its next stop.

You got the wrong person here. I'm not the one who is supposed to be strapped and confined like a prisoner. I'm a victim—the victim of no return. I've earned this right, damn it. I demand my rights to be heard.

"Not to worry princess, I will take care of you," a deep voice whispered close to her left ear.

How did he get in here? It's the middle of the night.

"Go now. Get off here, or these doors will close and you'll remain here forever," a soft feminine voice whispered in her right ear.

The dampness on Tara's cheeks saturated with fine particles of salt crystals slipped through Tara's lips and fed her parched mouth. The refreshing taste of tears made her tongue come to life. She swallowed and winced at the cheap, heavy cologne mixed with bad body odor, a smell she had to get away from.

Get me out of here!

She had to sneeze but held her breath. Playing possum was imperative with him around. He would leave if he thought she was dead.

"You are so beautiful lying here." She could hear the vinyl rubbing and pictured his arm brushing the sides of his jacket. He placed his hot, sticky palm on her forehead. The hair that draped over her face was now being tucked around her left ear. His breathing was in time to her rapid heartbeat.

"You remind me of Sleeping Beauty. My mom read me that story, you know. You'll have to meet her when you get out of here." His fingernail nibbled on her lobe, pinching and scraping each fold. "Don't worry. I'll make sure you get out of here."

"Who are you? Is that you, Josh?"

The rumbling inside her mind grew louder. The straps around her wrists tightened. Her naked body lay motionless on the cold steel of the tracks. The horn blasted. The vibration drifted up into her shoulder blades, into her back, and through her entire body. The train was getting closer.

"Time to wake up, Tara." The feminine voice took on a new tone with a tinge of alarm.

I've got to get out of here now! She tried to push the lid up, but it wouldn't budge. She expanded her shoulders, hoping the box would break. Nothing. Finally, she kicked up, and the gate to the tomb opened. But it was still so dark. She couldn't see her hand in front of her face.

How can I leave without knowing where to go?

His fingers lingered on the tip of her chin, his hand folded out like a fan around her neck. Fingers splayed on one side, and a thumb pushed on the other. He slid his open palm down her throat as if trying to smooth the wrinkles from the base of her neck. The hand stopped to manipulate her protruding collarbone.

Oh, my God. You're not Josh!

"Mom is so proud of me. I'll never forget the time when I brought home my first paycheck. Out for dinner, I insisted. The entire check spent on one meal, but I didn't care. The look on her face, the way she beamed. Her eyes sparkling with a huge grin from ear to ear."

Tara floated above her own corpse-like body and remained with her back up to the ceiling. This was the first time she had seen her small, private room. Floral paintings hung on each of the four sage green walls. Boxes of monitors surrounded the woman on the bed.

The unresponsive carcass was tucked into the bed with crisp white sheets. She looked so fragile, yet, threatening at the same time. The stupid, noisy machines hooked up all over her body and face made her look like a specimen being used for a scientific experiment.

No wonder I couldn't fall asleep.

Her eyes roamed from the machines back to her lifeless body. Nothing could have prepared her for who she saw hovering near ...

Oh, my God, it's him, the devil himself.

He looked as if he was ready to jack off at any moment.

She watched as his other hand reached behind her neck and used the edge of the cotton gown as a guide. He blindly searched, traveling with wide swipes across her shoulders and slowly down toward the surface of the bed.

He grasped the string to her gown while leaning in to her left ear, his breathing came in short bursts. He rolled the ends of the string around each fingertip as if he were doing a braid blindfolded.

"Just leave and trust yourself," the feminine-sounding voice spoke again, but the lips of the man hovering over her body hadn't moved.

Who's talking to me?

Well, this is crazy. I'm supposed to be the crazy one. Isn't that why I was admitted here in the first place? Now, you're telling me that I'm to either stay in this crate and fall to the bottom of doom or get off and trust some invisible existence to guide me back to safety?

"You have a choice," the soft voice replied.

Tara watched as the silent devil tugged on the knot. Her gown fell loosely over one shoulder. With one hand spanned around her throat, the other traveled across her collarbone where he outlined the long protruding bone with his fingertip. Stopping in the middle, he found the soft concave.

She watched his head bend toward the woman. His tongue splattered inside her ear, and then traced the entire length of her neck in a motion similar to the one he had just lead with his fingers. She heard his breath quicken as she watched him lick out the sternum as if it was an ice cream cone.

I don't want to die. Not like this.

"That's not a good enough answer. If you want to live, you must face him," instructed the soft feminine voice.

The pressure increased around her throat. His hand constricted and expanded the esophagus much like a doctor pulsating on an oxygen bulb. His breathing followed suit.

I can't. He's too strong. She willed for him to finish what he'd come for. If he wanted to take her, just do it.

"Just look at him. Look at you. Is this what you want, Tara?" The feminine voice questioned, still soft but with new firmness.

Lifting his mouth from her body, he remained standing over her like a coroner dissecting a body in a morgue. The hand around her neck traveled down and under her gown. Slowly, his fingers led and his mouth followed.

Dead center of her body, he stopped to rub the edge of each rib, groping the tautness of her skin. His nostrils flared as if he was sucking in the imaginary secretions of sexual moisture from their bodies. His head threw back as he flipped his chin high up in the air while he squeezed his eyes shut.

It's too late. The damage is done.

"It's never too late to face the one who has done you harm. You must stand up for yourself. Tell him how you feel and that he's never going to be able to hurt you again," instructed the unseen woman's soft voice.

His one hand remained on top of the cotton gown, finding her hardened nipple. He tweaked the erect bud. The other hand traveled under the thin cotton sheet on a blind mission to find her bare leg. He quickly traveled up the inside of her thigh.

I can't. I'm too scared.

"You're not alone," the soft voice continued. "Never will you be alone again."

Tara dropped from the ceiling and back into her own body. Her heart pounded, and her muscles tightened.

"Get off of me," she screamed. Her voice filled the hospital room. She coughed and sputtered, choking on her own phlegm.

Tara opened her eyes. She was alone in the room. But not all was quiet. Instead of the woman who belonged to the soft voice or the presence of the devil, the room squealed with beeping machines and an alarm set at high pitch.

The door banged open against the wall as Doctor Frances ran to her side.

"You finally decided to join the world." He checked her vital signs while staring into her eyes. He grinned.

His face wobbled and became fuzzy. "That's the best sound,"

Tara cleared her throat, "that door has made since I got here," she said, hearing her own words slur together.

"Shh, you shouldn't be talking," Doctor Frances responded, his voice deep but gentle.

Tara closed her eyes and pressed her lips together. She thought of the battle she had endured only moments before and sighed, knowing she had just escaped hell. She inhaled a deep, refreshing breath of fresh air and acknowledged her gratitude to the one who had helped her find the will to fight for her life. Ever so slightly, the corners of her mouth lifted as it all became clear. The unseen feminine voice belonged to no other than herself. ✦

THIRTEEN HOURS EARLIER

Chapter 13

THIRTEEN HOURS EARLIER

Tara grabbed Devin's hand, practically dragging him down the stairs. The second they stepped into her bedroom, Shadow bolted from under the bed and scurried between both their legs. The dog ran up the stairs looking more like a ball of fire than a fluffy snowball.

Tara giggled. She shrugged her shoulders while indicating the precise spot for him to sit. With the tip of her finger, she pointed out the lounge chair in the short distance.

He followed her gesture and sat, watching her every move.

She strolled to the far wall where he sat and looked down into his eyes. Slowly, she reached for the wand and closed the blinds, creating a dull gray appearance throughout her bedroom.

He rubbed his eyes and then opened them wide. "Tara," he rose from the soft cushions and stood just inches from her, "I think we should …"

Tara turned from the window and pushed him down. "You don't worry about anything. Let me do the leading. It's my specialty." She smirked at his young, naive expression of amazement.

She twirled toward the doorway. "I'll just be a few minutes. I need to freshen up a bit," she called over her shoulder. From across the short hallway, she shut the bathroom door.

Inside the tiny washroom, she leaned over the sink and rested her weight on the length of her arms. Gazing into the mirror, her smile dropped when she saw her reflection. Her usual sparkling eyes were dull and dead. Her shiny, black mane was now matted in snarls. The lines etched around her eyes and in the center of her eyebrows had deepened. She pressed the sides of her pounding head with both palms. She felt dirty, not filthy, but disgustingly dirty. What was she thinking to invite a total stranger into her bedroom? She needed love, but sex with Devin? What was she thinking?

There was only one man with whom she wanted to share passionate lovemaking in her bed. Her mind flipped back to Josh's wounded face when he barged into her home a few minutes earlier and saw her with Devin. He had left with that woman in the truck, the woman who knew Marvin so well, a stranger Kammy didn't even recognize.

"Think, Tara, think," She whispered to her reflection.

Suddenly, it was as if a light bulb had come on in her head. Her mouth gaped, eyes widened, and she sucked in a breath.

"Marvin's sister. Yes." Tara wagged her finger at the mirror. "Josh's niece, not his new girlfriend." But why hadn't Kammy explained that to her? She acted like she had never seen the girl before. Hadn't it always been Kammy who had encouraged her to break up with Josh, wanting to spend more time with her?

Tara flung open the bathroom door. She galloped the three steps into her bedroom. Devin had moved from the chair and sat on the edge of the bed. She practically knocked him over as she collapsed beside him.

"I can't blame Kammy for phoning Alex. Sure, I'm ticked, but she must think she's losing a friend. I've got it all figured out," she shouted as if he was clear across the room.

"I've got it figured out, too, Tara." Devin's voice was low, his face solemn. She stopped fidgeting and tried to slow her breathing. "What's wrong? You look ..." she cleared her throat, "different."

Devin rose and glared down.

Quickly, Tara found her feet and stood. With straight arms and the full weight of his body, Devin pushed her down hard. In the middle of the queen-sized bed, she lay sprawled on her back.

"No one pushes me." His low voice deepened with a hint of a drawl.

"No one controls me." He blocked the doorway with his widened stance. "I got enough of that with my old man—God *never* rest his soul." A blood-curdling laugh rose out Devin's mouth as he tipped his head back and squeezed his eyes shut.

Tara's head snapped up, and she bounced onto her elbows.

"Devin, I think there's been some misunderstanding." She stopped when she saw the look in his eyes. She swallowed hard before carefully finding the right words. "I should never have led you down into my bedroom."

"What are you saying, bitch?" he yelled, stepping closer.

Tara winced. The beating of her heart escalated, climbed into her ears where it pounded in time to her rapid breathing. "I'm saying this is my fault." Her voice shook as did her hands that now clutched the cotton bed sheet into her fists.

"Do you even know what you are blaming yourself for?" With straight arms and hands wrapped behind his back, he paced two steps and then half turned on his toes, much like a coach giving instructions in front of his team. "Here I thought you were going to be perfect for me. You accepted all of my attention. You just love the way I skate, don't you?"

Tara stared straight ahead as if mesmerized by his waltz, but she was actually terrorized by his psychotic actions.

He stopped in mid-motion. "I didn't fucking hear you," he screamed.

Startled, her head snapped up. Her eyes caught hold of his crazed face. "Yes, yes, yes," she said robotically.

Devin resumed his pacing. "Women are all the same, so irrational in their thinking. No plan for the necessary expectations of perfection."

Tara attempted to smile in his direction, but her lips only trembled. "I think I'd better get up and make you some coffee." Tara drew herself up into a sitting position, slowly sliding her stiff legs to the edge of the bed.

He stopped and glared at Tara. His eyes smoldered with a look of warning. "Did I say you could move?" He pointed at her as if she were a bad dog scolded to remain stationary.

She froze in position, eyes widened in alarm. Just for a second, he glanced down and stepped forward to resume the ritual march.

She flew up, running toward the tight opening between his body and the doorframe. Tara tried to squeeze by, but his hands grasped her around her waist and tightened. "You wanna die, bitch? I'll show you," he ground the words out through clenched teeth. His strong thighs sandwiched her legs. His body sliced into her back.

She dropped her head. His intent was to wrap his arm around her neck, but she dropped her head just in time. With all her strength, she lifted, heaving him up as if she was in a contest, and he was the heavy sack of flour. She continued to carry the tremendously heavy pack toward the finish line.

Taking a wobbling step, her legs buckled. She couldn't flip him off. He held on tight and reversed the hold, twirling her around and around.

She screamed.

He flung her body up and threw her down hard, slamming her face down on the bed. He flopped on top, pressing with all of his weight directly on her back.

With her mouth pressed into the mattress, she could barely breathe. Muffled screams escaped her throat.

"Shut up!" He commanded into the back of her head. He forced his hand between the sheets and her mouth, clamping her lips shut.

With the other hand, he wound his fingers through her tangled hair. As if repeatedly dunking her head under water, he pulled up on her head and plunged her nose and mouth deeper into the coils.

She bounced, sucked in, and parted her taut lips, prying them open. She bit down and clamped hard with her teeth, embedding them into his open palm.

He never even flinched. Instead, as if feeding off the excruciating pain, his hand pressed harder. He squeezed her lips shut, forcing her teeth to slice through her upper lip. Tara tasted her blood. His hand squeezed, choking her airway shut.

"You want to see what it's like to be bitten?" His weight lessened as he bit her right shoulder. A sharp stab of pain spread forth, heating her entire back as if lit on fire.

He jumped back on her body. There was no response from her lifeless body. Her lungs were depleted, empty, starved of all oxygen. Sparkles of light twinkled, becoming softer with each fading heartbeat. Complete darkness took over the sparks. She welcomed death:

The black curtain surrounds Josh's presence. He stands off in the distance, arms folded in front, shaking his head in total disappointment.

"Is that you? What are you doing here?" My voice sounds strange. His head stops, and he stares right through me.

"You have to fight for what you believe in," Josh responds with his own statement, rather than answering the question. His arms untangle and form fists in front of his face. "Fight, damn it. You must save yourself. You have the strength."

He falls to his knees. "Come back to me. We can make this work. Come back to me, Tara. Tara, come back to me," he pleads, his voice sounding more like someone yelling under water.

"I am strong. I do love myself, just as I am loved ..."

Behind closed lids, the darkness turned gray with shades of light. Tingling convulsions ran rapidly through her veins as fresh blood pumped, supplying her body with fresh oxygen and revived energy.

Suddenly, Tara bucked wildly, thrusting every ounce of power to dislodge Devin from her back. He flew up, his arms flailed high above his head. Coming down, his body splattered against the bare wall and crashed onto the floor.

Tara flipped off the bed and stood. The room spun. Now was her last chance. She staggered out of the bedroom and crashed into the hallway wall. She felt like she was on a moving ship during a hurricane. The floor shifted under her feet. She wavered, glancing back at Devin's crumpled form just as he rose to his feet.

She turned and ran to the stairs. She could hear his heavy breathing coming closer. She sprang up two steps, another two. Just two more and she'd be home free. Just as she lifted her foot for the last two steps, he grabbed her ankle and yanked hard. She crashed down the flight of stairs as he continued to pull her into his grasp.

She struggled in his arms, but this time he was stronger than before.

He threw her down onto the bed. Again, he pinned her face down. This time there was speed in his actions. He knew the path, and both hands clutched around her throat like talons gripping their prey. In a complete rage, he squeezed her neck with all his might.

Tara fell into complete darkness. ✦

TWELVE HOURS EARLIER

Chapter 14

TWELVE HOURS EARLIER

Josh watched Michael's shaking hands dump the contents of the first of the two bottles of vodka down the kitchen sink. His initial idea of bringing Tara on board had proved futile. His heart sank as he remembered the tight embrace of the two. Tara's appearance looked as if she'd been tousled in heated lust all morning with a man he had never seen before.

Everything is supposed to look better after a good night's sleep, but he had tossed and turned all night, with one nightmare after another. He recalled the worst: Margaret had been pleading with him not to leave her alone. She begged him to see her for who she was:

Her dark hair looked frizzy, haloed against the dark background. Her hands were clasped before her, squeezing her fists high above her head. "Please, accept me for who I am," she cried. "Help me."

Josh turned his head away, his eyes cast toward the night, refusing to look in his wife's direction. He walked away while gesturing for her to just go away. He left her behind, listening to her calls dissipate in the vastness of his world. This world ... he controlled.

He turned back for a final glance and blinked. She disappeared. He wiped his eyes with the back of his hand, but now Michael replaced her form. Something was between his pleading hands.

His son rose from his knees. Laughing, clutching the bottle, he tipped back the vodka, draining the transparent contents down his throat.

"No!" Josh screamed. Nothing came from his mouth.

Michael stopped drinking and chuckled while holding the empty bottle in front of his face. He flipped it over. Empty. Cocking the bottle upright, magically, right before his eyes, the bottle filled to the brim with more booze. The clear vodka turned into a deep, blood red liquid.

Josh hoisted both arms in the air, waving frantically, gesturing for Michael to stop. "Follow me!" Josh yelled. Still, no voice.

Michael glanced toward Josh and shook his head with a cryptic grin.

Suddenly, the muffled sound of sobbing came from behind him. He turned his head. Margaret reappeared on the other side of him.

He was caught in the middle, between the blending sounds of laughter and crying all rolled into one. The noise escalated in volume.

Josh turned his head from side to side. First, he stared at Margaret and then at Michael. They were like twins, both displaying a most crazy appearance. He couldn't keep up.

Dizzy from flipping his gaze one side to another, his hands pressed tightly against his head while his breathing took on the same urgency as the adrenalin that pumped through his veins. Body rigid, all muscles tight, the sweat bathed him until he was slippery like a bar of wet soap.

The noise increased.

Towering, he slumped forward, unable to keep the high pitched screams from bleeding through his fingers and penetrating his eardrums. His eyes bulged ...

"No! Stop!" Josh had yelled into the stillness of his bedroom. His body bolted upright in bed, lungs gasping for air.

Josh shook the cobwebs of last night's crazy dream from his head and watched his son drain the final bottle of vodka down the sink.

As requested, he must help Michael. He must keep his promise, just as he had to keep the promises he had made to both his sons about their futures. Josh clamped down on his molars and braced himself over the counter. There would be no more worries about their education. The signing of the papers would be complete. Assured of the position of Assistant Director of Education, he would never have financial concerns again. Finally, his dream was coming true. After tonight, all of his promises to his family would be fulfilled.

Josh grinned while staring into Michael's face, trying to read his solemn expression. Surely, the weekend would give him enough time to admit his problem and accept the reality of his illness. Agreeing to dump the liquor down the drain was a start.

Josh wished he could turn to Tara. She always stood behind him and had the answers. But after seeing her with *him*, he realized they were no longer a team. She had moved on without him. Hadn't that been what he wanted? Hadn't he told her that he could not fit her into his life, and it was time for them to move in different directions?

But, without Tara, he had no players on the ice to pass the puck. He would have to block all the opposition himself. There would be little glory scoring the winning goal with no one to cheer.

So, now he would have to handle his problems himself. No walking away as he had done with Margaret, pretending nothing was wrong. He would have to deal with the situation head on.

But what about the new philosophy of life he had gained when Marvin showed him that the world was not a place to be tackled alone? Josh recalled how Marvin had helped him thread the gigantic board through the table saw. And hadn't he just finished preaching to Glenda that the world is too difficult alone, and she should accept help from others?

Josh visualized Michael playing hockey as a lone player. The game was difficult, and the thrill was lost.

"I'm proud of you, son," Josh said as the water gushed from the tap, he placed his arm around Michael's drawn shoulders.

"Where are you going all spiffed up?" Michael scowled.

"I'm going to Alexandra Conway's." He straightened his shoulders in front of the entrance mirror and tightened his tie before fastening the button on the suit jacket. "This is my big night." He turned and grinned. "After tonight, I will be crowned Division Assistant Director of Education."

"Congratulations." Glenda appeared around the corner. "I'll hold down the fort." She smiled.

"Where's Marvin?" Josh asked as he bent to tie the matching black oxfords before donning the dress coat.

"He's playing in Michael's room. I heard the door slam closed about ten minutes ago. He must have found some real treasures," Glenda said.

"Treasures?" Michael's voice squeaked, "Well, good luck, Dad," his words flew out of his mouth. In the same instant, he rushed over, slapped his father's shoulder, and brushed by him running down the hallway.

Glenda gave Josh a skeptical glance.

Josh shrugged. "Sometimes, I just don't know about that boy." He shook his head. "But what I do know is that after tonight my wage will nearly double, and all our troubles will be over."

"Haven't you sacrificed too much for this promotion? Michael has been telling me about Tara. Sounds like she meant a lot to you."

"Well, I can't have both." He worked the muscle in his jaw back and forth. I made a choice, and it looks like we've both made the adjustments." Again, he saw the image of Tara and Devin at the top of her landing, huddled together, groping each other as if they were two teenagers with heated hormones.

From behind Glenda's back, she produced a second postcard. "Would you mind mailing this for me?" she asked. "Go ahead and read it if you like."

Josh looked at the picture of the Tiger Lily, the flower symbol of Saskatchewan, and flipped the card over to the back. He slid his glasses over his nose and read:

> *Dear Rochelle;*
>
> *In the last few years, I've been learning how not to trust people, and I'm glad I failed. Sometimes we depend on other people as a mirror to define us and tell us who we are. And each reflection makes me like myself a little more.*
>
> *I wonder how my family will remember me: as the small town wild girl, or the girl with a broken heart?*
>
> *All the best, and I hope to be back in the big city very soon.*
>
> *Love: Glenda*

Collapsing the arms and tucking his glasses back into his breast pocket, he glanced up into Glenda's face. She had a sense of inner peace about her that he had never seen before, and for the first time, he saw her years of wisdom double that of her age.

"When I get home, we need to talk." He grinned and placed his hand on her shoulder. "As a family, we need to come clean of all our past hurts and fears, and unite on the same page." He slid the tight gloves over his knuckles and fastened the Velcro around each wrist. "I'm going to need your help with Michael."

"What's wrong?" Her eyebrows furrowed.

Josh flipped the sleeve over the face of his watch. "I don't have time to get into everything right now. We'll hash it all out when I return." He turned and opened the door. A gust of wind mixed with snow icicles slammed against his cheeks. "Alexandra's number is listed on the fridge if you need to get hold of me," he called over his shoulder as he stepped outside and followed the snow-shoveled path toward his truck.

❖ ❖ ❖ ❖ ❖

Rounding Seventh Avenue and heading to the end of the street, Josh drove up the bare driveway in front of Alexandra's two-story house. The school board members must have been told to come at a later time, Josh thought, noticing the empty street as he rang the doorbell. He tried to peek into the side-panel window in the darkness but could see no movement at all. The entire house looked abandoned with no lights shining through any of the windows. He had expected lights, cars, and the cheer of voices to welcome him into her home by now. Instead, it was as if he had approached the wrong house and was trying to wake residents from their deep sleep.

The door opened almost as wide as his mouth when he saw Alexandra posing in a full-length, figure-flattering, low-cut gown. Her hair was pinned away from her heavily painted face with ringlets kissing the dangling diamond earrings. All details accentuated the gown and the glittered features of her face. His eyes couldn't help tracing the long gold chain down to the sparkling diamond pendant caught inside the deep cleavage between her exposed plumped breasts. His breath caught in his throat.

"You look stunning," he stammered, as he stood glued to the spot.

"Ah, just the reaction I was looking for." She smiled. "Come in." She gestured into the grand entrance.

Josh stepped inside and shook his head, attempting to clear the sudden rush of past memories. For just a second he had seen Margaret—how she appeared at the altar on their wedding day. Seeing Alexandra usually did not remind him of her, but at this particular time, he had seen a glimpse of Margaret's ghost.

"Trying to save on power?" Josh squinted, as he tossed his coat on the oak bench and made his way into the living room. There must have been twenty lit candles lining each table, and a candelabra centerpiece casting shadows over the dining room table and against the walls.

The table set for two was a dead give away.

He turned, and Alexandra was within inches of his face. Her eyes smoldered, and he could not read the suggestive smile on her face. He stepped back, and she stepped forward as if in a dance.

He noticed her long sharp nails as she reached for his hands. She wrapped her fingers around his wrist and pulled his body close. She lunged herself forward, and, before he knew it, she kissed him hard.

He grabbed her hands, locked his fingers around her wrists, and pasted her arms to her sides before pushing her away.

"What the hell are you doing?" Josh wiped his mouth with the back of his hand. He had the urge to spit, as if he had tasted dirt.

Alexandra cocked her head to the side with a smirk on her face. "Don't tell me you're as stupid as the rest of them." She strode up the two stairs from the sunken room and reached for the long-stemmed, crystal wine glasses from the table.

"Here," she said gently, "pour us some wine." She held up both glasses.

Taking a deep breath, Josh caught the aroma of Greek ribs, making his mouth water. Pushing out an audible breath, he climbed the stairs and took the offered glasses.

The corners of her mouth lifted, her eyes stared adoringly into his. "Tonight, we have so much to celebrate." She sauntered back down the stairs and perched in the middle of the floral couch, patting the seat next to her.

Ignoring her gesture, Josh placed the glasses down on the crafted oak coffee table before he sat in the chair parallel to the couch.

"Where is everyone?" he grumbled, as he pressed his shoulders back. "I thought the board was to meet here, and I was to sign my new contract."

"Please," she said, stretching for her glass and holding it up for a toast. "This is your night." She held herself erect and passed his glass to him, waiting for him to raise his arm. "I thought by us meeting first, we could discuss some of the extra benefits for you by accepting this position. After all, you will be *my* assistant." She winked. Bright red lipstick remained on the transparent glass after she gingerly took a sip.

Without taking a drink, he set his glass down and stood. "What exactly do you have in mind?" he questioned, his jaw becoming rigid.

"I really need you to sit and relax," she urged softly as she stood. Her eyes ranged freely up and down his body as she stepped closer. Her arm lifted, and she stroked the side of his face.

He caught her hand and gently squeezed. "Don't touch me, please." He released her hand and sat back down.

She twirled around, and when she faced him again, she wore a look of pure anger. "I don't get you, Josh Henderson." She threw her arms into the air. "I thought we had an understanding. You get rid of Tara, who has been holding you back for years, and you join my team of advancement." She turned and faced the closed curtains in front of the large picture window.

"Now, wait a minute here." In three easy strides, he was directly behind her. He grabbed her arm and turned her around, forcing her to face him. "Tara has never held me back. If anything, she was the one who supported me and respected my decisions."

"You cheating bastard." She spoke out the side of her pressed lips. Her eyes blazed as she looked like she was ready to attack.

"How would Margaret feel if she knew you were with Tara?" Alexandra's voice softened and was little more than a whisper. She glanced down at Josh's fingers pressing into the flesh of her bare arms, but she didn't try to break away.

"Margaret is dead." His words echoed off each wall and hit his ears. He released his hold and turned to face the curtain. "She is dead, and it's time I started living for the present. Stop dwelling on guilt and grief, and stop trying to change the past wrongs. It is me who has to be happy with who I am, where I am, and in the job I choose for myself. I know now that if I'm not happy, I can't be there for the people I love. And it's the people I love who are most important in my life." He turned back, stared straight into Alexandra's eyes. "Not this stupid job."

Josh stormed toward the front entrance.

"Where are you going?" Alexandra shrieked.

Josh grabbed his coat. His hand gripping the doorknob, he turned with a smile. "I have been so busy making amends to the people in my life and so wrapped up in thinking this promotion would solve all of my problems and make me happy that I forgot the most important love of my life: Tara."

"It will never work, Joshua. The community will never allow a school official to have a secret love affair with one of his teachers. You'll be fired on the spot."

Releasing the doorknob, Josh stomped back toward Alexandra and stopped within inches of her face. "But they can't fire me if we're married, now can they?"

"You can't marry Tara. What about Margaret?"

Josh opened his mouth to speak, and closed it quickly. Alexandra would have to come to terms with her sister's death on her own time.

He shook his head and left without another word. ✦

THREE HOURS EARLIER

Chapter 15

THREE HOURS EARLIER

An unbearably loud siren blared inside Tara's head. Her eyes fluttered open. The haze lifted enough for her to realize the siren came from the end table beside her bed. The telephone was ringing. She was not sure how many times it had rung, and her brain did not instruct her what to do about it. Her breathing was labored as she fought for oxygen to ignite her brain. Fragments of thoughts passed through a mental colander that sifted the remnants of terror and clumped them into a solidified manifestation of reality. Finally, the frantic bell stopped, and the siren softened to a faint roar.

All natural light from between the slits of the blinds had disappeared. The clock glowed red numbers that were fuzzy. Another blink forced her eyes to focus on 9:45. Had the day and most of the evening passed? Time was lost, dead, just as she felt at the moment.

Kammy's voice came through the phone speaker after the drawl of Tara's recorded cheery voice requested the caller to leave a message.

"Hon, I've been trying to get you all day, and now I'm worried. I need to talk to you. It's really important. The restaurant closes at midnight. If you're not down here by then, I'm coming over." The call ended with a click and the light flashing on the black phone.

"Looks like we're going to have company," Devin chuckled.

Tara moaned. She attempted to lift her chin, but the pain from her neck paralyzed her head to the pillow. Only her eyes moved as she scanned the bedroom in the direction of his eerie laughter.

"Now who's the boss?" Devin rose slowly from the corner chair, wiping the crusted blood from his hands onto the thigh of his faded jeans.

Like acid on steel, she felt his eyes burn holes through her entire body. She slowly curled up into a tight fetal position, much like a caterpillar protecting itself from the snout of a curious dog.

She felt the bed sink behind her. His body pressed tightly against her, molding to her back. His quick breathing heated her scalp with hot exhaled air. She tasted bile rising from her throat and swallowed.

"Oh baby, you know how I love you." His arm crawled over her shoulder to tighten the hold. She winced.

"Everything's going to be okay," he cooed, as her body shook like a tuning fork. "I've got everything under control."

All she wanted to do was die. She hated being confined, and she felt as though he had placed her in a body cast. Her breathing quickened as she realized she was trapped, suffocating in the arms of a madman. But she had to think of Kammy. His hands would wrap around her throat next.

"What's wrong, baby?" He grunted while shifting his body on top of her, flattening herself onto her stomach. His weight felt like a ton of bricks, crushing her spinal cord. "Don't you love me anymore?" His voice was soft, but rang in her ears like the sound of a baby crying out in pain.

"Perhaps I have to show you again who's in control here. Your lack of talk is making me think you're a tad confused." He kissed the back of her neck. Feeling like claw pinchers, his lips grazed over her bruises until he sucked hard. She thought of her flesh like the skin of raw vegetables, abrasively being flicked away with the many incisions of a bladed peeler.

"Devin," she coughed as her throat scratched, "I need to go to the bathroom. I need to wash up a little." Her voice was as soft as she could muster. With all her strength, she pushed herself up. He easily rolled off and to the side. She rose on her forearms, forcing herself to look at him. She needed to grin, but her numbed lips wouldn't move.

He brushed her hair up over her head as if he needed to see the truth in her eyes. She blinked and fought back the tears.

"Sure, honey, you go ahead and make yourself beautiful, but it would be impossible to look any more lovely than you do right now." His smile looked genuine.

She groaned as she slowly sat on the edge of the bed. Her head felt dizzy, and stars mixed with the blackness. Taking a deep breath, she pushed herself up and staggered to the bathroom doorframe. She paused.

"Don't even try to escape," he said ominously from where he lay stretched out on her bed. His arms were crossed under his head, his ankles were crossed, and a smile played on the edge of his lips.

She shut the bathroom door and locked it. She imagined him rehearsing her actions. He would know she couldn't go anywhere. His matching duplex had the same floor plan as hers. No window, a tub, toilet, vanity table, and a mirrored medicine cabinet. And the push-in door lock would only work temporarily if he attempted to gain entrance. She shuddered as his angry face flashed momentarily in her mind.

Tara braced herself with her hands on both sides of the single sink just before falling. She had little balance, her body felt numb, and her feet felt like they were floating off the linoleum floor. How would she ever face him without totally falling apart?

Stretching her shaking hand, she gripped the taps and turned the water on full blast. Collapsed onto her knees, she pulled both handles of the cupboard doors, and found her hard Samsonite make-up case. Opening the latch and lifting the lid, she spotted the broken mirror tucked safely within the satin ruffles. Carefully, she lifted the jagged four- by six-inch, razor-sharp glass from its binding. She turned the blade in her hand.

She squeezed her eyes shut and took a deep breath. Without exhaling and with eyes closed, she saw her steady hand grip the mirror and slice through the plum red artery pulsating up from her wrist.

Her hand dangles from her wrist as blood spurts like an erupted geyser, flying up and over her white skin, staining her robe. Sparkles dance in front of her eyes before dark clouds fog over her vision. Her heavy head falls onto her chest. She welcomes the warm liquid to blanket her body as she crumples onto the cold floor.

Tara's eyes sprang open. She lowered her chin to stare at the weapon. "No, then he would win," she heard her own voice whisper. She teetered back against the door. Leaning forward, she pulled her knees up and rested her elbows across them. She closed her eyes as she visualized the mirror slashing across the side of Devin's neck.

He staggers and falls, instantly dead.

Her heart fluttered as she sank back against the door. It was a better idea, but impossible. She was no match for his strength.
Like a zombie, she methodically placed everything back under the sink, dismissing her only weapon.
She crawled up the toilet and over to the running water rushing into the sink. Nothing could have prepared her for what she saw in the mirror. Glancing up, her mouth gaped open and her eyes grew wide. Blood covered her face. Her lips were swollen to twice their size.
Carefully, she lifted her fat top lip to analyze the depth of the cut. She knew her teeth had punctured both lips, but as she inspected each lip, she was amazed at how well the flesh had constricted. She washed the caked blood. How would she ever explain her appearance if she promised to remain silent? She was a public spectacle in Deerwood, and her girls would surely question.
She pushed the collar of her robe back and let it slide off her shoulders. Turning around to view her reflection, she gasped. The welts looked like ropes of hickeys all around her neck. On her back were big teeth marks the exact shape of his open mouth. She flipped the robe back over her shoulders and pulled the collar closed snugly around her neck.
She ripped a brush through her matted hair, and a final wiping with the face cloth cleaned the dried blood off her chin that had wandered down her neck. She was ready.
A sideward glance at the clock beside the soap dish, said 10:45. She would have to move quickly. She had just over an hour.
"What are you doing in there?" Devin bellowed, as the door banged and vibrated to the pounding of his fist.

She flushed the toilet. "I'll be right out. Just have a little bit more washing up to do," Tara answered in a soft voice. She was dizzy. Bending over the toilet, she grabbed the open seat and heavily leaned forward. She willed the bile to stay down as the blood drained from her thumping heart up into her head.

"One more minute, and I'm coming in," Devin yelled. She visualized his ear against the wood.

She lifted her body upright and took a step toward the door handle. Her legs wobbled, and her hands shook in the same degree. She sucked in a deep breath, turned the knob, and exhaled.

She pushed past his solid stance back into the open space in her bedroom. She ignored his eyes raping her body from head to toe.

Reaching for the light switch, she flicked it on. "You want to see what you did to me, Devin?" she questioned in a slow drawl.

His mouth opened, "I never ..."

"Look at my mouth," she shouted, curling her swollen lips back with the tips of her fingers. "Look at the strangulation marks your hands left on my neck," her words firing as if they were bullets in a machine gun. She undid the top three buttons, exposing her bare neck and pointing at the inflicted welts. "Is this what you wanted to do to me?" she questioned, even louder than before. "Did you want to hurt me?" she screamed. Her eyes sought out those of the mad man who had tried to kill her.

His shoulders dropped with his chin. "Tara, you know I never wanted to hurt you." He stepped forward with his hand outstretched as if he were a beggar on a side street. His face looked empty, and his eyes filled with tears.

She stepped back, crossed her arms across her chest, and tilted her head to the side.

"You just have to learn not to fight me so you don't get hurt." Again, he came forward, but this time his arms stretched out wide as if taunting her to hug his mistakes away.

She stood her ground, tapping her foot as she made a disgusted expression. "Well, I am hurt. Last night, you spoke of how you wanted to make your mother proud. Is this something she would admire if she were to find out? What about the people of Deerwood and your skating reputation? Did you even think what would happen if someone saw me disfigured? It wouldn't take long for everyone to figure out who hurt me. You might as well kiss your jobs good-bye."

"I'm so sorry, Tara." Dropping his head into the palms of his hands, he bawled like a baby. "I'm sorry, I'm sorry, I'm sorry," he sputtered.

"Your father would be so disappointed," she scolded.

"It'll never happen again. I promise," he begged, as he dropped to one knee and pleaded up to her rigid structure. His cheeks were streaked with tears.

"You really hurt me. You are VERY bad," Tara repeated while wagging her finger. Her breathing was labored and grew unsteady. She swallowed air while glaring down onto his crumpled form as if she were punishing a dog.

Devin rose and began to pace. He stopped. "Oh, my God, does this mean I'm going to lose you?" He shook his head. "I couldn't live without you." He cupped these invisible words to his chest and sobbed with dry tears.

"You bet you're going to lose me," she said through clenched teeth. "I'm never going to let you come close to me again. Do you hear me, Devin? Never!"

His once soft, droopy brown eyes blazed. His body began to shake uncontrollably. Had she gone too far? Her throat began to constrict.

"I'm going to have to kill myself, Tara."

She exhaled loudly and watched him pace across the floor to the bedroom entrance door.

"I'm going into *that* bathroom, and I'm *never* coming out. You'll find me dead." He turned and stomped over the threshold. "Do you hear me?" He called over his shoulder, watching her reaction as if expecting her to stop him. "I don't deserve to live." He took two steps outside the room and out of sight.

She listened for the sound of the door. No voice dared to come forth. The clock turned 11:15. If she escaped now, she would have plenty of time to reach *The Hutt,* to get help for herself, and to warn Kammy.

Suddenly, Devin splattered his body against the doorframe like a spider on a web.

Tara screamed. Her fists clutched her heart as if attempting to trap the organ from pounding out of her chest. She stepped back, tripping on the leg of the bed, and falling onto the mattress. Breathing heavily, she quickly sat up and stared into the eyes of a crazy man.

Devin strode into the room and stood within inches of her, looking down as if viewing her body just before the coffin lowered into the deep cold ground. She squeezed her eyes shut and could feel him lower himself close beside her, then slide off and position himself in front of her. She assumed he was on his knees as she felt the weight of his arms resting on the full length of her thighs, the pressure of both hands cupping around her hips.

His gentle voice broke the silence. "You know, killing myself would be too easy." The hot air from his breath filtered through her hair that cascaded across her face, his soft lips pressed on her open forehead. Surprisingly, his anger had disappeared as if it never existed. Her head remained down, unsure of his next move, scarcely able to breathe.

"Instead, I'm going to feel your pain, Tara," he growled, as his voice became condescending. "I'm so sorry for all I've done. I don't know how I could be so ... stupid!" Her eyes flew open, not to the sound of the word, but she heard the excruciating smashing of bone connecting with bone at the same instant he had said stupid. His fist hit dead center of his forehead. She sprang to her feet and stared in total disbelief as she watched him crush his face with his fist. Each time he chanted: "I'm so stupid. I'm so stupid. I'm so stupid."

"Oh, God," a low moan escaped from her lips. Her hands hugged her face as she peeked through the splayed fingers.

"I'm so stupid. I'm so stupid. I'm so stupid," he repeated, and with full force pummeled his fists into his face.

"Stop it!" she screamed at the vehemence of his assertion.

His actions and voice ceased. He looked at Tara in pity. "See, baby, now I'm hurt just like you are." His lips quivered as he spoke. The open cracks around his mouth quickly expanded, blood poured from each nostril, and his eye sockets filled with instant swelling and discoloration.

Tara turned away. He had smashed his face as if he were merely swatting flies. Her temples pulsated to the same fluctuation as her heart. Her breathing was ragged and labored. And the uncontrollable shaking of her hands continued deep within her gut. She spotted the clock reading 11:25.

"Devin, just let me go," Tara announced, forcing an upbeat inflection into her voice that made her sound somewhat excited and a lot crazy. Her head turned in the direction of his battered face, looking past his stone brown eyes.

"Let you go?" he replied with a derisive snort. "I'm never going to let you go." His voice deepened, growing louder as if ready to explode. He jumped to his feet.

Quickly, she changed the subject and looked sympathetically into his eyes. "I'm tired." She lifted her arms above her head and gave her body a stretch high into the air." Would you mind comforting me while I sleep for a while?" Like a cat, her body arched and curled itself on the mattress. She gathered the sheet around her like a giant shawl.

She watched his face lighten with the request as he climbed in behind her. His motion brought tears to her eyes. She blinked them away. Even though her stomach felt like it had been through a meat grinder, she forced her muscles to relax. She fought to keep her teeth from clattering, and tightened her mouth to stop the scream from slipping through.

"Now, this feels better, doesn't it?" she questioned, her voice smooth. She was careful to choose her words wisely for fear of him usurping them and taking her thoughts as his own.

Can he hear what I'm thinking? She swallowed hard, barely breathing. His body was like a metal chain, curling tighter around her back. She recoiled at his touch, fought the urge to squirm away from his heat.

It wasn't that long ago when she had felt comforted in a man's arms. Josh's aroma of spice mixed with the tantalizing fragrance of pure man. His strength lifted and quenched her needs of passion until she was totally satisfied. But this ...

Her nightmares had never compared to this type of reality. When she dreamed, she was the heroine and was always victorious, and total pleasure was the outcome. Josh would have the power to lead but would always submit to her control in the end. He was at her beck and call. She could run out the door anytime she wanted. She had freedom. He never trapped her or made her feel confined.

But this was anything but freedom. This was worse than any nightmare. Devin had taken away the dreams forever.

"Yeah," he exhaled, "this is great, isn't it, Tara?" he seductively whispered. His lips smacked, and she imagined him tasting the crimson blood as a dog would lap up its wounds.

She tried to move, but it felt as though her body was being held down by anchors. His one arm was draped heavily around her torso, slightly rubbing the base of her breast through the terrycloth material of her robe. She felt like she was under a slab of heavy metal that was weighing her down.

Oh, my God, what do I do if he wants to have sex, or even if he kisses me? The question came to her mind in full force. A question with no answer ... she hated not knowing.

Tara fought back tears, wondering what she would do next. She felt the warm liquid of his blood trickling down the back of her neck and envisioned it mixing with her own. Again, the contents within her stomach rose and threatened to break free into her mouth.

No time to focus on the fears. If Devin were to rape away her dignity, she would have to deal with that when the time came. She had no time for the possibilities or the uncertainties; only time to follow through with the plan. Unfortunately, her usual ability to structure actions existed only in spurts of fragmented information. Her head throbbed like a massive migraine.

Please, God, give me my mine and my full memory, just for tonight. Keep me strong, Tara prayed.

While listening to Devin wheeze, and smelling the staleness of his breath, she had rehearsed her speech until it was absolutely perfect. She had prepared herself for possible glitches that he could throw her way, reasons for keeping her away from others and confined to the dungeon inside her own home. She had decided to carefully guide him into her world of his hell, the dominating woman leading the insecure pupil toward codependent crowds of overeager enablers. Everything she had preached herself to stay clear had suddenly become attractive and necessary for survival.

"You know, Devin, I'd love to show you off."

"You don't expect me to let you go, do you?"

"That's not what I'm asking you. I know how much you want to please me and, right now, I'm starving. We could go to *The Hutt* as a couple. Isn't that what we always wanted?" As if the thick links had broken loose, his arm lifted.

"If we go, you'll squeal on me, and then I'm screwed."

She flipped her body around and forced her eyes to make direct contact with his, trying not to wince at the appearance of his angry, self-inflicted wounds. "Oh, Devin, you have my word. I won't tell anybody. That's not what two people do when they," she paused briefly, "when they love each other." She smiled, hoping it passed for complete admiration.

He grinned and hugged her tightly. Releasing her, he looked down at his bloody clothes and touched his face.

"I can't go like this."

She glanced at the clock. "*The Hutt* closes in half an hour. We'll go over to your place, you can change and tidy up, and then we'll leave."

He shook his head.

"Come on, now." She jumped to her feet, biting down on her molars to keep from screaming out in pain. "Where's your sense of adventure?" Careful not to push him out the door, she sprang on her toes as if full of energy and excitement, arms flailing, hands clapping as she chirped, "You're the young pup here."

"Okay, okay, if it's that important to you, it's that important to me." ✦

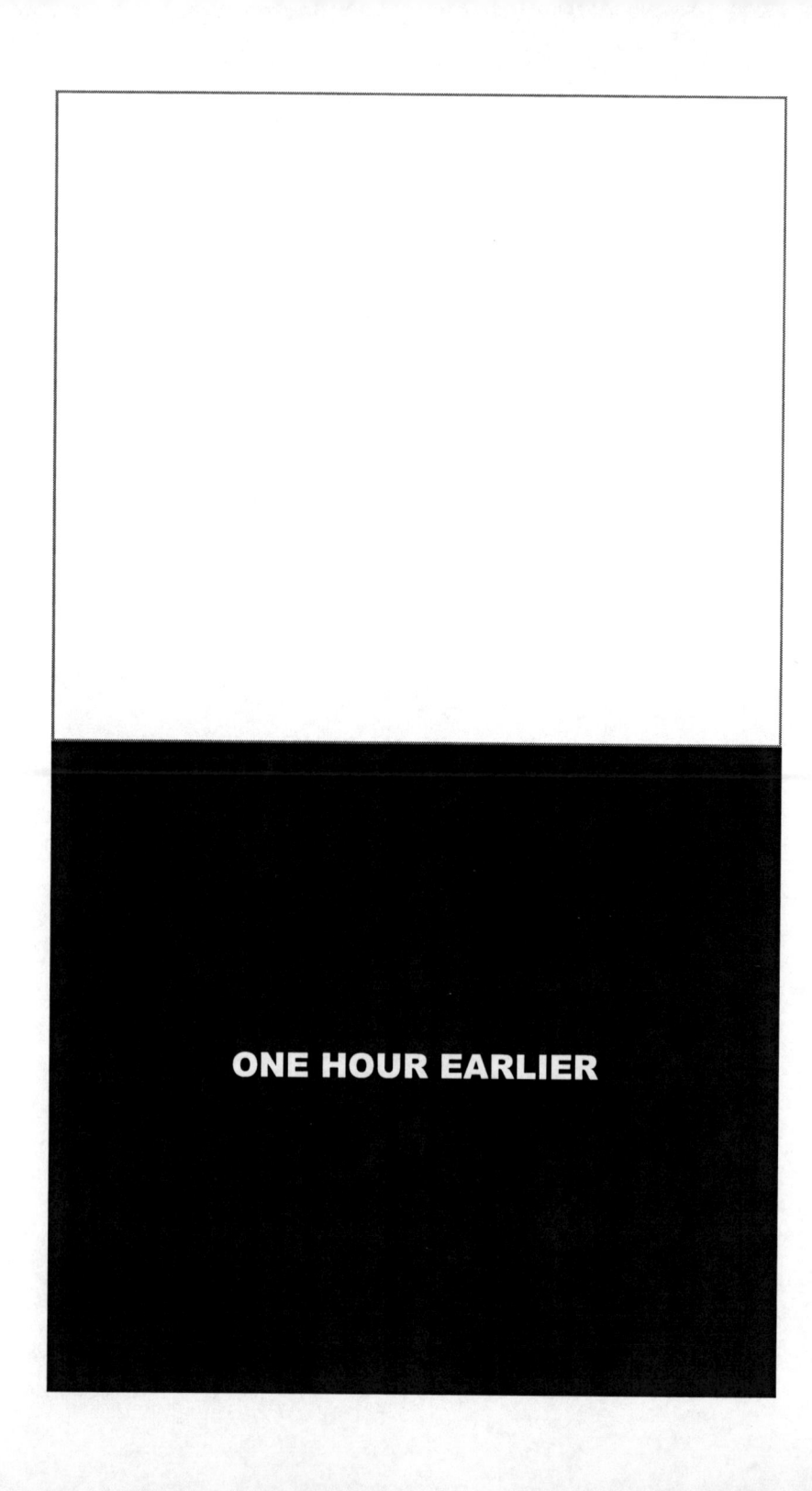

ONE HOUR EARLIER

Chapter 16

ONE HOUR EARLIER

Throwing his truck keys down on his kitchen table, Josh turned and strode down the long hallway carrying the paper-covered bundle of roses. Entering his office, he dropped the roses on the side table and collapsed in his black leather swivel chair.

The drive to the florist in Gladstone and back to Deerwood had done wonders to straighten his thoughts.

He stretched down and fought to pull open the drawer in the left column of his desk that always stuck. Finally, it opened wide, and he fished below the binders searching for a silky sensation to swim around his fingers. Snagging the mint-green chiffon scarf, he brought it to his face and closed his eyes. Taking in a deep breath, he smelled her sweet fragrance, felt her soft skin.

He smiled and exhaled an audible sigh and shoved the scarf deep within his front coat pocket. Reaching back into the drawer, he lifted the colored binder and felt to the deepest far end of the drawer. He grasped the object he had intentionally come for. A small velvet box sat in the palm of his hand. He lifted the lid. The sparkle from the medium-sized diamond immediately caught his eye. He plucked out the thick band from its slot and slipped it onto his little finger.

There was a soft knock. "It's me, can I come in?" Glenda asked, as she peeked around the partially open door.

"Come on in," Josh answered, as he sat twirling the engagement ring with his thumb.

Glenda's eyes grew wide when she saw the ring. She sat across from him and watched his actions. "Can I see?" she asked, stretching across his desk and opening her hand.

The ring easily slid off his finger and into her palm. "I had no idea you were this serious about Tara." Her eyes shone as she slipped it on her finger and brought her hand up into the light. She tilted it this way and that.

"I was sure Tara was the right woman in my life the first year after we had started seeing each other," Josh said while he watched Glenda admire the ring. "I had fallen in love with her immediately, but I wanted to make sure my feelings weren't confused with the need for her to replace Margaret. Then this promotional job opportunity came up and Alexandra spent more time in my office than ever before."

"Things didn't go as planned tonight?" Glenda asked softly while lowering her hand to divert her attention back to Josh.

"No, not at all." His head dropped, and he stared at his clasped hands stretched over the top of his desk. "I've always wanted more for the boys and to be able to cover all the expenses for Nathan and Michael. I planned to move up the corporate ladder so I could make more money. I had my sights set, and it seemed like a good plan until this past year." He swallowed and paused, "Alexandra has been encouraging me to seek this new job and kept reminding me about the financial gain and how much my family would prosper. Margaret's name came into our conversations more and more."

He let out a sigh and looked into Glenda's searching eyes. "I regressed. Rather than letting Margaret go, I started to base all of my decisions on what Margaret would have wanted. I forgot about what I wanted, what made me happy. As if Margaret was still alive, I became guilt ridden until I was sick with my true feelings about Tara."

Glenda touched and patted the top of her uncle's hand. "You did what you thought was best at the time," she said gently, mimicking the piece of advice he'd given her not so long ago.

"Well, tonight was a wake-up call. It seems Alexandra had personal motives for getting me on board. And falling into that trap wasn't worth it." He worked his jaw. "Everything I was told about getting this promotion to Assistant Director has been a lie." He slammed his fist down on the flat surface of his desk. "Alexandra lied about everything!" His chin dropped. "And now I've lost Tara forever." His mind flashed back to the loving embrace between Tara and her new lover.

"It's not too late." Glenda looked over at the thin flowered wrapping in the shape of a bunch of flowers. "You've got everything in place for what I can see is the *big* proposal." She smiled.

"I thought I had the courage, but suddenly, I'm losing my nerve." He shook his head. "Tara has Devin now." He recalled her disheveled appearance as she stood in Devin's arms and their brief introduction at Tara's front entrance.

"Who?" Glenda shouted. Josh's head snapped up at the sudden change in Glenda's voice. Her hands immediately started to shake like a massage vibrator against the back of his hands.

"Devin. Devin Tucker," Josh repeated.

She jumped up. "Oh, my God." She lunged toward the door and flung it open. "Tara is with Devin Tucker?" she said again, slightly louder, marching out into the hallway. She turned and stomped back into the room. Michael's bedroom door opened, and suddenly Marvin and Michael stood across from the office, backs pressed against the wall as an audience for her performance.

Josh rose and peered around Glenda's upright stance. "Guys, go back to the room. This is no concern of yours." He gestured by a wave, and they obediently turned back down the hallway. He sat, hoping Glenda would do the same and calm down. He had never seen her react like this.

"We've got to stop her, Josh." She fell back down into the chair, grabbed both his hands that had repositioned themselves above the desk. Her hold tightened, squeezing hard enough that his skin was turning white. "Devin is the man who's had me fearing for my life." Her nails punctured his flesh.

"I don't understand." He winced as he withdrew his hands and rubbed them together.

"To make a long story short, he's crazy—psycho crazy," Glenda said. She made circles with her fingers up to the side of her head like the hands of a clock, and then she took the ring off and placed it back in the box.

Josh shook his head. "Tara would never get mixed up with someone like that." He snapped the lid shut and slipped the velvet box deep inside the same pocket as the silk scarf.

"Do I look like someone who would fall for a man who gets off on abusing women?" Her fists slammed down like a gavel, and she stooped over like a linebacker ready for a rush play on the line of scrimmage.

Without waiting for Josh to comment, Glenda continued, "He's smart, normal looking, comes across as someone who is caring and loving, but once he knows he has you in his control, he turns animal. He's dangerous."

Josh glanced at his Rolex, and jumped to his feet. "It's just about midnight, she should be at home." He rushed to the doorway of his office. "Come on." He waved, beckoning her to follow, but she remained in her stance and dropped her head.

He could hear her heavy breathing, and could only imagine what would be going through her mind: the chances of her coming face to face with a man who had physically assaulted her not so long ago.

"You stay." Josh suddenly changed his mind, leaving Glenda in the office. He ran down the hallway, and briefly turned into Michael's room. He would need to tell Marvin and Michael to shut down their play and turn in soon. It was getting late, and both where like bears if they didn't get enough sleep.

"You guys need to …" His voice trailed off. They weren't there. "Michael? Marvin?" He yelled from Michael's room as his eyes grew wide. His hands suddenly broke out in a sweat as he slowly walked toward Michael's bed and towered over a crumpled towel. He picked up the pink neck warmer and, like a yo-yo, it unrolled to reveal an empty bottle of vodka.

"What's wrong?" Glenda asked from the doorway. Josh watched her head cranking around in search of her brother and Michael, and then he could hear her footsteps as she approached his frigid stand.

"Oh, my God." Her hand flew to her mouth. Now it was her turn to yell, "Marvin? Michael?"

There was no answer. The only sound came from the constant hum of the furnace fan.

Josh ran to the front entrance, then to the back door. "Their boots and coats are missing," he yelled over to Glenda.

She was close on his heals and stopped. When Josh turned around, she looked as if she had seen a ghost.

"He heard," Glenda's voice quivered. She fell back against the bare wall and slowly shrank as if her legs wouldn't hold her.

"What are you talking about?" Josh asked, watching her body deflate as if she was a punctured balloon.

Slowly, she looked up. "I told Marvin that Devin was bad and if he was ever to see him to run the other way." Josh held out his hand and hoisted Glenda up.

"Well, that's good," Josh said.

"No," she said quietly. "You don't understand." Her brows furrowed as she spoke with worry lines all over her face. "Marvin's very protective. He's got a temper, and he'd better not have had any liquor. Mixing his medication with booze will make him go ballistic."

Josh didn't know which was greater, his anger at Michael or his worry about Marvin. Michael's alcoholism was not only affecting him, but those around him. And he felt full responsibility. If he hadn't made his priority to go to Alexandra's and seek this promotion, he would have had Michael in rehab by now. Again, the choice he had made was wrong.

He knew by the size of Marvin that he could take care of himself. But how mad would Marvin get if he found Devin after what he'd just heard? What would he do to Devin?

"Is there anything Marvin could use to seriously hurt Devin? He wouldn't think of taking a weapon, would he?" he asked.

Glenda stared straight ahead as if in deep thought, then glued her eyes onto Josh's. Her legs wobbled. Josh reached forward and caught her just before she fell. Her face became a mask of terror. Her glossy eyes made her blink many times.

In Josh's arms, she whispered, "Dad's gun."

Josh shook his head. "Your father keeps his guns locked."

Pushing him away, Glenda stood tall and placed both hands on her hips. "Yes, but Marvin knows where the key is hidden." She clutched her stomach with both hands and scowled. "I have this awful sick feeling." She covered her mouth with one hand.

"We have to go find her. Tara's in danger." Josh said.

He ran out the door, his heart racing faster than his feet. His gut rolled as if flipping ahead of him. He jumped into his truck and started the engine.

Glenda climbed in the passenger side just as her uncle threw the gear into reverse. They backed out and raced down the street. "We have to find Marvin. Your son is with him. They've been drinking, and God knows what they could be doing. If Marvin finds Devin, after what I've told him, he'll kill him." Her hands clutched the dashboard as he rounded the corner. "Where are we going?" she yelled.

"Tara's." As Josh turned the wheel, whipping around the corner and down the street where Tara lived, he glanced over at Glenda. Her face etched in desperation, she sat high on the edge of her seat, staring at the set of duplexes. Her fingers turned white as they remained glued to the front dash.

"But what about Marvin?"

"We'll find Tara first, then go find Marvin and Michael." He pulled behind Tara's car in front of her place. She had to be home, and once he got his hands on that psycho, Devin would wish he'd never have stepped into this town.

Josh looked over at Glenda. She sat frozen, staring with numbed fear at the next duplex. Unlike Tara's, her neighbor's place was completely dark.

Glenda pressed her lips together and just shook her head.

"Good idea. It's best you stay here in case Devin's inside."

Speechless, she nodded her head.

Josh opened the front door of Tara's duplex. "Tara? Tara, are you here?" he yelled from the front landing. Suddenly, there was a commotion of barking getting louder by the second. The door behind him sprang open. He jumped and twirled around, fists ready for attack. Glenda's hands shot up.

"Whoa, it's me," Glenda said, "I decided to follow you and …" The barking stopped and was instantly replaced with high-pitched whines. Glenda stepped back and almost fell down the three stairs leading up to the front entrance. Regaining her balance, she stepped back up and into the duplex. Her pale face turned a bright red and her mouth dropped as she fell to her knees.

Josh looked up the stairs and watched as a white fluffy dog scampering at high speed ran down the stairs and jumped into Glenda's arms. Its tongue lapped repetitiously across her face as if she was the best tasting sugar treat it had ever tasted.

"Shadow. Shadow. You're alive!" Glenda's face beamed, and she giggled while rubbing the underside of the dog's upturned belly.

Josh had never seen a dog so excited, and he had never seen Glenda so happy. The tears streamed down her cheeks as she kept repeating its name.

"I thought Devin had killed her, but he didn't. She's alive. Shadow is alive." Glenda explained, looking up into Josh's eyes. For a moment their eyes locked.

"Let's hope we can say the same for Tara."

❖ ❖ ❖ ❖ ❖

Josh couldn't find Tara anywhere. He ran down the stairs, skirting around Glenda's crumpled form on the landing where she cuddled her dog. Tears of happiness streamed down her cheeks as she chanted "thank you" and kept repeating its name.

"I can't find her. I'm going to look downstairs," he called up over his shoulder.

The basement in Tara's house was dark. He found the switches on the walls and flipped each one as he hurried by. There were only three rooms. The doors were open to each. The first was the storage room where he could see a washer and dryer at the far end. There was no movement. The second was a bedroom. He guessed it to be hers from the frills of the queen-sized bed and clothes that he recognized strewn over a chair.

Running into her room, he glanced down onto her tousled bed. His heart skipped a beat. Crimson blood spotted the white sheets. The one pillow was saturated as if someone spilled a blood donor bag. He quickly searched for other clues. Next to the overturned and smashed lamp, he reached down and pulled the other pillow up from the floor. He squeezed it hard into his gut. He was too late. His chin sank into his chest.

"What did you find?" Glenda spoke at the doorway. Her eyes widened. "Oh, my God." Her face paled.

"The blood doesn't stop here." Josh pushed past her, pointing down, and into the bathroom across the hall. It trails from her room into here."

Glenda shook her head. "The more she struggles, the worse he becomes." She hugged her dog tighter.

"I wonder where they've gone?" he questioned, running up the stairs and outside, Glenda following close behind.

Jumping into the truck, Glenda shrugged and slammed her door. "No lights on at his place." The truck revved forward down the street.

"How do you know there are no lights at his place?"

"Devin lives right next door." Her thumb pointed back over her shoulder. "His car's still in the driveway, so they must have walked somewhere."

Josh glanced down at his watch. "It's five to twelve. Only two places are open: the bar and *The Hutt*. Knowing Tara, she would've talked him into taking her to see Kammy."

"Who's Kammy?"

"Tara's best friend. She waitresses there."

"But if Devin had his way, he would choose the bar."

"We'll check them both out, but, on the way, I want to check at your mom and dad's place for Marvin and Michael." ✦

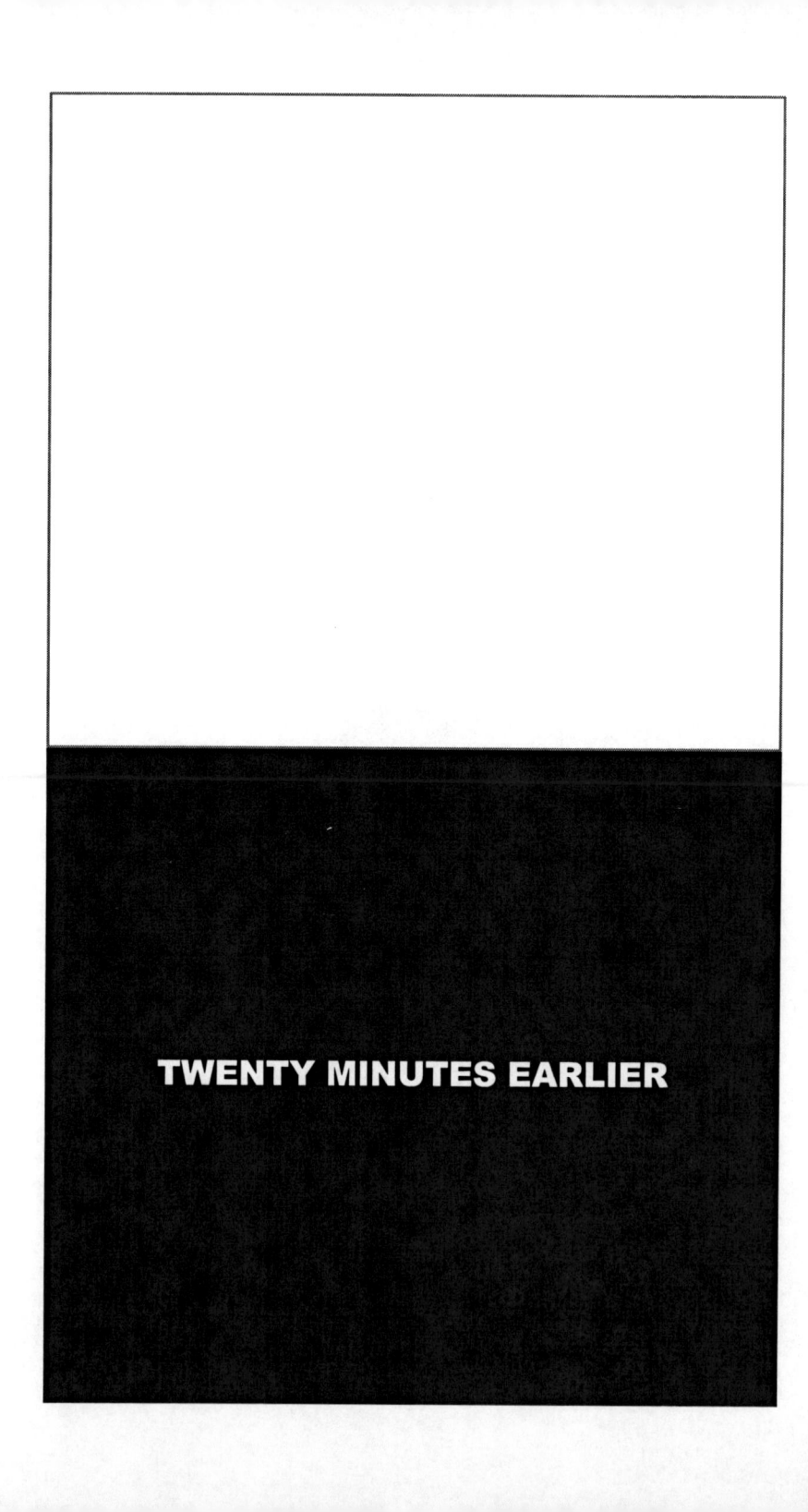

TWENTY MINUTES EARLIER

Chapter 17

TWENTY MINUTES EARLIER

Without letting go of Tara's hand, Devin shut the front door to his duplex. He had made good use of the short time at his place and raced down the stairs into his bedroom. He had quickly changed his clothes, washed up, and plunked a hat over his tousled hair. He never took his eyes off of Tara the entire time, and continued to chat about their future, reassuring himself of how proud his mother and father would be to see him take a gorgeous woman out on the town.

Tara scanned the front yard. Across to the neighbors and down the street there wasn't a soul. She spotted the tail lights of a truck barely stopping at the end of the street and then hightailing it around the corner. If only they had left his place seconds earlier, perhaps she could have flagged down the kid who was obviously joy riding in his father's fancy truck and somehow signaled that she was in danger.

She would have to stick to her original plan of action. Once they got to *The Hutt* and were comfortable around the table, she would lull Devin into a false sense of security and pretend she was madly in love with him. She would somehow signal Kammy of the danger she was in, so she would call for help. There was no way Devin was going to let her out of his sight or let her go. This plan was simple enough; it just had to work.

Without tipping her chin, she glanced down, felt him squeezing her hand with his, and saw him turning the key with the other. Nonchalantly, she coughed into her other hand. She scanned the snow-covered path and couldn't miss the huge tips of the boots extending out that felt more like a pair of skis. He had insisted she wear the boots to keep her feet warm, but since they were three sizes too big for her, it was an obvious tactic to contain her so she couldn't run away from him.

"You're not going to lock your door?" he questioned, as they turned to get into his car.

"I never lock my door," she answered with a smile, then clapped her hands quickly, giggling excitedly while thinking that she would never leave her door unlocked again. "I just can't wait to get to *The Hutt*. Kammy's going to love you once she sees us together."

"This is the way our life together is going to be from now on," he said, tipping his cap as he backed the car out of the driveway and headed down the street. He patted her knee, grinning up into her face. "Just you and me, babe."

Her legs shook, her entire body vibrating with tension. "You must be cold." He frowned and stretched to turn the heater on full.

"You're so perceptive." She watched his face light up.

The red glow on the digital clock read 11:55. They pulled into the empty parking lot. From inside the car, Tara could see through the large front windows. Kammy was kneeling on the bench, stretching across the table to pull the cord, directing the horizontal blinds to slide down to the base of the sill.

"Looks like we missed the boat." Devin reached for the gear shift to pull the car into reverse.

"No," she squealed, her voice rushed. "I mean, let's go in. She's used to having me come in late." Tara reached over and rubbed Devin's thigh. "Please," she stretched the plea into a playful request while batting her eyelashes and forming a pout with her lips.

He laughed and shut the motor off. "You're just too much fun." He opened his car door and walked around the car to open hers. "After you, my pretty lady." He gestured for her to lead while he followed.

The bell over her head chimed loudly when she opened the restaurant door, but it went nearly unnoticed. The thumping in her chest deafened Tara to most of its ring. Kammy glanced her way but continued her task of closing the blinds.

"Honey, it's about time!" Kammy spoke into her reflection. "I was hoping I didn't have to make that long hike to your place in this cold weather. So tell me about this new man you've been bragging about."

Tara cleared her throat while shuffling her butt across the bench. Devin crushed her body against the wall. This was not what she had planned. She wanted to hug Kammy, whisper in her ear, signal about the danger she had gotten herself into. Now what would she do? She couldn't move.

This time, Kammy looked over her shoulder, and her eyes widened. "Oh, my, I'm sorry." She scooted down from her elevation and dropped the cord for the final blind. She left the last window exposed to the outside. "There goes my big mouth again." She placed her hand over her mouth to cover her up-turned lips.

Devin remained seated, head down, his brim covering most of his bruised face.

"Never even saw you come in." She walked over to their booth and stretched out her hand for Devin. "I'm Kammy." She smiled.

His tight grip loosened around Tara's hand so he could shake Kammy's hand. Slowly, he tipped up his chin ...

The bells above the door rang again. Kammy's head cranked around to check out the next customer arriving at this late hour.

The bulk of his body filled the doorway. Marvin looked as if he was ready for a showdown. His stance was wide. One arm held the door open, and the other was hidden, down at his side. His head turned to the only customers. His usual glistening eyes were cold stone blue, and his face lacked the crinkles of smiling dimples. Tara had never seen this expression before. His body language screamed pure anger. Shivers crawled up her spine.

Marvin stared into Devin's dark eyes. Devin jumped up from his seat. Tara's arm felt as if it was going to rip from her shoulder as he yanked her up with him. She gasped.

"Let her go," Marvin's deep voice yelled as his arm rose. The long barrel of a shotgun extended at his waist, pointing in Devin's direction.

Immediately, Devin dropped Tara's hand and lifted both arms above his head. His eyes widened, and his body shook.

"Kammy!" Tara teetered, steadying herself against the table. She was sure she could feel Devin's eyes on her back as she ran across the room and flew into Kammy's open arms. They huddled together behind the counter. "Phone the cops," Tara whispered into her friend's ear before she released her. She stared toward Marvin, unsure of what he would do next.

"Hey, buddy. Don't think I know you," Devin's voice quivered, but remained light. Nothing moved except his feeble attempt to grin.

"Bad. You're a bad man," Marvin said. With his finger on the trigger, he took a step forward, only a few feet from Devin's solid stance.

Never taking his eyes off of Marvin's face, Devin took several steps backwards until his back sprawled up against the wall. "You got the wrong guy," he pleaded.

The door behind Marvin flew open. For the first time, Devin's eyes darted to the main entrance, but Marvin's didn't move. It was as if no one or nothing else existed in the room.

"Michael!" Tara yelled.

Michael ran past Marvin and into Tara's arms. Kammy used this perfect opportunity to sneak around the corner to the back kitchen. Tara knew it would take almost twenty minutes for the police to drive into Deerwood from Gladstone—too much time to stop Marvin and save Devin. By the time help arrived, it would be too late.

"You don't need to see this," Tara whispered as she attempted to keep Michael's attention away from the scene. But Michael wiggled free from her hold. He turned and stared at the gun Marvin pointed just a few feet from Devin's body.

"Bad man," Marvin said and stepped closer to Devin. "You hurt Glenee, you killed my doggie, and now I'm *not* going to let you hurt Taree."

Devin blinked, his eyes moistened. "Please, I can explain." He fought back the tears. "Shadow's not dead."

"Liar," Marvin shouted. "Glenee told me."

"I can prove it." Devin's head turned to Tara. "Tell him. Tell him Shadow's not dead, and I'm not going to hurt you."

Tara swallowed. It was as if the words were stuck in her throat. She just couldn't spit them out. Had she no respect for human life? Could she actually allow Marvin to pull the trigger and watch Devin die before her eyes? Her mind flashed back to a few hours ago when Devin's hands were around her throat. All of the air had depleted from her lungs and left her starving for life. But what about Marvin? He would go to jail for life. His soul would wither away locked up with no freedom. She shook her head and licked her dry, swollen lips.

"Marvin, it's true. Just put the gun down," Tara said.

"Hon, Tara's right. Come on over and sit in your chair. I'll make you hot milk, and you can eat some cookies," Kammy said from behind Tara as she stepped out from around the corner.

Devin's head was nodding up and down, his eyes now staring at the end of the gun barrel. Sweat was coming down his forehead and dripping off his chin. Slowly, the barrel of the gun lowered.

"Michael," Devin said, his hands lowering at the same speed as the gun, "tell this guy, I mean, tell Marvin what great friends we are." His voice gained strength while his lips lifted.

Silence.

"Hey, Mike, tell the fellow how we're such good buddies."

A long pause followed.

Michael cleared his throat as if he was ready to announce a grad speech to an audience without a microphone.

"You ain't no friend of mine," Michael growled. The descent of the gun stopped, and the barrel rose up to Devin's chest. Marvin lifted the butt to rest on his shoulder.

Devin's arms shot back up into the air.

Marvin peered down the open sights. "Should I kill him, Mikie?"

A cryptic smile grew on Michael's face. ✦

FIFTEEN MINUTES EARLIER

Chapter 18

FIFTEEN MINUTES EARLIER

The truck stopped in front of the home of Glenda's mother and father. Glenda ran past Josh and down the stairs.

"Marvin? Michael?" Josh called through the house. No response.

From behind, Glenda grabbed his forearms, her breathing labored. Her hands trembled on his sleeve.

"The gun's missing," she said.

"Let's go."

The road was empty of moving vehicles. Rounding the corner, Josh could see the end of Main Street. There were half a dozen vehicles parked in front of the corner bar but only one car in *The Hutt* parking lot. Without pulling in, Josh braked on the street and threw the truck into park.

"That's Devin's car," Glenda said, her voice shaking. In her arms, the dog cried as if sensing the danger. It fought her grip, wiggling to free itself from her tight hold.

Except for the interior light peeking through the slats of the side window, the entire building was shadowed in blind darkness. "I'll be able to see in the side window," Josh said. "You wait here." He turned the ignition off and quietly shut his door.

He crouched, side-stepping, then attached his back to the side of the jagged bricks like a fly caught in a sticky web. Slowly he crept toward the light. He lifted his head and peeked into the restaurant.

Tara! Josh wanted to scream, his heart thumped loudly.

Tara and Kammy stood bundled behind the counter, while Michael stood in front. His lips moved, but his body remained still. Just by their fearful expressions and their guarded appearance, Josh didn't dare move. But where was Devin?

Josh squeezed his hands into fists and clamped down on his molars. The blood throughout Tara's house flashed into his mind. *I'll kill him.*

Josh followed the direction where Michael's eyes glared. In the middle of the room, Marvin stood tall with his legs a shoulder width apart. He could only imagine Marvin's expression. As Josh stared at the back of his head, it was obvious that all of Marvin's attention was concentrated toward the far wall.

Josh ran around to the front entrance. Before entering the restaurant, he gave Glenda a thumbs up that Devin was nowhere in sight. He would have much to discuss with Michael. He thought of the empty bottle of vodka found on his bed. The time had come. He couldn't wait for Monday to admit him into recovery. This was the final sign that his son needed professional help, and he would be there to see to it.

Josh opened the door and heard the bells clang. He stopped, frozen like a statue. His heart sank, and his cheeks numbed. Marvin had Devin trapped against the wall, with the barrel of a shotgun inches from his nose. Marvin's finger shook on the trigger, ready to squeeze.

"Marvin, no!" Josh shouted.

Marvin's finger relaxed as his shoulders dropped. He stepped back.

The door behind Josh flew open.

"Hey, Marvin," Glenda said with sheer excitement as she entered. "Guess who I brought for …" The dog squirmed and jumped out of her arms. Yelping and wagging its tail, it ran to Marvin.

As if in slow motion, Marvin twirled around. His face lit up as his smile broadened. Opening his hands, the gun crashed to the floor as Shadow sprang up, jumping into his arms.

Glenda screamed, clutching her throat with both hands.

Devin instantly lunged forward and scooped up the gun, landing back on his feet in a single motion.

Oblivious to his surroundings, Marvin sat sprawled on the floor with his legs straight out, shoulders forward, head down, with the dog licking his face.

"Shadow," Marvin giggled, hugging his dog as if he was a little boy playing with a toy in the middle of his mother's kitchen floor.

"Now the real show begins." Devin grinned mischievously. "All of you," he yelled, "against this wall." He swung the gun around the room much like a pointer stick in a teacher's hand.

Tara, Kammy, Michael, and Josh held their hands up and quickly lined up against the same wall where Devin had been imprisoned mere seconds ago. Marvin did not move.

"You dumb idiot," Devin sneered, staring at Marvin's sprawled form on the floor. With both hands on the gun as a discus thrower in the warm-up swing, he bashed Marvin across the back of his head with the edge of the gun stock.

Marvin's head cracked as the sword-like stock slashed open his flesh, nearly hacking off the top of his head. His chin lifted, his eyes rolled back in his head, and he fell over. A growing pool of blood crawled from under his head. Remaining inches from Marvin's limp body, the dog whimpered and licked his face, coaxing the lifeless form of its best friend to awaken from a dead sleep.

"Shut up, you dumb mutt." Devin flipped the gun around and aimed it at the dog.

"Stop!" Glenda screamed.

An eerie laugh escaped Devin's mouth. "Should have killed him the first time." His finger tightened on the trigger.

"Please, no." Tara's voice was soft as she stepped out from the line of the firing squad. With her arms held wide, she smiled a lopsided grin. Josh now noticed her swollen lips. His heart pounded in his ears. He wanted to stop her, take her place, but he knew he had to trust her. Tara never did anything without a plan. And she had always succeeded.

"Your mother would never approve." Tara's voice took on a tone much like the one she used when disciplining her students.

The gun wavered as if battling against a strong wind. Devin's hands shook. Slowly, his finger released the trigger.

"You don't want to be like your father. This is something he would do." Her hands clutched at her waist and then crossed in front of her chest. "You'd end-up in jail like your old man." She spat the words.

Devin's eyes began to water and grew instantly red around the rims. His nose started to run. He stared at Tara. "I don't care about nothing. Nothing but you, Tara." He sniffed. "I love you, just like you love me."

"You can't have me," Tara said softly, she untangled her arms and let them fall to her side.

"Don't you love me anymore?" Devin asked, his shallow voice squeaked. His brows furrowed, and he appeared as though he would start to bawl at any second.

Her head shook from side to side. Sirens screamed in the distance.

"If I can't have you," Devin whispered, just loud enough to be heard. He glanced down and turned the barrel up under his chin.

Josh leaped forward, tackling Devin.

The gun fired.

"Josh!" Tara screamed. The echoes of the gunshot sounded like an explosion. Her ears rang and her screams were muffled against the blast as if listening under water. Josh and Devin lay on the floor intertwined and motionless a few feet from Marvin's crumpled heap, their faces turned downward.

Tara ran toward Josh, jumping over Marvin's still body. Her knees buckled, and she collapsed on her haunches beside the pile of bodies. She grabbed Josh's shoulder. Her breath was trapped in her lungs, her eyes huge and dry. She tugged on his coat.

"Josh?" her voice quivered. She shook his arm, but there was nothing. She flipped him over and watched him topple off Devin. Josh's head fell into her lap. He was soaked in blood. "Oh, Josh, come back to me," she cried, tears now streaming down her face. Gently, she pushed his hair back from his forehead. Her hands shook as she wiped his face and cradled his head while rocking back and forth.

His eyes fluttered and opened. "Hey, beautiful," he whispered. His lips pressed as he attempted to grin.

She lifted her chin, squeezing her eyes shut: "Thank you." She smiled up to the ceiling and then glanced down.

Josh coughed. "I love you." His words emerged in gentle waves.

His eyes glazed over, filling with tears.

She wiped her face with the back of her hand.

"I love you," he said in a deep, hoarse voice. She clutched her chest, feeling his words form a blanket and cover her body. Her heart soared, finally hearing the exact phrase she had been waiting for from the man she loved. Now, somehow, the words doubled in meaning and became bigger than life itself.

She felt a hand tighten on her shoulder and looked up into Michael's flushed face. She took his hand and led him down beside her. Josh slowly hoisted himself to a sitting position and widened his arms. Michael, on his knees before him, fell into his father's arms.

"I was so scared, Dad," Michael cried. "I'm so sorry. This is all my fault." His body racked with sobs.

Josh pulled away. With both hands on his son's shoulders, he looked deep into his eyes. "No. This is not your fault." He grunted and winced. He glanced over to Tara's searching eyes. "This is no one's fault." His one hand lifted and motioned for Tara to join the embrace. "We need to be thankful we're all okay."

Glenda sobbed behind Tara. Tara lifted her head and turned to see Glenda with Marvin's head in her lap. Josh scooted himself closer to them.

Tara rose and walked toward Devin while listening to Glenda cry.

"There's so much blood." Glenda spoke clearly as if she was the only one in the room. In shock, she teetered back and forth. "He's breathing, but he's out cold."

Tara stood over Devin. She kicked the gun from his side, nudging him with the toe of the big boot.

No response.

Bending down, she grabbed his shoulder and pushed him over. His head toppled on a weird angle from his shoulders. There was no face. A gaping hole was all that was left. His chin hung by threads down his neck and the skin of his forehead lifted back over his hairline.

Tara turned, eyes wide in horror. "Oh, my God," she shrieked, shaking uncontrollably. Not bothering to cover her mouth, the bile refused to remain down. She wrenched away and coughed, distancing herself from the corpse before sinking to the floor.

The bell above the door rang, and in rushed two police officers.

"Where is he?" the first of the two shouted, gun drawn, and pressed up against his chest. The second officer followed suit, twisting his head from side to side.

"Better late than never," Kammy said as she pointed with her chin in the direction of Devin's body. Her hands were busy wrapping Marvin's head with a towel, the white cloth turning red within seconds.

The screams of more sirens ceased, and three paramedics charged through the doors. Using his son as a crutch, Josh rose to his feet. "I'm fine." He waved one of the paramedic away to join his partner. "It's Marvin. You'd better tend to him first."

"We'll need a stretcher for this one," the first paramedic called to his partners while quickly checking Marvin's vital signs. "He's lost a lot of blood. We'll have to hurry."

"Just a body bag for this one," the third paramedic answered his partners while dropping Devin's wrist.

Tara slowly rose to her feet. Her legs wobbled. She grabbed the back of a chair and sank down. The first police officer sat across from her. She glanced up and saw his face widen and blur as if she was watching his reflection on the side of a steel kettle. His lips moved faster than his words.

"I'd—like—to—ask—you—a—few—questions," Tara heard him say. Her head felt as if it was being plowed by a bulldozer. Her eyes were unable to focus.

Everything darkened to nothing. ✦

NOW

Chapter 19

NOW

Glenda had no trouble keeping up with the ambulance on the way to Gladstone Hospital. The quick-flashing red lights exploded into the black sky and ricocheted off the banks of the snow-lined ditches. The square-shaped vehicle ahead looked as if it was in a battle of fireworks. The sparks flew high and shot off into the fields.

"I see you have your mother's heavy foot," Josh said grinning, attempting to break the silence and the horrible worries that swallowed his mind.

Ignoring his statement, Glenda kept her eyes on the road. "Marvin's lost a lot of blood," her voice trembled, "and they can't seem to make him come to." Her fingers gripped tighter around the steering wheel. She turned her head to view her passenger. "What's with Tara? If she just fainted, why can't they revive her?" Her head turned back so she could focus on the road in front of her.

Josh listened to Glenda's words. It was the last question, the same question Glenda had just asked him, that had bothered him the most. What was really wrong with Tara?

"Both Marvin and Tara are in good hands. They'll be fine." Josh tried to reassure her.

Glenda snapped her head toward Josh as her eyes hooked onto his. "Are you for real?" she asked in a condescending tone. "Tell me you're just trying to make me feel better, and you *are* with the program."

Josh's grin dropped as he lowered his chin. "I'm," he swallowed, "I'm kind of new to this."

Glenda's eyes lifted to the rear view mirror. "Don't worry. They're going to be fine," she spoke over her shoulder to Michael who sat rocking back and forth in the back seat.

"Dad, I need you to check me in," Michael said, staring straight ahead, face pale as he sat on his hands.

There was too long of a pause.

"Dad, did you hear me? I need you to check me into rehab."

"We'll deal with that later," Josh said without turning around, speaking to the windshield in front of him.

"No, I need to go in now!" Michael's voice rose and sounded close to panicking. "I can't deal with this anymore!"

"I'm here to help you, son."

"You're not listening. I need you to help me get checked in. I can't stand this anymore. Too much has happened because of my drinking. I've got to stop, but I can't." Michael's voice softened. "Look what happened to Marvin. And you. You were almost killed. For a second, I thought you were shot."

"That wasn't your fault," Josh said, shaking his head.

"Will you quit trying to cover up for me and my addiction? I'm not stupid, you know! I've been reading, and I remember what happened to Mom," Michael shouted as if trying to yell over loud music.

Josh stared into his lap. His thoughts flew to all the situations that had happened in the last six months. Had everything happened because he couldn't get real and admit what was really going on? His mind wandered to Margaret and all the times she had pleaded for him to see her drinking problem, her cries for help, and him just shrugging everything off. He had been so blind. But hadn't he vowed to change?

He thought of Michael and shook his head. Even with the promises he made to himself, he still found excuses to put off the inevitable. Waiting to admit him into the rehab center was just another tactic to put off the problems in front of him.

"I'm sorry," Josh said. "We'll get you settled as soon as we get there. There's a ward right in the hospital." His heart took on an extra beat, and he squeezed his eyes shut.

"Are you okay?" Glenda asked.

Josh squeezed the bridge of his nose with his finger and thumb, squinting, then springing his eyes wide open, along with his mouth.

"Let's just say that I'm glad you're driving." ✧

NOW

NOW

Gladstone Central Hospital
Mental Health Division
Gladstone, Saskatchewan

When she opened her eyes, Josh was sitting beside her. His hand wove through the steel bars at the side of the bed, intertwining her fingers with his own. Everything slowed. Josh's breathing, her heartbeat, and the ticking of the monitors. All action became suspended, hung by an invisible trap within the confines of the four walls. Surely, her overactive imagination had conjured up her thoughts. Her will must have been controlled by someone other than herself. Had Devin even existed? Wasn't he the psycho actor from some famous horror movie? None of this had really happened. Impossible.

Marvin … no, it just wasn't possible. It was an impossible sequence of events that had simply been recalled from her nightmare.

Had Josh really said he loved her? If Devin never existed, then Josh must be a mirage—a ghost. She blinked several times as she watched the man of her dreams sit hunched over, patiently waiting for his lover to wake up.

Now, if only Josh, the handsome prince, would kiss me as if I were Sleeping Beauty, I'd wake up. He could whisk me away, and we could live happily ever after.

Through the odor of disinfectant, she could smell Josh's spice cologne. His breathing came in spurts of rapid succession with the odd heavy sigh. She found his eyes, and willed hers to remain open. She never wanted to close them, fearing he would disappear and be replaced by the evil image. Devin, the monster, haunted her thoughts, as he had hunted his prey. And she was the victim through her nightmares. Would she ever allow herself to sleep again?

Tara squeezed her eyes shut, and let her lids spring open. His actions threatened to consume her. Her screams ricocheted inside her head.

That bastard! He's spoiled my life. How could she possibly accept Josh's love when Devin haunted her every second? *Damn him.*

Her muscles tightened as she thought of the woman's voice throughout her dreams. The choice was hers, she had said. Tara had the power to determine her life. *I want to live! I refuse to be a slave to a dead soul.*

Tara breathed deeply as she glanced at Josh. He looked as if he had not slept for days. The stress showed on his face. His shriveled cheeks sank under his bloodshot eyes. His skin blotched like hives, and his hair was a disheveled mess. The swollen bags under each rim showed nothing but a defeated man.

Did the wall still exist between them? Maybe it was more like a blockage, as she thought of the drawbridge to her castle closing between them. Her chest throbbed spastically, constricting her lung capacity.

I'm not worth it. I don't deserve you. Her stomach turned and flipped into a corded knot. She wasn't worth being there for anyone. She hadn't been there for Josh when he came to the house, hadn't been there for Marvin—unable to stop him as she recalled his head floating in the pool of blood. She had failed everyone who had been part of her life, even her daughters. She had failed to keep her first marriage with their father in tact.

Tara studied the image sitting next to her. *We worked so well as a team.* God, she spent a lot of wasted time in pointless reveries, consumed too much energy on men who sucked every ounce of life out of her, hid her true feelings of how much love she felt toward Josh. Wasn't it time to have the secret exposed so she could celebrate and openly rejoice with everyone around her? Did he really want her?

"Hey, beautiful," Josh whispered. His breath feathered her cheek, feeling like a soft rose petal. His eyes twinkled as his lips lifted into a huge smile. Without any further ado, his lips caressed hers in a soft kiss.

"Can I call you Prince Charming?"

"Only if I can break the evil spell."

"I think it's working. You may have to kiss me again."

"First, I've got something that may do the trick." Josh reached into his coat pocket and held a small black velvet box in the palm of his hand. Flipping up the lid, a twinkle caught her eye and instantly ignited a fire that spread throughout her body. She smiled.

Josh lifted her left hand up, and slipped the diamond engagement ring on her finger. "Tara, will you marry me?"

Tara blinked back the tears threatening to roll down her cheeks. Finally, she felt warm as heat washed over her body. "Does this mean I will discover how you like your eggs cooked?"

The door squeaked open. Tara slid her hand under the white sheet and lay frigid.

Josh shook his head, fished her hand out from under the sheet, and held it gently within his warmth. "Not to worry, my love. I've learned a lot since we've been apart. Let's just say I'm tired of 'faking it 'til I make it.' No more faking it. As far as I'm concerned, if you will accept me in your life, I *will have* made it. It's time for me to be real. And for my life to be complete, I need you permanently with me. I will be happy only then. Tara, will you share your life with me?"

Tara's head turned toward the entrance door to her room. Streams of people marched through and lined themselves in rows, surrounding her and Josh. The faces beamed, some waved, others gently touched her shoulder as they crowded around. Nicole and Stephanie pushed past and jumped up on either side of her bed and hugged her tightly. Unable to hold back the tears, she felt the wetness saturate through the cotton and stick to her chest. "I …"

Josh's chin dropped. The crowd froze, and the room became silent as if empty.

Doctor Frances brought up the rear of the line. His deep voice broke the code. "I just came from Marvin's room." Tara searched for a grin, a glint in his eyes, anything that would answer her final prayer of the day. His face was unreadable, empty of good news.

Marvin had to be alive. Somehow she'd felt responsible. He was just trying to protect her. She held the air tight in her chest.

Stephanie and Nicole sat up. From behind Nicole's back, she produced a pink wool scarf.

"Mom," she extending her hand and laid the fabric touching Tara's cheek, "Marvin asked me to give this to you." She grinned. "He wants you to get better so the two of you can share a cookie."

Tara exhaled loudly. Her muscles relaxed and tingles spread from her inner core. Her head sank lower into the pillow as she closed her eyes and said a silent prayer of thanks.

She opened her eyes and smiled. "Oh, honey." Tara's hand extended out to wrap her daughter within the crook of her arm.

Nicole fell into her body and sobbed, "I'm sorry, Mom. I feel so terrible. I should be helping you."

Tara lifted Nicole's chin. She stared into her eldest daughter's bright blue eyes. "Sweetheart, please don't blame yourself. I should never have tried to do everything myself." She glanced over at Josh. "Sometimes I take over like no one else is capable, and then I end up hurting myself because I have nothing left for myself."

Tara turned her head toward Stephanie. "I hope you can learn from my mistakes."

Stephanie nodded her head.

Tara couldn't help but think of how much Stephanie was like her, and Nicole was like their father. There had to be a middle ground somewhere, a balance between doing too much and too little.

"Help me," Tara asked, as she extended her arm toward Josh. His brows shot up in surprise. Had she never asked for help before? He stepped close. "I need to sit up." With Josh's arm around her back, she hoisted herself up to a sitting position.

"I don't think I heard what you asked me, Josh." Tara's voice took on a tone of playfulness. Her eyes sparkled as she turned from Josh back to the crowd.

"Well, I'd better do this properly," he chuckled as he went down on one knee while holding her left hand. He smiled at all the audience.

Tara looked around and then focused on their children. Nicole, Stephanie, Michael, and Nathan stood staring at them with wide eyes and open mouths.

"Tara, will you marry me?" Josh's deep brown eyes sparkled as he grinned into Tara's loving eyes.

"Yes," Tara responded and laughed.

While the crowd cheered, Michael hugged his dad, and Nathan slapped him on the back in manly fashion. "About time," they echoed each other. Nicole and Stephanie flew up onto the bed and into their mother's arms. ✦

TWENTY-EIGHT DAYS LATER

Chapter 20

TWENTY-EIGHT DAYS LATER

Tara teased her long, thick eyelashes with the mascara wand while staring into her dresser mirror. She had chosen to wear a simple off-white lace dress for her wedding day. The crowned veil lying over the corner chair would be a perfect accessory to complete her attire. A soft knock interrupted her last minute preparations.

"Hey, Hon, can I see you for a minute?" Kammy poked her head around the door.

Tara swiveled around and stood, gesturing for her Maid of Honor to enter. "You know I'll always have time for you," Tara grinned.

"Oh, my, girl, you look beautiful." Kammy's eyes shone as her head nodded up and down.

Tara blushed and ran into her best friend's open arms. She pulled away. "I'm so happy. Everything is so perfect."

Kammy stepped back. Her mouth still smiled, but her eyes had lost their sparkle. "Yes, Michael just got out of rehab and is a whole different kid."

"And Marvin is back in his Care Home. He was so excited when I spoke with him about the wedding. You'd think he was the one getting married." Tara giggled. "He wants the first dance with me."

Kammy turned around and chuckled.

"I hear Glenda's got her SUV packed and is ready to head back to the big city," Tara added.

"I've got something I want to tell you," Kammy spoke to the far wall while walking farther away from Tara.

"Well, before we get into a heated chit chat, I promised myself and everyone around me that I would no longer hesitate if I needed help."

"Kammy twirled around. "What's wrong? Are you feeling okay?" Her words flew from her mouth.

Tara slowly lowered herself onto the bench. "I'm fine." She held her hand up as a stop sign. "I'm in great health, so Doctor Frances says, as long as I take these new meds and keep up with my regular visits for check-ups."

Kammy frowned. "I don't understand. What do you need? This is so strange. You are usually the one helping me."

Tara smiled. "I need you to help me with my veil."

An audible breath came from Kammy as she carefully picked up the long lace veil from the chair. Tara faced the mirror as Kammy placed it on her head and worked magic on her hair to frame her face. Once finished, both ladies stared into the mirror at each other's reflection. Kammy stood behind Tara and remained serious. Tara was the only one smiling.

"I need to ..." Kammy started to say.

"I already know," Tara interrupted.

Kammy scooted over next to Tara, sitting right next to her on the bench. Tara grinned at Kammy's reflection. "I figured out it was you who had called Alex that day."

Kammy's head dropped to her chest.

Tara placed her arm around Kammy's shoulders and tipped her chin up. "It's okay. I forgave you ... once I figured out your motive."

Kammy's eyes widened, and she turned toward Tara. "I'm so sorry. I didn't mean to hurt you."

"I know. But you have to know that I won't abandon you. My time will have to be shared, just like with my children. There will be times when there's nothing like talking with another woman, if you know what I mean."

Kammy threw her arms around Tara. "Gosh, girl, I love you." She squeezed her hard. "You don't know how scared I was. I thought I'd lose you for sure."

"You won't lose me. Just don't hold on too tightly. You know how I hate to be confined."

Both laughed together just as the door swung open.

Stephanie and Nicole barged into the room wearing full length blue satin dresses to match Kammy's. Their bouquets danced in the air.

"Mom, do you need any help?" Nicole asked.

"No, sweetheart. My best friend has taken care of everything." Tara winked at Kammy.

Nicole skipped over to her mother and thrust the gathering of flowers less then an inch from Tara's face. "Mom, smell. Aren't they beautiful?"

Tara obediently sucked in.

"Mommy, look," Stephanie called from the corner of the room.

Tara's eyes darted to her youngest daughter, toward the voice she could swear was her own. Suddenly, her breath caught high in her chest.

"I'm Cinderella." Stephanie's dress flared out from the base as she stood on the blowing register.

No longer did the flowers carry the fragrance of tranquility. All Tara could smell was mold and mildew.

Tara's face twitched as the metallic smell of trapped minerals scratched her nose. She squeezed her eyes shut.

Images behind closed lids splashed vibrant colors against the pitch black walls of the tunnel.

A dull throb pulsated inside her head. Could she not contain this haunting gene to herself? For once, accept confinement as a necessity and lay in her coffin like a good girl?

Stephanie cackled.

Where are my baby's giggles?

"Mommy, you're not watching," Her daughter's voice from the other side of the room morphed inside Tara's head.

No! My child cannot be strapped to a single bed at Gladstone Mental Hospital. She cannot ride down the same shaft, slide into a coffin, and listen to the squeaky door that I forgot to name.

Tara's stomach curled into a knot. She wanted to know. She needed to know. She swallowed and licked her moist lips.

"Why do you do that, Steph?"

Stephanie stopped and starred back into the matching blue eyes of her mother. Her mouth opened to form the words—the same words Tara already knew by heart.

In unison, the response thundered through the room …

"I like to feel … nothing at all." ✦

Alan Stupak, Photogapher

JO-ANNE VANDERMEULEN

JO-ANNE VANDERMEULEN graduated from the University of Saskatchewan with a degree in Education and an English Literature major. She taught for the Moosomin School Division for twenty years before starting her full time writing career in 2006.

Jo-Anne produces and hosts a live weekly Blog Talk Radio (BTR) show, "Authors Articulating," where she shares marketing and promotional tips with other writers and answers questions from her extensive and ever-growing list of followers. She is an owner of Premium Promotional Services, a company that supports and markets fellow writers.

Her next book, a non-fiction resource titled *Premium Promotional Tips for Writers*, will be released in the fall of 2009.

Jo-Anne has two grown daughters and resides in Yorkton, Saskatchewan, with her husband, Randy, and their mini-dachshund, Oscar. ✦

Jo-Anne's personal and professional websites are listed on the following page.

JO-ANNE VANDERMEULEN

Owner and Marketeer of
PREMIUM PROMOTIONAL SERVICES
You Write – We Promote
www.premiumpromotions.biz

Professional Online Network Support
MARKETING TIPS FOR WRITERS
www.joconquerobstacles.com

Produces and Hosts a Live Radio Show
AUTHORS ARTICULATING
www.blogtalkradio.com/prempromotions

Prolific Author
• *CONQUER ALL OBSTACLES* (Suspense/Romance)
• *PREMIUM PROMOTIONAL TIPS FOR WRITERS*
(Non-fiction/Resource)

Visit Her Personal Sites
Journey to Publication – www.joconquerall.com
Conquer All Obstacles – www.joconquerobstacles.com

Jo-Anne welcomes new fans to request friendship at:
www.facebook.com/joanne.vandermeulen